Sidonie Gabrielle Colette was born in 1873 in the small Burgundian village of Saint-Sauveur-en-Puisaye. Her father was a pensioned army officer with unfulfilled literary ambitions; her mother, Sidonie, was a woman of extraordinary character, to whom Colette later was to pay memorable tribute. In 1893 Colette married Henri Gauthier-Villars, alias "Willy," fifteen years her senior, a music critic, hack writer, and *bon vivant;* she moved to Paris, leaving the countryside she loved. On her husband's prompting, she jotted down recollections of schoolgirl days, which, "spiced up" by Willy, appeared under his name as the first of the highly successful Claudine Series. Divorcing Willy in 1906, Colette took to the stage as a dancer, then, in 1910, married Henri de Jouvenel, journalist and diplomat. This, too, ended in divorce, after the birth of a daughter; not until 1935, when she married Maurice Goudeket, many years her junior, did she attain a lasting union. However, these and other fluctuations in her personal life nourished her unceasing creative output, which came to include more than forty works of fiction, criticism, reminiscence, and meditation. By the time of her death, in 1954, she had won the devotion of an immense reading public, and was universally regarded as one of the supreme prose artists of the age. Colette was elected the first woman member of the Goncourt Academy; she was an honorary associate of the American National Institute of Arts and Letters . . . and the second woman in history to be made a grand officer of the Legion of Honor.

GIGI
And Selected Writings

by
COLETTE

With a Foreword by ELAINE MARKS

A SIGNET CLASSIC

Published by THE NEW AMERICAN LIBRARY

Contents

Foreword

Sidonie Gabrielle Colette is one of the most representative of French writers. Her literary work has affinities with the medieval fabliaux and the irreverent humor of *l'esprit gaulois,* with Rabelais and the stoic gaiety of Pantagruelism, with La Fontaine and the classical insistence on stylistic perfection, with the Symbolists and the metaphorical transcription of sensuous experience. Yet, unlike the creations of her predecessors and successors, Colette's work is not embued with the seriousness that characterizes much of the best French literature: a preoccupation with man's metaphysical relation to God, to other men, to himself, and to art. It would be a mistake to attribute this absence of abstract and theoretical thought to the fact that Colette was a woman. It can be explained rather by the very particular milieu into which she was born and in which she was raised, a milieu that had little taste or time for philosophical speculation.

Life in a small provincial French village like Saint-Sauveur-en-Puisaye during the 1870's and 1880's, the period of Colette's childhood and adolescence, was solidly anchored in tradition, routine, and perpetual activity. For the children there were the discoveries to be made in the garden and in the woods, and a freedom of movement that city children rarely know. Colette's own family was quite unorthodox. Her one-legged father, Captain Jules-Joseph Colette, an avid reader of periodicals and a would-be writer, was her mother's second husband. Colette had one half brother, one half sister, and one brother. But most important, she had a mother, Sido (Sidonie), whom she adored and whom she described in some of her books.

It is of course difficult to distinguish the "Sido" about whom Colette writes—the character "Sido" whom she created—from the real woman Sido. However, the facts of Sido's life and the letters she wrote to her daughter seem to corroborate what Colette tells us about her. Sido, unlike many a "petite bourgeoise," was broad-minded and tolerant. She was not a religious woman, although she attended church services because they were a part of her village's way of life. Her infirm husband, her children, and her household and garden duties were for Sido a sufficient *raison d'être*. She required no spiritual revelations or philosophical justifications to make bearable or to explain her own existence. Sido's capacity to accept joy and sorrow, health and sickness, birth and death, as natural and inevitable rather than as miraculous or calamitous events greatly influenced her younger daughter, Sidonie Gabrielle Colette. Sido functioned with the greatest of ease, despite financial and domestic worries, despite sickness and old age, in a world in which the forces of nature, rather than the Judeo-Christian God, reigned supreme. Sido was a nineteenth-century French pagan in a Catholic village. Her children, who received the teachings of both traditions, all tended toward paganism, but a paganism that was embedded in the orthodox rituals of village life. Thus Colette was at an early age the rightly proud possessor of an inexhaustible fund of practical knowledge and human wisdom. She coped with the trials and vicissitudes of her life—her first marriage and divorce; her years as a music-hall dancer; her second marriage and divorce; her many liaisons and friendships; her varied careers as actress, journalist, mother, beautician, and writer; two world wars and arthritis; a third marriage to a much younger man—in a manner that bears the mark of Sido's bequest to her daughter: with honesty, with patience, and with more pleasure than pain. Colette always remained Sido's daughter and disciple. This fidelity is evident in her writings.

Colette's world is suffused with blue and smells of flowering herbs. It is peopled by animals who talk like humans and by humans who frequently look and behave like animals. It is a world dominated by "Colette," the first-person narrator who appears in about half of the fifteen volumes of Colette's complete works. Colette's particular sensitivity is the key to an understanding of what she created. Colette is a sensuous writer. Her realm is one of colors, odors, sights, and smells as perceived by herself and by her animal and human creations. In this world, moral superiority is always equated with intensity of perception and feeling. Perception is comprehension. This anti-Cartesian comprehension, which does not involve intellectualization, requires an extreme and unself-conscious attentiveness to oneself and to the physical world. It is not surprising that for Colette, children, the experiences of childhood, the relation between the child and the universe, are accorded a privilged place and role. Colette belongs to a literary tradition that from Jean-Jacques Rousseau to Marcel Proust exalts the lost paradise of childhood and attempts to recapture and to reconstruct, within the work of art, an eternal present, the living intensity of things past.

And yet Colette is not obsessed by the quest for "time lost." Sido's presence confirms the possibility of retaining the child's complete absorption in things during the entire course of a human life. Sido is an exemplary figure, both for Colette and for the reader. Through Sido we discover that the immediate relation between the child and the world can be preserved beyond the limits usually assigned to childhood and that this relation is a constant source of moral strength and aesthetic pleasure.

The lesson of Sido is deceptively simple and partially Voltairean: cultivate your garden and prefer it to yourself. For Sido the garden was a real French garden at Saint-Sauveur-en-Puisaye, with plants, trees, flowers, vegetables, insects, and pets. The garden was also Sido's family: her four children and her second husband. Sido tended these gardens with fidelity, tenderness, and detachment, with a certain maternal anxiety but without sentimentality. This detachment and this absence of sentimentality constitute the source of Sido's moral strength and the source of her daughter's aesthetic originality. Colette's style is a literary prolongation of her mother's sensitivity and vision. Thus Sido is present in all of Colette's works, giving them the fundamental unity that the varied extracts in this anthology reveal. In several of Colette's writings—and regardless of the diversity of genre: novel, short story, fictionalized autobiography, journal—the couple Sido-Colette, mother-daughter, teacher-disciple, reappears. Colette's first-person writings are, in a sense, inner dialogues between herself and her mother, dialogues in which, using Sido as her model, Colette appraises her own worth, her own image. Léa and Chéri in *Chéri*, Madame Alvarez and Gigi in *Gigi*, perhaps even Saha and Alain in *The Cat*, are fictionalized transpositions of this essential mother-daughter relationship. As the chronological order chosen for the presentation of the selections indicates, this relationship became most important to Colette in the 1920's, when she had reached the halfway mark in her life and in her work.

Colette both transforms into aesthetic terms her mother's sensitivity and endeavors to imitate her moral virtues. To be worthy of Sido and of childhood is one of the leitmotifs of Colette's world. It is as if Colette's marriage to Monsieur Willy, in 1893, and their subsequent installation in Paris constituted a rupture with Sido, childhood, and nature. In Colette's first literary efforts, the four novels of the Claudine Series, executed as a form of forced labor, sexuality is presented as perversion and is opposed to the country, to peace, and to love. A duel is being waged in these novels between the lesson of Sido and the temptations of Monsieur Willy, between country life and city life, between being and appearing. Claudine is an ambiguous character who moves from the country to the city and then back again to the country. Colette has not yet assimilated these two worlds, and the novels seem contrived and often gratuitous.

Colette's animal stories, of which "The Journey" (1905) is an early example, were among her first independently inspired works. Their originality lies in the fact that for Colette "There is only one animal." Cat, dog, man, and woman are different species of the living animal, and Colette's preference is accorded to the felines and the canines rather than to male and female Homo

sapiens. Undoubtedly what attracts Colette to animals is
their individuality, their beauty, and their intense reactions to life. Kiki-the-Demure and Toby-Dog are more
aware of things, more involved in the present moment—
in this case the adventure of a journey by train—than are
the anonymous He and She. One need not be an animal
lover to appreciate the lamentations and the pride of
Kiki or the fears of Toby-Dog. Colette revels in the
transcription of minutiae, of those little details that have
become so much a part of our lives that we no longer
see them or feel them or touch them or hear them.

Music-Hall Sidelights (1913) is based on lived experience. In at least half of Colette's writings the line between
fact and fiction is extremely tenuous. Since even the most
sincere attempt at autobiography is doomed, as past
fact tends to become fiction in the present, words suggesting words, rhythms suggesting rhythms, and images
suggesting images, these works all bear the equivocal
generic title of fictionalized autobiography. Colette became a music-hall mime in order to earn her living after
her divorce from Monsieur Willy. In this marginal world
of struggling acrobats and would-be stars, Colette discovered more suffering than success, more dowdiness than
glamour, more courage than weakness. Colette's music-
hall experiences reiterate the lesson of Sido in a completely new and different context.

"The Old Lady and the Bear" (1914) is a transitional
piece. It combines the chatty quality of Colette's journal-
ism with the tendency to draw a moral lesson based
either on a childhood episode or on an animal anecdote.
The old lady is possibly an early and an unintentional
sketch of Sido.

My Mother's House (1922) is the first of Colette's
major works dominated by Sido. It is composed of short
short-stories, a series of anecdotes that cover many facets
of childhood experience. The child's vision of the world
is coupled with the adult's nostalgia for and understanding of the past. *My Mother's House* is a tribute to Sido
and a reconstruction of the child's world. The opening
chapter—"Where are the children?"—presents the im-
posing maternal figure of Sido, the earth goddess in
search of her lost, silent children. The wealth of concrete

detail, of precise description, situate this semimythological scene in a particular time and place. The particular and the universal are fused, through the double perspective of the "I," into a poetic entity. In "Jealousy" we have a very different image of the parents: a jealous, grumpy, middle-aged father and a bustling, round mother, worried about her husband and quite oblivious of her seductive charms. The final jealous outburst comes as a surprise after the child's realistic description of the butcher shop and her sudden, pained realization that her parents are growing old.

In "The Priest on the Wall" the parallel between Colette's daughter and Sido's daughter reinforces the notion of the impenetrability of the child's world. The sound of an unknown, mysterious word initiates a series of fanciful word-thing associations that create an illusory but, for the child, real world. "The Priest on the Wall" is a kind of parable on the aesthetic use of language.

Sido's vivacious monologue in "My Mother and Illness" exemplifies the humor, the femininity, the wisdom, and the courage that were Sido's weapons in the inevitably lost battle against sickness and death.

In "The Seamstress" Colette now is the mother and Bel-Gazou is her daughter. Yet Colette, with a generous dose of modesty, attributes something of the wisdom of Sido to Bel-Gazou as well as to herself. With her daughter as with her mother, it is Colette, the observer, who learns. "The Seamstress" begins with an apparently insignificant and gossipy dialogue on the virtues of sewing. It ends with a lyrical statement that describes the child's intuitive awareness of the sexual instinct. The image of the words that pass like a bridge over Bel-Gazou's head suggests the playful manner in which Colette constructs her anecdotes; the reader, like Bel-Gazou, is charmed by the often elliptical sentences from which the hidden content must be deduced.

"The Savages," from *Sido* (1929), is really a continuation of *My Mother's House*. Colette concentrates on her brothers and the savage purity of their childhood, which they never lost. Her attempts at understanding her brothers, at re-creating their childhood, constitute again a means of comprehending herself. Mingled with Colette's affection for her siblings is the superior feeling that she alone successfully survived the passage from Sido's garden to her own.

The Last of Chéri (1926), a sequel to the more famous novel *Chéri* (1920), relates the torments and suicide of a spoiled and handsome young man who loves an older woman. *Chéri* tells of the birth, the flowering, and the mutually accepted termination of that love. At the end of *Chéri,* Chéri marries a sweet young thing, and Léa, not without regrets, courageously prepares to face a life more suitable to her wrinkles and her girth. When we see Chéri again in *The Last of Chéri,* he is a discontented husband and a disconsolate war veteran. It appears at first as if the experience of the First World War were responsible for Chéri's anguish. In reality, Chéri is suffering from the absence of Léa, from his inability to live and to love in a world so different from the perfume-scented paradise of Léa's bedroom.

The pages that have been selected for this anthology describe the last meeting between Chéri and Léa. Despite the appalling evidence, Chéri refuses to abandon his image of Léa, his search, under the voluminous folds of this asexual, good-natured monster, for the Léa he loved. The blue of her eyes, the warm laughter, and the pearl necklace allude to another world, painful and deceptive reminders of the grandeur that was Léa. The obsessive image of Léa, the beautiful inaccessible Léa, triumphs over the real Léa, whom Chéri never accepts. This obsession thrives on anecdotes and old photographs. When he has heard them all and seen them all, Chéri kills himself. It is interesting to compare Chéri's inability to face reality with both Léa's and Sido's acceptance of the inevitable. In Colette's world the female is always the superior human animal.

The pink cactus of which Sido speaks in the opening letter of *Break of Day* (1928) is one of the most significant of Colette's many images. It is not by chance that this image appears at the chronological and perhaps the qualitative center of her work. The pink-cactus image proposes an aesthetic-moral solution to the problems that confront the aging Colette. To prefer the possible vision of the pink cactus to a visit with one's beloved daughter is to prefer one's garden, one's creation, to oneself. It implies the difficult awareness of the time when certain human ties must be severed, when love, whether maternal or sexual, must be replaced by an even deeper absorption in the natural rhythms of life, in the seasonal changes, in the perpetual metamorphoses of day into night and night into day. Sido's pink cactus finds its equivalence in Colette's writing. We see Colette writing throughout the *Break of Day*, noting the transformations in the outer landscape of Provence and in the inner landscape of her heart. It is because of her fidelity to her mother and to her pen that she finally emerges as triumphant as the break of a new day.

"Look!" (1929) is a more direct statement of the pink-cactus image. If one were to choose the single word that best summarizes Colette's world, it would be this simple imperative, which commands us to devote a loving and faithful attention to those things in the world around us that solicit it.

The Cat (1933) and *Gigi* (1944) are novelettes; "The Photographer's Missus" (1944), "Armande" (1944), and "The Sick Child" (1944) are long short stories. With the exception of "The Photographer's Missus," in which "Colette" is the narrator, they are all written in the third person. The most popular of these works is *Gigi*, which has been made into a play and twice into a film. *Gigi* is a modern version of "Cinderella," a love story that is also a success story. The contrast between the socially ambiguous milieu of Gigi's courtesan female family and its rigid notions of proper and improper behavior provides much of the humor of this tale. Morality and immorality are juxtaposed in a way such that we are incapable of judging the characters. We accept them with much the same kind of tenderness that Colette must have felt when she created them.

Gigi herself is the lily in a garden of red roses, a moral phenomenon in her morally immoral home. Despite the careful coachings and plans of her grandmother and her aunt, despite their highly developed techniques and strategy, Gigi commits the unpardonable sin of falling in love with Gaston and of wanting to marry him. Love finally conquers all, and Gigi prevails over her family's and Gaston's natural aversion to the bourgeois marital state. The tale is saved from the mire of sugary sentimentality because of the fact that Gigi is herself so very unconventional. Colette has created a very special type, an adolescent, French Lolita, ambiguously feminine, impertinent and wise. The reader is constantly titillated by Gigi's presence, by the description of her family and its antics.

Life is not nearly so simple for the characters in *The Cat* or for the Photographer's Missus. Both Alain, in *The Cat*, and the Photographer's Missus are unable to live the humdrum, routine lives that they find themselves leading. Alain discovers a more mysterious and poetic world with Saha, the cat, than with his young wife, Camille, and the Photographer's Missus hopes but fails to discover that world in the moments that precede death. The two protagonists are very much like Chéri, who cannot live without Léa. They create their own uninhabitable private worlds.

Armande and *The Sick Child* are stories with happy endings: in the former, love is acknowledged after a crisis; in the latter, health is restored after a crisis. The different techniques employed by Colette in the writing of these two stories are indicative of her technical mastery of the craft of fiction. *Armande* is written in a more traditional vein of storytelling, a form of slice-of-life realism in which characters and events are presented by the omniscient author. *The Sick Child* tends toward symbolism in its descriptions of the child's inner world, the metamorphosis of everyday objects into instruments that serve his private mythology.

"Orchid" (1949) is a portrait. Colette excels in this minor genre whether the objects of her portrait be an animal, a flower, or a human being. Colette is like the jaguar hunter she describes in "Orchid," who was "dazzled" by just such a flower. Colette's orchid is an exotic creature that spellbinds the observer and forces him to abandon, at least momentarily, all other objects and occupations. It is one of the functions of literature to provide us with occasions for this kind of magical concentration.

"Orchid" contains strikingly contracted sentences and hence achieves an antithetical equilibrium. The orchid is scientifically observed and deciphered with the aid of a blade, the human palate, and a magnifying glass; it is described as resembling an "octopus, wooden shoe, silvery beard, owl, dried blood." Scientific analysis and description by association are combined with a series of questions that allude to the unresolved mystery of creation: ". . . someone—but who?" ". . . a hand—but whose?" "Who? Where? Under what skies? According to what design? By what license is the exercise of this mimesis permitted?" Colette wisely does not propose solutions for this great enigma, an enigma that excites but in no way upsets her.

The electric light bulb shaded by a piece of blue paper that gives its name to *The Blue Lantern* (1949) burns both day and night, illuminating the familiar objects and the room that the aging Colette rarely leaves. *The Blue Lantern* is Colette's last major work, a rambling promenade through the riches of her past experience and the distractions of her bedridden arthritic existence. Colette chats with us, writes to us, in her own inimitable style, personal and objective, chock-full of past and present details. Almost until the very end, Colette celebrates *"Rhythme, parfum, lueur, ô mon unique reine!"*—the fire of the hearth and heart that glowed in *My Mother's House,* the fire that she nourished with care and that, although the *"fanal bleu"* has been turned off, glows still in the complete works of Sidonie Gabrielle Colette.

ELAINE MARKS
UNIVERSITY OF WISCONSIN (MILWAUKEE)

The Journey

KIKI-THE-DEMURE, TOBY-DOG, SHE, *and* HE *have set-tled themselves in a first-class carriage. The train is heading for the far-off mountains and all the freedom of summer.* TOBY-DOG, *on a leash, turns an inquisitive nose to the window.* KIKI-THE-DEMURE *is silent and invisible in a closed basket, which is* HIS *particular charge.* HE *has already opened twenty newspapers and strewn them all over the carriage.* SHE *is lost in dreams, her head against the dusty upholstery of the carriage, her thoughts flying ahead to that dearest of all mountains, the one that bears on its flank a low house nestling under vines and jasmine.*

TOBY-DOG

How very fast this carriage is going! It isn't our usual coachman. I didn't see the horses, but they smell horrid and the steam they're giving off is black. You, there, dreaming away in silence and never looking at me, tell me, will we get there soon?
(*No answer.* TOBY-DOG *gets agitated and begins to whine through his nostrils.*)

SHE

Quiet!

TOBY-DOG

I've hardly said a word. Will we get there soon?
(*He turns toward* HIM, *absorbed in his reading, and puts a discreet paw on the edge of his knee.*)

HE

Quiet!

TOBY-DOG (*resigning himself*)

I'm out of luck, no one wants to talk to me. It's a bit boring in this carriage, where I don't feel at home. I'm tired, too, because they waked me early and I amused myself by running all over the house. They'd hidden the armchairs under dust covers, swathed coverings around the lamps, and rolled up the rugs. Everything looked white and different and alarming and there was a musty smell of camphor everywhere. It made me sneeze till my eyes were full of water whenever I went under an arm-chair, and in my efforts to stick close to the maids' white aprons wherever they went, I kept skidding on the bare parquet floor. They were very busy with the trunks dotted all over the place, and the mere sight of such unusual zeal was enough to warn me that something out of the ordinary was happening. Then at the last minute when, all flushed with her exertions, She called out, "Toby's collar! And the cat's basket, quick, put the cat in his basket!"—at that very moment, just as She was saying that, my chum disappeared. I can't tell you what a rumpus broke out after that. He was so furious because they'd let his Kiki escape that He swore blue murder and looked really terrifying, pounding on the floor with his stick. She kept calling "Kiki!" in a voice sometimes beseeching and sometimes threatening, and the two maids brought in plates to pretend—though they were really empty—and stained wrapping paper from the butcher's. I really thought my friend the cat had departed this life! Then suddenly we all caught sight of him, perched on the top shelf of the bookcase, watching us with green eyes full of contempt. She reached up her arms to him and said, "Just you come down this very minute, Kiki. You'll make us miss the train!" But he didn't come down, and it made me giddy to look up from the floor and see him standing right up there, padding up and down with his paws and turning around on himself, all the time mewing shrilly to explain how impossible it was for him to obey. As for Him, He was nearly frantic and kept repeating, "Good heavens, he's going to fall!" But She gave a cynical smile and left the room, returning with a whip in her hand. She made it go "clack!" just

twice, and as if by a miracle, the cat bounded down on
the floor, looking softer and more elastic than the woolen
ball we play with. If it had been me, I would have broken
every bone in my body.

Since then he's been in his basket. . . . (*He goes up to
it.*) I can see him through a little peephole. The tips of
his whiskers look like white needles. My goodness, what
a look! I'd better move back. I'm a little frightened. With
a cat you never can be quite sure it's shut in. But he
must be feeling wretched. Perhaps if I speak gently to
him . . . (*He calls to him, very politely.*) Cat!

KIKI-THE-DEMURE (*spitting like a wild beast*)

Khhh . . .

TOBY-DOG (*backing away a little*)

Oh, you used a bad word! What a terrible expression
on your face! Do you have a pain somewhere?

KIKI-THE-DEMURE

Go away! Can't you see what a martyr I am? Go away,
I tell you, or I'll spit fire at you!

TOBY-DOG (*innocently*)

Why?

KIKI-THE-DEMURE

Because you're free and I'm in this basket, and because
the basket's in a filthy carriage that jolts me, and because
their Serene Highnesses are getting on my nerves.

TOBY-DOG

Would you like me to go and look out and tell you
what's to be seen through the window?

KIKI-THE-DEMURE

I don't care. Everything's equally obnoxious to me.

TOBY-DOG (*comes back, having had a look*)

I didn't see anything. . . .

KIKI-THE-DEMURE (*bitterly*)

Thanks all the same.

TOBY-DOG

What I mean is, I didn't see anything easy to describe. There are some green things passing so close and so quickly that they give you a slap in the eye. And a flat field that's turning around and a little spire in the distance running as fast as the carriage. Now something red has clouted me in the eye: it's another field, of deep pink clover this time. Now the earth's dipping down, or perhaps we're climbing, I'm not quite sure which. Far away below I can see green lawns dotted with white daisies, which may be cows. . . .

KIKI-THE-DEMURE (*bitterly*)

Or holy wafers, perhaps, or something else.

TOBY-DOG

Aren't you enjoying?

KIKI-THE-DEMURE (*with a hollow laugh*)

Ha! ask a soul in hell . . .

TOBY-DOG

Ask who?

KIKI-THE-DEMURE (*more and more melodramatically, but without the slightest conviction*)

Ask a soul in hell, in his vat of burning oil, whether he's having a nice time! The torments I'm suffering are all moral. I'm enduring imprisonment, humiliation, darkness, neglect, and a pitching motion, all at the same time.
(*The train stops. An employee on the platform bawls: "Aoua, aouaoua, ioua . . . ouain!"*)

TOBY-DOG (*in a panic*)

Someone's calling! There's been an accident! Let's run!
(*Muzzle thrust out, he hurls himself against the closed door, which he claws desperately.*)

SHE (*drowsily*)

My little Toby, you're a bore.

TOBY-DOG (*scared out of his wits*)

Oh, how can you sit there so calmly, You whom I'll never understand? Don't you hear those cries? Now they're growing fainter. The accident's moved away. I'd like to have known . . .
(*The train starts again.*)

HE (*putting down his paper*)

This beast's hungry.

SHE (*now wide awake*)

D'you think so? I am too. But Toby mustn't eat much.

HE (*anxiously*)

And Kiki-the-Demure?

SHE (*firmly*)

Kiki-the-Demure's sulking. He hid this morning. He'll have less still.

HE

He's not saying anything. Ill?

SHE

No, only annoyed.

KIKI-THE-DEMURE (*as soon as they begin speaking of him*)

Meow!

HE (*fondly and eagerly*)

Come, my beautiful Kiki, my prisoner, come, and you shall have cold roast beef and breast of chicken.
(*He opens the basket jail. Out comes* KIKI-THE-DEMURE'S *head, flat as a serpent's, followed by such a length of striped and wary body as to give the impression of emerging by the yard.*)

TOBY-DOG (*kindly*)

Ah, there you are, Cat! Now you must celebrate your freedom!
(KIKI-THE-DEMURE, *without answering, smooths some of the ruffled silk of his coat back into place with his tongue.*)

TOBY-DOG

Come on, celebrate your freedom. We always do. Every time a door's opened, one should run and jump and chase one's tail and cry out.

KIKI-THE-DEMURE

One should? Who d'you mean by "one"?

TOBY-DOG

We Dogs.

KIKI-THE-DEMURE (*sitting down with dignity*)

Will I have to bark too? We've never had the same code of manners, as far as I know.

TOBY-DOG (*hurt*)

Oh, well, I won't insist. What d'you think of this carriage?

KIKI-THE-DEMURE (*sniffing it carefully*)

Frightful. But the upholstery's not bad for doing one's claws.
(*Suiting the action to the word, he begins fraying it.*)

TOBY-DOG (*aside*)

Now if I were to do that . . .

KIKI-THE-DEMURE (*keeping on fraying*)

Hnnn! Hnnn! This spongy gray stuff's just the thing to soothe my rage. Ever since this morning, every blessed thing's gone against me, and He, of all people, the one I love and who worships me, hasn't stood up for me. I've had to put up with jolts and humiliating contacts, and more than once a whistle has pierced my brain from ear to ear. Hnnn! What bliss to let one's nerves relax and to pretend that one's claws are busy tearing to ribbons the bleeding, stringy flesh of an enemy! Hnnn! I could go on treading and fraying this seat forever. I'll lift my paws higher than need be to show my utter contempt. . . .

SHE

Now then, Kiki, that's enough.

HE (*full of indulgent admiration*)

Let him be. He's doing his nails.

KIKI-THE-DEMURE

He's taken my part! I forgive him. But now that they allow me to tear the cushion, I don't want to do it any more. When am I going to get out of here? It isn't that I'm afraid, because after all They're both here, and so is the Dog, looking just as usual. Oh, what hunger pains I have!

(*He yawns. The train stops, and an employee on the platform bawls:* "Aaahhh, ouah . . . aouaouh, haiii . . .")

TOBY-DOG (*in a panic*)

Someone's yelling! There's another accident! Let's run!

KIKI-THE-DEMURE

Good Lord, how tiring this dog is! What's it matter to him if there is an accident? Besides, I don't believe there is. It's only some men calling out, and they do it just for the pleasure of hearing their own voices.

TOBY-DOG (*calming down*)

I'm hungry. O You who are my one hope, are we going to eat? In this strange land I no longer know what time it is, but all the same it seems to me . . .

SHE

Come on now, we'll all have lunch.

(*She unpacks the picnic things, crumples up the papers, and breaks pieces off a long bread with a crackling golden crust.*)

TOBY-DOG (*chewing*)

What She's just given me must have been extra good because it seemed so small. It melted in my mouth and now I can't even remember it.

KIKI-THE-DEMURE (*chewing*)

It's breast of chicken. Frrr . . . Goodness me, I'm purring without realizing it! I mustn't do that, or They'll think I've stopped minding about this journey. I must look grim and disillusioned and eat slowly, as if I were doing it only to keep alive.

SHE (*addressing the animals*)

Do let me have some lunch too! I also happen to like cold chicken and lettuce hearts dipped in salt.

HE (*anxiously*)

However will we manage to get this Cat back in the basket?

SHE

I don't know. We'll see when the times comes.

TOBY-DOG

Is it over already? I could have eaten three times as much. You know, Cat, for a martyr you're eating pretty well.

KIKI-THE-DEMURE (*hypocritically*)

Grief has taken it out of me. Go away for a while. I want to sleep now—or at least to try to sleep. Perhaps a merciful dream will waft me back to the house I've left and the flowered cushion that He gave me. Home! sweet home! Carpets of just the colors I most enjoy looking at, huge porcelain vase from which springs that little palm whose shoots I nibble, deep armchairs that I hide my woolen ball under, to give myself a surprise. Cork hanging by a string from the doorknob, and precious objects on tables to give my paws the pleasure of breaking some delicate glass thing. And then the dining room, holy of holies! The hall full of mystery whence, invisible myself,

I keep an eye on all who come and go. The narrow staircase where the milkman's footstep has for me the ring
of the angelus. Farewell, my fatal destiny is bearing me
hence and who knows if ever . . . Oh, it's really too sad!
All those beautiful sentiments I've uttered have made me
feel genuinely upset.

(*In a mood of deep gloom he begins a very thorough
toilet. The train stops. An employee on the platform
bawls:* "Aaahhh . . . ouah . . . aouaouh . . .")

TOBY-DOG

Someone's yelling! There's been an acci— Oh darn
it all, I'm fed up with the whole thing.

HE (*anxiously*)

We'll have to change in ten minutes. What shall we
do about the Cat? He'll never let himself be shut up.

SHE

Let's think. What if we put some meat in the basket?

HE

Or perhaps while we're stroking him . . .
(*They go up to the formidable creature and both address him at the same time.*)

HE

Kiki, my beautiful Kiki, come sit on my knee, or perch
on my shoulder the way you like. You shall doze there
and then I'll lay you gently in this basket. There's a cushion in it to protect you from the sharp wickerwork, and
after all, you can see through it. . . . Come, my sweet!

SHE

Now listen, Kiki, you must learn to face facts. You
can't stay as you are. We're going to change trains and a

terrifying trainman will appear and say offensive things about you and all your tribe. And apart from that, you'd better obey because if you don't, I will give you a good slap. . . .

(*But before any hand can touch his sacred fur,* KIKI *gets up, stretches, arches his back into a bridge, yawns to show his rosy lining, and then, going over to the open basket, lies down in it with a calm deliberation so insolent as to compel admiration.* HE *and* SHE *exchange significant looks.*)

TOBY-DOG (*with his instinct for the right moment*)

I have to lift my leg.

[TRANSLATED BY ENID McLEOD]

From *Music-Hall Sidelights*

ON TOUR

The Halt

Here we are at Flers. . . . A bumpy, sluggish train has just deposited our sleepy troupe and abandoned us, yawning and disgruntled, on a fine spring afternoon, the air sharpened by a breeze blowing from the east, across a blue sky streaked with light clouds and scented with lilac just bursting into bloom.

Its freshness stings our cheeks, and we screw up our smarting eyes like convalescents prematurely allowed out. We have a two-and-a-half-hour wait before the train that is to take us on.

"Two and a half hours! What shall we do with ourselves?"

"We can send off picture postcards. . . ."

"We can have some coffee. . . ."

"We might play a game of piquet. . . ."

"We could look at the town. . . ."

The manager of our touring company suggests a visit to the Park. That will give him time for forty winks in the restaurant, nose buried in his turned-up collar, heedless of his peevish flock bleating around him.

"Let's go see the Park!"

Now we are outside the station, and the hostile curiosity of this small town escorts us on our way.

"These people here have never seen a thing," mutters the ingenue in aggressive mood. "Anyhow, the towns we don't play are always filled with hicks."

28

"And so are those where we do," observes the disillusioned duenna.

We are an ugly lot, graceless and lacking humility: pale from too hard work, or flushed after hastily snatched lunch. The rain at Douai, the sun at Nîmes, the salty breezes at Biarritz, have added a green or rusty tarnish to our lamentable touring "outer garments," ample misery-hiding cloaks that still pretentiously boast an "English style." Trailing over the length and breadth of France, we have slept in our crumpled bonnets, all of us except the *grande coquette,* above whose head wave pompously —stuck on the top of a dusty black velvet tray—three funereal ostrich plumes.

Today I look at them as if I had never seen them before, these three hearse-trappings, and the woman beneath them.

She seems out of keeping in the "town we don't play," rather ludicrous, with her Bourbon profile and her recurrent "I don't know why everyone tells me I resemble Sarah! What do you think?"

A gay little squall tugs at our skirts as we turn the corner into a square, and the carefully waved tresses of the ingenue's peroxide hair stream out in the wind. She utters a shriek as she clutches her hat, and I can see across her forehead—between eyebrows and hair—a carelessly removed red line, the trace of last night's makeup!

Why don't I have the strength to look away when the duenna's bloomers brave the light of day! They are tan-colored bloomers and fall in folds over her cloth boots! No mirage could distract my attention from the male star's shirt collar, grayish-white, with a thin streak of "ocher foundation" along the neckline. No enchanted drop curtain of flowers and tremulous leafage could make me overlook the comic's pipe, that fat, old, juicy pipe; the assistant manager's cigarette butt; the purple ribbon, turning black, in the makeup man's buttonhole; the senior lead's matted beard, badly dyed and in part discolored! They are all so crudely conspicuous in "the town we don't play"!

But what about myself? Alas, what made me dawdle in front of the watchmaker's shop, allowing the mirror there time to show me my shimmerless hair, the sad twin-shadows under my eyes, lips parched with thirst, and my flabby figure in a chestnut-brown tailor-made suit whose limp flaps rise and fall with every step I take! I look like a discouraged beetle battered by the rains of a spring night. I look like a molting bird. I look like a governess in distress. I look—Good Lord, I look like an actress on tour, and that speaks for itself.

At last, the promised Park! The reward justifies our long walk, dragging our tired feet, exhausted from keeping on our boots for eighteen hours a day. A deep, shady park; a slumbering castle, its shutters closed, set in the midst of a lawn; avenues of trees, just beginning to unfurl their sparse, tender foliage; bluebells and cowslips. . . .

How can one help shivering with delight when one's hot fingers close around the stem of a live flower, cool from the shade and stiff with newborn vigor! The filtered light, kind to raddled faces, imposes a relaxed silence. Suddenly a gust of keen air falls from the treetops, dashes off down the path, chasing stray twigs, then vanishes in front of us, like an impish ghost.

We are tongue-tied, not for long enough.

"Oh, the countryside!" sighs the ingenue.

"Yes. If only one could sit down," suggests the duenna. "My legs are pressing into my body."

At the foot of a satin-boled beech we take a rest, inglorious and unattractive vagrants. The men smoke; the women turn their eyes toward the blue perspectives of the alley, toward a blazing bush of rhododendrons the color of red-hot embers, spreading over a neighboring lawn.

"For my part, the country just drains me . . ." says the comic with an unconcealed yawn, "makes me damned sleepy!"

"Yes, but it's healthy tiredness," decrees the pompous duenna.

The ingenue shrugs her plump shoulders: "Healthy tiredness! You make me sweat! Nothing ages a woman like living in the country. That's for sure!"

Slowly the assistant manager extracts his pipe from his mouth, spits, then starts quoting: " 'A melancholy feeling, not devoid of grandeur, surges from——' "

"Oh, shut up!" grumbles the *jeune premier,* consulting his watch as if terrified of missing a stage-entrance.

A lanky boy, tall and pale-faced, who plays bit parts, is watching the movements of a little "dung beetle" with steel-blue armor, teasing it with a long straw.

I take deep, exhaustive breaths, trying to detect and recapture forgotten smells that are wafted to me as from the depths of a clear well. Some elude me, and I am unable to remember their names.

None of us laugh, and if the *grande coquette* hums softly to herself, it is bound to be a broken, soulful little tune. We don't feel at ease here: we are surrounded by too much beauty.

At the end of the avenue a friendly peacock appears, and behind his wide-spread fan we notice that the sky is turning pink. Evening is upon us. Slowly the peacock advances in our direction, like a courteous park attendant whose task it is to evict us. Yes, yes, let's get going! My companions are by now almost on the run.

"What if we missed it, children!"

We all know well enough that we will not miss our train. But we are fleeing the beautiful garden, its silence and its peace, the lovely leisure, the solitude of which we are unworthy. We hurry toward the hotel, to the stifling dressing rooms, the blinding footlights. We scurry along, pressed for time, talkative, screeching like chickens, hurrying toward the illusion of living at high speed, of keeping warm, working hard, shunning thought, and refusing to be burdened with regrets, remorse, or memories.

Arrival and Rehearsal

Toward eleven o'clock we arrive at X, a large town (whose name is of no consequence) where we are fairly well paid and have to work hard; the pampered audiences demand "Star Numbers" straight from Paris. It is raining, one of those mild spring showers that induce drowsiness and take the starch out of your legs.

The heavy lunch and the smoky atmosphere of the tavern, after a long night on the train, have turned me into a sulky little creature, reluctant to face the afternoon's work. But Brague stands no trifling.

"Put a wiggle on; let's go! The rehearsal's at two."

"Oh, shut up! I'm going back to the hotel to get some sleep! Besides, I don't like you to address me in that tone of voice."

"Apologies, Princess. I simply wanted to beg you to have the extreme kindness of stirring up your wits. Fresh plasters await us!"

"What plasters?"

"Those of the 'Establishment.' We're opening tonight."

I had forgotten. This evening we are to inaugurate a brand new music hall, called the Atlantic or the Gigantic or the Olympic—in any case, the name of a liner. Three thousands seats, an American bar, attractions in the outer galleries during the intervals, and a Gypsy band in the main hall! We'll read about all these glories in to-morrow's papers. In the meantime it makes no difference to us, except that we are certain to cough in the dressing rooms, since new central heating never works, making the place either too hot or not warm enough.

I meekly follow Brague, who elbows his way along the North Avenue, cluttered with workers and factory girls, hurrying, like ourselves, to their factories. A nipping March sun makes the rainy air smoke, and my damp hair hangs limp, as in a steam bath. Brague's too-long overcoat flaps over his heels, gathering mud at each step. Taken at our face value, we are just worth ten francs per evening: Brague, speckled with dirt; myself, drunk with sleep, sporting a Skye terrier's hairdo!

I let my companion guide me and, half dozing, I turn over in my mind a few comforting facts and figures. The rehearsal is set for two o'clock sharp; with delays, we can count on half-past four. One and a half to two hours' work with the orchestra and we should be back at the hotel about seven o'clock, there to dress and dine and return to the joint by nine; by a quarter to twelve I'll be in my own clothes again and just in time for a lemonade in the tavern. Well! Let's be reasonable and hope, God willing, that within ten little hours I shall once again be in a bed, with the right to sleep in it until lunchtime the next day! A bed, a nice fresh bed, with smoothly drawn sheets and a hot-water bottle at the end of it, soft to the feet like a live animal's tummy.

Brague turns left—I turn left; he stops short—I stop short.

"Good Lord," he exclaims, "it isn't possible!"

Wide awake, I too judge at a glance that it really is not possible.

Huge rubbish carts, laden with sacks of plaster, obstruct the street. Scaffolding screens a light-colored building that looks blurred and barely condensed into shape, on which masons are hastily molding laurel wreaths, naked females, and Louis XVI garlands above a dark portal. Beyond this can be heard a tumult of inarticulate shouts, a battery of hammers, the screeching of saws, as though the whole assembly of the Niebelungen were busy at their forges.

"Is that it?"

"That is it."

"Are you certain, Brague?"

In reply I receive a fulminating glance that should have been reserved solely for the Olympic's improvident architect.

"I just meant, you're certain we rehearse here?"

The rehearsal takes place. It passes all comprehension, but the rehearsal takes place. We go on through the dark porch under a sticky shower of liquid plaster; we jump over rolls of carpet in the process of being laid, its royal purple already bearing marks of muddy soles. We climb a temporary ladder leading, behind the stage floor, to the artists' dressing rooms, and finally we emerge, scared and deafened, in front of the orchestra.

About thirty performers are putting on a real effort here. Bursts of music reach us during lulls in the hammering. On the conductor's rostrum a lean, hairy, bearded human being beats time with arms, hands, and head, his eyes turned upward to the friezes with the ecstatic serenity of the deaf.

There we are, a good fifteen "numbers," bewildered, and already discouraged. We have never met before, yet we recognize each other. Here is the *diseur,* paid eight francs a night, who doesn't give a hoot what goes on.

"D'you think I care?" he says. "I'm engaged as of this evening, and get paid as of this evening."

There is the comic, with a face like a sneaky solicitor's clerk, who talks of "going to the law," and foresees "a very interesting case."

There is the German family, athletes of the flying trapeze, seven Herculean figures with childish features, affrighted, amazed, already worried by the fear of being thrown out of work.

There stands the little "songstress," who's always "out of luck," the one who's always "in trouble with the management," and is supposed to have been robbed of "twenty thousand francs' worth of jewelry" last month, Marseilles! Naturally she is also the one who's lost her wardrobe trunk on her way here and has had "words" with the proprietor of her hotel.

There is even, out in front, an extraordinary little man, looking worn, his cheeks furrowed by two deep ravines, a "star tenor" in his fifties, grown old in goodness-knows-what outlandish places. Indifferent to the noise, he rehearses—implacably.

Every other minute he flings his arms wide to stop the orchestra, rushing from the double bass to the kettledrums, bent in two over the footlights. He looks like a stormy petrel riding the tempest. When he sings, he emits long shrill notes, metallic and malevolent, in an attempt to bring to life an obsolete repertory in which he impersonates, in turn, Pedro the Bandit, the light-hearted cavalier who forsakes Manon, the crazed villain and his sinister cackling at night on the moors. He scares me, but delights Brague, who instinctively reverts to his nomad fatalism.

Risking his luck in the general confusion, my companion lights the forbidden "cig" and lends an amused ear to the "vocal phenomenon," a dark lady who spins out almost inaudible high C's.

"She's a scream, isn't she? Makes me feel as if I were listening through the wrong end of my opera glasses."

His laughter is infectious. Mysteriously, a comforting cheerfulness starts to spread among us. We feel the approach of night, of the hour when the lamps are lit, the hour of our real awakening, of our glory.

"ANANKE!" suddenly shouts the litigious comic, a high-brow in his way. "If we go on, we go on and if we don't—well we don't."

With a ballet dancer's leap he skims over the edge of the stage box, ready to give the electricians a helpful hand. The "out-of-luck" girl is chewing on fruit drops with the Herculean septet. My drowsiness has left me and I settle down on a roll of linoleum, side by side with the "vocal phenomenon," who is all set to tell my fortune! Still another carefree hour ahead, empty of thought or plans.

Happy in our obtuse way, devoid of intuition or foresight, we give no thought to the future, to misfortune, to old age—or to the impending failure of this altogether too new and luxurious "Establishment," which is due to take place one month from today, precisely on "Saint Payday."

A Bad Morning

Not one of us four feels fit to face the harsh light that falls from the glass roof like a vertical cold shower. It is nine in the morning; that is, dawn for those who go to bed late. Is it really possible that there can still exist, within a mile or so, a warm bed and a breakfast cup still steaming with the dregs of scented tea? I feel as if I will never again go to bed. I find this rehearsal room, the scene of our reluctant and too early foregatherings, utterly depressing.

"Aah . . ." the lovely Bastienne yawns expressively.

Brague, the mimic, throws her a fierce look, as much as to say, "Serves you right." He is pale and badly shaven, whereas the lovely Bastienne, battered and shrunk to nothing inside her sentry box of a coat, would wring the heart of anyone other than a fellow player, by the pink swellings under her eyes and her bloodless ears. Palestrier, the composer, his nose bright purple on a wan countenance, is the personification of a drunk who has spent the night unconscious in a police station. As for myself, good God, a saber slash across one cheek, limp skeins of hair, and skin left dry by my lazy bloodstream! One might think we are showing off, exaggerating our disgrace in a fit of witless sadism. "Serves you right," say Brague's eyes, probing my sunken cheeks; while mine retort, "You're just such another wreck yourself."

Instead of shortening the rehearsal of our pantomime, we fritter time away. Palestrier starts on a salacious story, which could be funny were it not that the dead cigarette he keeps masticating imparts a most obnoxious smell to his every word. The stove roars yet does not heat the hall, and we peer into its small mica window, like chilled savages hoping for some miraculous sunrise.

"What do they burn in it, I wonder?" Palestrier hazards. "Newspaper logs, maybe, bound together with wire thread. I know how to make that stuff. I learned how from an old lady, the year I won my prize at the *Conservatoire*. She used to cough up three francs to make me play waltzes for her. There were times when I'd turn up, and she'd just say, 'We'll have no music today. My little bitch is nervous, and the piano puts her on edge!' So she would invite me to help with the fuel provision—nothing but newspapers and wire. It was she, too, who taught me how to burnish brass. I certainly didn't waste my time with her. In those days, providing I could get a meal for it, I would have clipped dogs and doctored cats!"

In the now-glowing square of mica he gazes at the vision of his needy youth, the period when his talent struggled within him like a splendid, famished beast. As he sits staring his pale-faced, hungry youth becomes so alive that he reverts to the juicy slang of the suburbs, the drawling accent and thick voice; and sticks both hands in his pockets as his shoulders shake.

On this harsh winter morning we lack courage, lack all incentive to face the future. There is nothing inside us to burst into flame or blossom amid the dirty snow. Crouched and fearful, we are driven back by the hour, the cold, our rude awakening, the momentary malevolence in the air, to the most miserable, most humiliating moments of our past.

"The same goes for me," Brague breaks out suddenly. "Just to be able to eat one's fill. . . . People who've always had plenty can't imagine what that means. I remember a time when I still had some credit at the bar, but never a chance to make any dough. When I drank down my glass of red wine—well, I could have cried just at the thought of a fresh little crust to dip into it."

"The same goes for me. . . ." the lovely Bastienne says, picking up her cue. "When I was a mere kid—fifteen or sixteen—I'd all but faint in the mornings at the dancing class because I hadn't had enough to eat; but if the ballet mistress asked me whether I was ill, I'd brag and answer: 'It's my lover, madame, he's exhausted me.' A lover indeed! As if I'd even known what it meant to have one! She'd throw her arms in the air: 'Ah, you won't keep your queenly beauty for long! But what on earth have you all got in those bodies of yours?' What I didn't have in my body was a good plateful of soup, and that's for sure."

She speaks slowly, with assiduous care, as if she were spelling out her reminiscences. Sitting with her knees wide apart, the lovely Bastienne has sunk into the posture of a housewife watching her pot boil. Her "queenly beauty" and her brassy smile have been discarded, as if they were mere stage props.

A few slammed chords, a run up the scale by stumbling numb fingers, excite a superficial thrill. I shall have to move out of the posture of a hibernating animal, head inclined on one shoulder, hands tightly clasped like cold-stricken paws. I was not asleep. I am only, like my companions, emerging from a bitter dream. Hunger, thirst—they should be a full-time torture, simple and complete, leaving no room for other torments. Privation prevents all thought, substitutes for any other mental image that of a hot, sweet-smelling dish, and reduces hope to the shape of a rounded loaf set in rays of glory.

Brague is the first to jump to his feet. Rough-and-ready advice and inevitable invective assume, as they flow from his lips, a most familiar sound. What a string of ugly words to accompany so graceful an action! How many

traces of trial and error are to be seen on the faces of the
three mimes, where effort sets a too quickly broken
mask! Hands that we compel to speak our lines, arms
for an instant eloquent, seem suddenly to be shattered,
and by their strengthless collapse transform us into muti-
lated statues.

No matter. Our goal, though difficult to attain, is not
inaccessible. Words, as we cease to feel their urgency,
become detached from us, like graceless chips from a
precious gem. Invested with a subtler task than those
who speak classical verse or exchange witticisms in lively
prose, we are eager to banish from our mute dialogues
the earthbound word, the one obstacle between us and
silence—perfect, limpid, rhythmic silence—proud to give
expression to every emotion and every feeling, and accepting no other support, no other restraint than that of
music alone.

[TRANSLATED BY ANNE-MARIE CALLIMACHI]

The Old Lady and the Bear

(*Spring, 1914*)

We are in a restaurant near the Madeleine. It is half-past twelve, the hour when the deputies usually lunch. At the table next to ours are two men whose names I do not know; but it is not difficult to foresee that when they have finished their cigars, their coffee, and their brandy, they will cross the bridge and take their places once again in the Chamber opposite. Although they are well enough dressed, they behave badly, like people who never relax except at mealtime; they put their elbows on the table, sit any which way, play with a fruit knife as if it were a paper knife, display complete indifference to everything happening around them, and talk politics; and though they lower their voices and adopt a cautious and weary manner, I catch words that have already appeared in the press a hundred times that week, and have been repeated over and over again on all sides: "The Viviani Plan . . . approach to Doumergue . . . Peytral . . . Ribot . . . Bourgeois . . ."

They get worked up and in spite of myself I begin to take in the drift of the conversation.

"Normal debating methods, you call them? Normal debating methods, I like that!"

"Well, I try to——"

"My dear sir, *they* don't debate. Each of them merely issues an ultimatum, and in what a tone! It all goes to show what extraordinary people they are, each more unequivocal than the other. One of them *does not admit,* another *cannot tolerate*; if you question *So-and-So* you offend him mortally. Thingummy threatens you, though on what authority it's hard to make out; if you attempt to contradict him, he bawls and substitutes for arguments a kind of war dance accompanied by a frenzied dirge. As for Whats-His-Name, he utters nothing but verdicts, which are generally decrees of banishment.

"And the joke of it all is that if only we inquired a little closely, we should discover that hardly anyone has ever heard of Whats-His-Name, that Thingummy has no sort of political past, not even a financial one, that So-and-So's coffers are empty and his thunder a mere sound effect. Only we don't inquire, we merely quail. This is the heyday of the Peremptory."

Exhausted, the two men fall silent for a moment, and I control my indiscreet desire to butt into their conversation and tell them a perfectly true story of which their last words have just reminded me: the story of the old Polish lady and the bear.

An old Polish lady once lived in Austria—I am speaking of fifty years ago—on an estate in a forest where, among the tall and very ancient trees, there were still to be found wolves and bears. One day a she-bear, slightly injured, was caught there. The lady had it cared for and cured in her house, and it became as tame as could be, so much so that it followed her like a bitch and slept on the drawing-room carpet.

One day when the old lady was taking a forest path to one of her farms, she saw that Masha, her pet bear, was following her.

"No, Masha," she says to her, "you mustn't come to the farm. Go back to the house."

Refusal on the part of Masha, who persists, so the Polish lady takes her back herself and shuts her up under close supervision in the drawing room.

In the forest she hears once more a muffled trot on the pine needles; she turns around and whom does she see hurrying after her but Masha, who quickly catches up with her and stops dead in front of her.

"Oh, Masha," cries the old lady, "I forbade you to follow me! I'm very angry with you! I order you to go home! Go on now. Get along with you!"

She punctuates this speech with two little raps of her umbrella—pan! pan!—on Masha's muzzle. The bear looks at her mistress with an undecided eye, gives a jump sideways, and disappears into the forest.

"I shouldn't have done that," thinks the old lady. "I've made Masha angry, and now she'll never want to come back again. She'll terrorize the sheep and cattle. I'll go back to the house and send them to look for Masha."

She retraces her steps, opens the drawing-room door, and finds—Masha, Masha who had not budged, innocent Masha dozing on the carpet! The beast in the wood was simply a different bear, who was hurrying after the old lady to eat her, but who, on receiving two little raps from an umbrella and being scolded like a mere poodle, said to himself: "This commanding person obviously wields mysterious and limitless power. I'm getting out of here!"

But all the same, if the other bear, the wild bear, had known that the lady, the peremptory old lady, was armed with nothing but a little pink cotton umbrella, what then?

[TRANSLATED BY ENID McLEOD]

Where Are the Children?

The house was large, topped by a lofty attic. The steep gradient of the street compelled the coach houses, stables, and poultry house, the laundry and the dairy, to huddle on a lower level all around a closed courtyard.

By leaning over the garden wall, I could scratch with my finger the poultry-house roof. The Upper Garden overlooked the Lower Garden—a warm, confined enclosure reserved for the cultivation of eggplants and pimentos—where the smell of tomato leaves mingled in July with that of the apricots ripening on the walls. In the Upper Garden were two twin firs, a walnut tree whose intolerant shade killed any flowers beneath it, some rosebushes, a neglected lawn, and a dilapidated arbor. At the bottom, along the Rue des Vignes, a boundary wall reinforced with a strong iron railing ought to have ensured the privacy of the two gardens, but I never knew those railings other than twisted and torn from their cement foundations and grappling in midair with the invincible arms of a hundred-year-old wistaria.

In the Rue de l'Hospice, a double flight of steps led up to the front door in the gloomy facade with its large bare windows. It was the typical burgher's house in an old village, but its dignity was upset a little by the steep gradient of the street, the stone steps being lopsided, ten on one side and six on the other.

A large solemn house, rather forbidding, with its shrill bell and its carriage entrance with a huge bolt like an ancient dungeon, a house that smiled only on its garden side. The back, invisible to passersby, was a sun trap, swathed in a mantle of wistaria and bignonia too heavy for the trellis of worn ironwork, which sagged in the middle like a hammock and provided shade for the little flagged terrace and the threshold of the sitting room.

42

Is it worthwhile, I wonder, seeking for adequate words to describe the rest? I shall never be able to conjure up the splendor that adorns, in my memory, the ruddy festoons of an autumn vine borne down by its own weight and clinging despairingly to some branch of the fir trees. And the massive lilacs, whose compact flowers—blue in the shade and purple in the sunshine—withered so soon, stifled by their own exuberance. The lilacs long since dead will not be revived at my bidding, any more than the terrifying moonlight—silver, quicksilver, leaden gray, with facets of dazzling amethyst or scintillating points of sapphire—all depending on a certain pane in the blue glass window of the summerhouse at the bottom of the garden.

Both house and garden are living still, I know; but what of that, if the magic has deserted them? If the secret is lost that opened to me a whole world—light, scents, birds, and trees in perfect harmony, the murmur of human voices now silent forever—a world of which I have ceased to be worthy?

It would happen sometimes long ago, when this house and garden harbored a family, that a book lying open on the flagstones of the terrace or on the grass, a jump rope twisted like a snake across the path, or perhaps a miniature garden, pebble edged and planted with decapitated flowers, revealed both the presence of children and their varying ages. But such evidence was hardly ever accompanied by childish shouts or laughter, and my home, though warm and full, bore an odd resemblance to those houses that, once the holidays have come to an end, are suddenly emptied of joy. The silence, the muted breeze of the enclosed garden, the pages of the book stirred only by invisible fingers, all seemed to be asking, "Where are the children?"

It was then, from beneath the ancient iron trellis sagging to the left under the wistaria, that my mother would make her appearance, small and plump in those days when age had not yet wasted her. She would scan the thick green clumps and, raising her head, fling her call into the air: "Children! Where are the children?"

Where indeed? Nowhere. My mother's cry would ring through the garden, striking the great wall of the barn and returning to her as a faint and exhausted echo. "Where . . . ? Children . . . ?"

Nowhere. My mother would throw back her head and gaze heavenward, as though waiting for a flock of winged children to alight from the skies. After a moment she would repeat her call; then, grown tired of questioning the heavens, she would crack a dry poppyhead with her fingernail, rub the greenfly from a rose shoot, fill her pockets with unripe walnuts, and return to the house, shaking her head over the vanished children.

And all the while, from among the leaves of the walnut tree above her, gleamed the pale, pointed face of a child, who lay stretched like a tomcat along a big branch and never uttered a word. A less shortsighted mother might well have suspected that the spasmodic salutations exchanged by the twin tops of the two firs were due to some influence other than that of the sudden October squalls! And in the square dormer, above the pulley for hauling up fodder, would she not have perceived, if she had screwed up her eyes, two pale patches in the hay —the face of a young boy and his book?

But she had given up looking for us, had despaired of trying to reach us. Our curious turbulence was never accompanied by any sound. I do not believe there can ever have been children so active and so mute. Looking back at what we were, I am amazed. No one had imposed upon us either our cheerful silence or our limited sociability. My nineteen-year-old brother, engrossed in constructing some hydrotherapeutic apparatus out of linen bladders, strands of wire, and glass tubes, never prevented the younger, aged fourteen, from disemboweling a watch or from transposing on the piano, with never a false note, a melody or an air from a symphony heard at a concert in the county town. He did not even interfere with his junior's incomprehensible passion for decorating the garden with little tombstones cut out of cardboard, and each inscribed, beneath the sign of the cross, with the names, epitaph, and genealogy of the imaginary person deceased.

My sister with the too-long hair could read forever and with never a pause; the two boys would brush past her as though they did not see the young girl sitting ab-

stracted and entranced, and never bother her. When I
was small, I was at liberty to keep up as best I could with
my long-legged brothers as they ranged the woods in pur-
suit of swallowtails, white admirals, and purple emperors,
or hunted for grass snakes, or gathered armfuls of the tall
July foxgloves, which grew in the clearings already aglow
with patches of purple heather. But I followed them in
silence, picking blackberries, bird cherries, a chance wild
flower, or roving the hedgerows and waterlogged meadows
like an independent dog out hunting on its own.

"Where are the children?" She would suddenly appear
like an oversolicitous mother-bitch breathlessly pursuing
her constant quest, head lifted and scenting the breeze.
Sometimes her white linen sleeves bore witness that she
had come from kneading dough for cakes or making the
pudding that had a velvety hot sauce of rum and
jam. If she had been washing the Havanese bitch, she
would be enveloped in a long blue apron, and sometimes
she would be waving a banner of rustling yellow paper,
the paper used around the butcher's meat, which meant
that she hoped to reassemble, at the same time as her
elusive children, her carnivorous family of vagabond cats.

To her traditional cry she would add in the same anxious and appealing key a reminder of the time of day.
"Four o'clock, and they haven't come in for their
snack! Where are the children . . . ?" "Half-past six!
Will they come home to dinner? Where are the children . . . ?" That lovely voice; how I should weep for joy
if I could hear it now! Our only sin, our single misdeed,
was silence, and a kind of miraculous vanishing. For
perfectly innocent reasons, for the sake of a liberty that
no one denied us, we clambered over the railing, leaving behind our shoes, and returned by way of an unnec-
essary ladder or a neighbor's low wall.

Our anxious mother's keen sense of smell would discover on us traces of wild garlic from a distant ravine
or of marsh mint from a treacherous bog. The dripping
pocket of one of the boys would disgorge the bathing
shorts worn in malarial ponds, and the "little one," cut
about the knees and skinned at the elbows, would be
bleeding complacently under plasters of cobweb and wild
pepper bound on with rushes.

"Tomorrow I shall keep you locked up! All of you, do you hear, every single one of you!"

Tomorrow! The next day the eldest, slipping on the slated roof where he was fitting a tank, broke his collarbone and remained at the foot of the wall, waiting, politely silent and half unconscious, until someone came to pick him up. The next day a fifteen-foot ladder crashed right onto the forehead of the younger son, who never uttered a cry but brought home with becoming modesty a lump like a purple egg between his eyes.

"Where are the children?"

Two are at rest. The others grow older day by day. If there be a place of waiting after this life, then surely she who so often waited for us has not ceased to tremble for those two who are yet alive.

For the eldest of us all, at any rate, she is through with looking at the dark windowpane every evening and saying, "I feel that child is not happy. I feel she is suffering." And for the elder of the boys she no longer listens, breathlessly, to the wheels of a doctor's carriage coming over the snow at night or to the hoofbeats of the gray mare.

But I know that for the two who remain, she seeks and wanders still, invisible, tormented by her inability to watch over them enough.

"Where, oh where are the children . . . ?"

[TRANSLATED BY UNA TROUBRIDGE AND ENID MCLEOD]

Jealousy

"There's nothing for dinner tonight. Tricotet hadn't yet killed this morning. He was going to kill at noon. I'm going to the butcher's myself, just as I am. What a nuisance! Why should one have to eat? And what shall we eat this evening?"

My mother stands, utterly discouraged, by the window. She is wearing her "at home" dress of dotted sateen, her silver brooch with twin angels encircling the portrait of a child, her spectacles on a chain and her lorgnette suspended from a black silk cord that catches on every door key, breaks on every drawer handle, and has been re-knotted a score of times. She looks at each of us in turn, hopelessly. She is well aware that not one of us will make a useful suggestion. If appealed to, my father will reply, "Raw tomatoes with plenty of pepper."

"Red cabbage and vinegar" would have been the contribution of my elder brother, Achille, whose medical studies keep him in Paris.

My second brother, Léo, will ask for "A big bowl of chocolate!" And I, bounding into the air because I so often forget that I am past fifteen, will clamor for "Fried potatoes! Fried potatoes! And walnuts with cheese!"

It appears, however, that fried potatoes, chocolate, tomatoes, and red cabbage do not constitute "a dinner."

"But why, Mother?"

"Don't ask foolish questions!"

She is absorbed in her problem. She has already seized hold of the black cane basket with a double lid and is about to set forth, just as she is, wearing her wide-brimmed garden hat, scorched by three summers, its little crown trimmed with a dark brown ruche, and her gardening apron, in one pocket of which the curved beak of her pruning shears has poked a hole. Some dry love-

47

in-the-mist seeds in a twist of paper in the bottom of the other pocket make a sound like rain and fingernails scratching silk as she walks.

In my vanity on her behalf, I cry out after her, "Mother, take off your apron!"

Without stopping, she turns toward me that face, framed by its bands of hair, which looks its full fifty-five years when she is sad and when she is gay would still pass for thirty.

"What for? I'm only going to the Rue de la Roche."

"Can't you leave your mother alone?" grumbles my father into his beard. "By the way, where is she going?"

"To Léonore's, for the dinner."

"Aren't you going with her?"

"No. I don't feel like it today."

There are days when Léonore's shop, with its knives, its hacking knife, and its bulging bullocks' lungs, pink as the pulpy flesh of a begonia, iridescent as they sway in the breeze, delight me as much as would a confectioner's. Léonore cuts me a slice of salted bacon and hands me the transparent rasher between the tips of her cold fingers. In the butcher's garden, Marie Tricotet, though born on the same day as myself, still derives amusement from pricking the unemptied bladders of pigs or calves and treading on them to "make a fountain." The horrid sound of skin being torn from newly killed flesh, the roundness of kidneys—brown fruit nestling in their immaculate padding of rosy lard—arouse in me a complex repugnance that attracts me while I do my best to hide it. But the delicate fat that remains in the hollow of the little cloven pig's foot when the heat of the fire bursts it open, that I eat as a wholesome delicacy! No matter. Today I have no wish to follow my mother.

My father does not insist, but hoists himself nimbly onto his one leg, grasps his crutch and his stick, and goes upstairs to the library. Before going, he meticulously folds the newspaper, Le Temps, hides it under the cushion of his armchair, and thrusts the bright blue-covered La Nature into the pocket of his long overcoat. His small Cossack eye, gleaming beneath an eyebrow of hempen gray, rakes the table for printed provender that will vanish to the library and be seen no more. But we, well trained in this little game, have left him nothing to take.

"You haven't seen the *Mercure de France?*"

"No, Father."

"Nor the *Revue Bleue?*"

"No, Father."

He glares at his children with the eyes of an inquisitor. "I should like to know who it is in this house who——"

He relieves his feelings in gloomy and impersonal conjecture, embellished with venomous expletives. His house has become *this* house, a domain of disorder, wherein *these* "base-born" children profess contempt for the written word, encouraged, moreover, by *that* woman. . . .

"Which reminds me, where is that woman now?"

"Why she's gone to Léonore's, Father."

"Again?"

"But she just left. . . ."

He pulls out his watch, consults it as though he were going to bed, and for want of anything better, grabs a two-day-old copy of *L'Office de Publicité* before going up to the library. With his right hand he keeps a firm grip on the crosspiece of the crutch, which acts as a prop for his right armpit: in his other he has only a stick. As it dies away I listen to that firm, regular rhythm of two sticks and a single foot, which has soothed me all my childhood. But suddenly, today, a new uneasiness assails me because for the first time I have noticed the prominent veins and wrinkles on my father's strikingly white hands, and how the fringe of thick hair at the nape of his neck has faded just lately. Can it really be true that he will soon be sixty years old?

It is cool and melancholy on the front steps, where I wait for my mother's return. At last I hear the sound of her neat little footsteps on the Rue de la Roche, and I am surprised at how happy it makes me feel. She comes around the corner and down the hill toward me, preceded by the dog—the horror from Patasson's—and she is in a hurry.

"Let me pass, darling! If I don't give this shoulder of mutton to Henriette to roast at once, we shall be eating shoe leather. Where's your father?"

I follow her, vaguely disturbed for the first time that she should be worrying about my father. Since she left him only half an hour ago and he scarcely ever goes out, she knows perfectly well where he is. There would have been more sense, for instance, had she said to me, "Minet-Chéri, you're looking pale. Minet-Chéri, what's the matter?"

Without replying, I watch her throw off her old garden hat with a youthful gesture that reveals her gray hair and her face, fresh colored, but marked here and there with ineffaceable lines. Is it possible—why, yes, after all, I am the youngest of the four children—is it possible that my mother is nearly fifty-four? I never think about it. I should like to forget it.

Here comes the man on whom her thoughts are centered. Here he comes, bristling, his beard tilted aggressively. He has been listening for the bang of the closing front door; he has come down from his aerie.

"There you are! You've taken your time about it." She turns on him, quick as a cat.

"Taken my time? Are you trying to be funny? I've simply been there and come straight back."

"Back from where? From Léonore's?"

"Of course not. I had to go to Corneau's for——"

"For his sheep's eyes? And his comments on the weather?"

"Don't be tiresome! Then I had to go get the black-currant tea at Cholet's."

The small Cossack eye darts a piercing look.

"Aha! At Cholet's!"

My father throws his head back and runs his hand through his thick hair, which is almost white.

"Aha! At Cholet's! And did you happen to notice that he's losing his hair and that you can see his pate?"

"No. I didn't notice it."

"You didn't notice it? No, of course not! You were far too busy making eyes at the village beaux having a drink at the café opposite, and at Mabilat's two sons!"

"Oh! This is too much! I, I making eyes at Mabilat's sons! I honestly don't know how you dare! I swear to you I didn't even turn my head in the direction of his place. And the proof of that is . . ."

Indignantly my mother folds her hands, still pretty although aging and weather-beaten, over a bosom held up

by a whalebone corset. Blushing beneath the strands of
her graying hair, her chin trembling with resentment, this
little elderly lady is charming when she defends herself
without so much as a smile against the accusations of a
jealous sexagenarian. Nor does he smile either as he goes
on to accuse her now of "gallivanting." But I can still smile
at their quarrels because I am only fifteen and have not
yet divined the ferocity of love beneath his old man's
eyebrows, or the blushes of adolescence upon her fading
cheeks.

[TRANSLATED BY UNA TROUBRIDGE AND ENID McLEOD]

The Priest on the Wall

"What are you thinking about, Bel-Gazou?"

"Nothing, Mother."

An excellent answer. The same that I invariably gave when I was her age, and was known by the same name in the intimacy of my home. Whence comes the name and why did my father call me by it, long ago? No doubt it is the Provençal form of *beau gazouillis*—pretty prattle —but it would not disgrace the hero or the heroine of a Persian fairy tale.

"Nothing, Mother." It is not a bad thing that children should occasionally, and politely, put parents in their place. All temples are sacred. How dull and tactless I must sometimes seem to my Bel-Gazou of today! My question falls like a stone and cracks the magic mirror that reflects, surrounded by its favorite phantoms, the image of a child that I shall never see. I know that in her father's eyes my daughter is a kind of little female paladin who rules over her own lands, brandishing a hazel spear, cleaving haystacks, and driving the flock before her as though she were taking it on a crusade. I know that a smile from her enchants him, and that when he whispers "Doesn't she look adorable right now?" it is because, at that particular moment, he sees on her childish features the amazing resemblance to a certain masculine face.

I know that to her faithful nurse, my Bel-Gazou is alternately the center of the universe, a consummate masterpiece, a possessed monster from whom the devil must hourly be exorcised, a champion runner, a dizzy abyss of perversity, a *dear little one*,* and a baby rabbit. But who will tell me how my daughter appears to herself?

---

* These three words are in English in the original.

52

At her age—not quite eight years old—I was a priest on a wall, the thick, high wall that divided the garden from the farmyard, and of which the flat, tiled summit, broad as a pavement, served me as promenade and terrace, inaccessible to the ordinary run of mortals. Yes, I mean it; a priest on a wall. Why should it seem incredible? I was a priest without religious duties or parish, without any irreverent travesty, but nonetheless, unknown to all, a priest. A priest just as you, sir, happen to be bald, or you, madam, arthritic.

The word "presbytery" had chanced that year to drop into my sensitive ears and had wrought havoc.

"It's undoubtedly the most cheerful presbytery that I know of. . . ." someone had said in my hearing.

Far from asking one of my relations: "What is a presbytery?" I had absorbed the mysterious word with its harsh and spiky beginning and the brisk trot of its final syllables. Enriched by a secret and a doubt, I slept on the *word* and bore it off to my wall. "Presbytery!" I would shout it over the roof of the hen house and Miton's garden, toward the perpetually misty horizon of Moutiers. From the summit of my wall, the word rang out as a malediction: "Begone! You are all presbyteries!" I shouted to invisible outlaws.

Later on, the word lost some of its venom and I began to suspect that "presbytery" might very possibly be the scientific term for a certain little yellow-and-black-striped snail. A chance remark was to be my undoing, in one of those moments wherein a child, however solemn or fanciful she may be, fleetingly resembles the picture made of her by grown-up people.

"Mother! Look what a lovely little presbytery I've found!"

"A lovely little—what?"

"A lovely little presb—"

I broke off, but too late. I had to learn—"I sometimes wonder if this child is all there"—that of which I was so anxious to remain in ignorance, and to "call things by their proper names . . ."

"Come now, a presbytery is a priest's house."

"A priest's house . . . Then Monsieur Millot, the priest, lives in a presbytery?"

"Why, of course he does. . . . Keep your mouth shut and breathe through your nose. . . . Of course he does. . . ."

I still tried to react. . . . I fought against the intrusion, closely hugging the tatters of my absurdity. I longed to compel Monsieur Millot to inhabit, for as long as I wished him to, the empty shell of the little "presbytery" snail. . . .

"When will you learn to keep your mouth shut when you're not speaking? What are you thinking about?"

"Nothing, Mother. . . ."

And then I yielded. I was cowardly and I compromised with my disappointment. Throwing away the fragments of the little broken snail shell, I picked up the enchanting word and, climbing on to my narrow terrace, which was shaded by the old lilac trees and adorned with polished pebbles and scraps of colored glass like a thieving magpie's nest—I christened it the Presbytery and inducted myself as priest on the wall.

[TRANSLATED BY UNA TROUBRIDGE AND ENID MCLEOD]

My Mother and Illness

"What time is it? Eleven o'clock already! Didn't I say so? He'll be here in a minute. Give me the eau de cologne and the rough towel. And give me the little bottle of violet perfume too. Did I say violet perfume? There isn't any real violet perfume nowadays. They make it with orrisroot. Or do they even use that? But you don't care about that, Minet-Chéri. You don't like essence of violet. What's come over our daughters that they don't like essence of violet any more?

"Time was when a really refined woman never used any perfume but violet. That stuff you drench yourself with isn't respectable. You simply use it to put people off the scent. Yes, that's exactly it, to put them on the wrong scent! Your short hair, the blue you put on your eyelids, the eccentricities you indulge in on the stage—it's all, just like your perfume, to put people on the wrong scent. Yes it is. It's so that they will think you an unusual person with no prejudices. . . . Poor Minet-Chéri! But you don't take me in. . . . Take out my two wretched little braids. I put them up very tightly last night so that I would have a wave this morning. D'you know what I look like? An elderly indigent poet without talent. It's pretty hard to retain the characteristics of one's sex after a certain age. In my decline, two things distress me: the fact that I can no longer wash my little blue saucepan for boiling milk myself, and the sight of my own hand on the sheet. You'll understand later that one keeps on forgetting old age up to the very brink of the grave.

"Even illness can't force one to remember it. Every hour I say to myself: 'I have a pain in my back. The nape of my neck aches atrociously. I have no appetite. That digitalis goes to my head and makes me feel sick! I'm going to die, tonight, tomorrow, no matter when.

. . .' But I'm not always thinking of the ways in which age has altered me, and it's when I look at my hand that I realize the change. I'm astonished not to see under my eyes my little hand as it was when I was twenty. . . . Hush! Be quiet a moment and let me listen. I hear singing. . . . Ah! It's old Madame Lœuvrier's funeral. A good thing they're burying her at last! No, no, I'm not being brutal. I say 'a good thing' because she won't any longer be able to bother her poor fool of a daughter, who is fifty-five and has never dared to get married, for fear of her mother. Ah, parents! I do say it's a good thing that there should be one old woman the less on this earth.

"No, decidedly, I can't accustom myself to old age, neither my own nor other people's. And, seeing I'm seventy-one, I'd better give up trying, for I shall never succeed. Be a darling, Minet-Chéri, and push my bed nearer the window so that I can see old Madame Lœuvrier go by. I adore watching funerals pass. One can always learn something from them. What a crowd! That's because of the fine weather. It's a good excuse for a pleasant walk. If it had rained, she'd have had three cats for an escort, and Monsieur Miroux wouldn't have risked wetting that fine black-and-silver cope. And what piles of flowers! Oh, the vandals! They've simply massacred the sacron rose tree in the Lœuvriers' garden. Imagine killing all those young flowers for the sake of an old woman.

"And look, look at that great idiot of a daughter; I was sure of it: she's crying her heart out. Of course, that's only common sense; she has lost her torturer, her tormentor, the daily poison, the lack of which may well kill her. After her come what I call the vultures. Oh, those faces! There are days when I congratulate myself that I haven't got a cent to leave you. The very thought that I might be followed to my last home by a great redheaded lout like that nephew there; look at him—he'll spend his time now waiting for the daughter to die. . . .

"You children, at any rate, will miss me, I know. Whom will you write to twice a week, my poor Minet-Chéri? But it won't be so bad for you. After all, you've left me and built a nest for yourself far from me. But what about your elder brother, when he has to pass in front of my little house on his way back from his rounds and no longer finds his glass of red-currant syrup there and a rose to carry off between his teeth? Yes, yes, of course you love me, but you're a girl, a female creature of my own species, my rival. But in his heart I never had any rival. Is my hair all right? No, I won't wear a cap, only my Spanish lace kerchief; he'll be here in a minute. All that dingy crowd has kicked up the dust. It's hard to breathe.

"It's nearly noon, isn't it? If no one has held him up, your brother must be less than two miles away by now. Let the cat in; she too knows that it's nearly twelve o'clock. Every day after her morning walk she comes back afraid of finding me well again. To sleep on my bed, night and day, what an earthly paradise for her! This morning your brother had to go to Arnedon, Coulefeuilles, and then home by Saint-André. I never forget his rounds. I follow him, you see. At Arnedon he's taking care of the small son of the fair Arthémise. Those love children always suffer because their mothers have crushed them under their stays trying to hide them, more's the pity. Yet after all, a lovely unrepentant creature, big with child, is not such an outrageous sight.

"Listen—listen! There's the carriage at the top of the hill! Minet-Chéri, don't tell your brother that I had three attacks last night. In the first place, because I forbid you to. And if you don't tell him I'll give you the bracelet with the three turquoises. Now I want none of your reasons—they bore me. It has nothing whatever to do with honesty. To begin with, in any case, I know better than you do what honesty is. But at my age there's only one virtue: not to make people unhappy. Quick now, put the second pillow behind my back so that I shall be sitting up when he comes in. And the two roses there, in the glass. It doesn't smell like a shut-in old woman in here, does it? Am I flushed? He'll think I'm not so well as I was yesterday. I know I ought not to have talked so much. Close the shutter a little, and then be a dear, Minet-Chéri, and lend me your powder puff."

[Translated by Una Troubridge and Enid McLeod]

The Seamstress

"Do you mean to say your daughter is nine years old," said a friend of mine, "and she doesn't know how to sew? She really must learn to sew. In bad weather sewing is a better occupation for a child of that age than reading story books."

"Nine years old? And she can't sew?" said another friend. "When she was eight, my daughter embroidered this doily for me. Look at it. . . . Oh, I don't say it's fine needlework, but it's nicely done all the same. Nowadays my daughter cuts out her own underclothes. I can't bear anyone in my house fixing holes with pins!"

I meekly poured all this domestic wisdom over Bel-Gazou.

"You're nine years old and you don't know how to sew? You really must learn to sew, etc. . . ."

Flouting truth, I even added: "When I was eight years old, I remember I embroidered a doily. . . . Oh, it wasn't fine needlework, I dare say. . . . And then, in bad weather . . ."

She has therefore learned to sew. And although—with one bare sunburned leg tucked beneath her, and her body at ease in its bathing suit—she looks more like a cabin boy mending a net than an industrious little girl, she seems to experience no boyish repugnance. Her hands, stained the color of tobacco juice by sun and sea, hem in a way that seems contrary to nature; their version of the simple running stitch resembles the zigzag dotted lines of a road map, but she sews buttonholes and scallops with elegance and is severely critical of the embroidery of others.

She sews and kindly keeps me company if rain blurs the horizon of the sea. She also sews during the torrid hour when the spindle trees gather their circles of shadow

directly under them. Moreover, it sometimes happens that
a quarter of an hour before dinner, black in her white
dress—"Bel-Gazou, your hands and frock are clean, and
don't forget it!"—she sits down solemnly with a square
of material between her fingers. Then my friends ap-
plaud: "Just look at her! Isn't she good? That's right!
Your mother must be pleased!"

Her mother says nothing—great joys must be controlled. But should one feign them? I will speak the
truth: I don't much like my daughter sewing.

When she reads, she returns all bewildered and with
flaming cheeks from the island where the chest full of
precious stones is hidden, from the dismal castle where a
fair-haired orphan is being persecuted. She is soaking up a
tested and time-honored poison, whose effects have long
been familiar. If she draws or colors pictures, a semi-
articulate song issues from her lips, unceasing as the hum of
bees around a hedge. It is the same as the buzzing of
flies as they work, the slow waltz of the house painter,
the refrain of the spinner at her wheel. But Bel-Gazou
is silent when she sews, silent for hours on end, with her
mouth firmly closed, concealing her large, newly cut in-
cisors that bite into the moist heart of a fruit like little
saw-edged blades. She is silent, and she—why not write
down the word that frightens me?—she is thinking.

A new evil? A torment that I had not foreseen? Sitting
in a grassy dell or half buried in hot sand and gazing out
to sea, she is thinking, as well I know. She thinks rapidly
when she is listening, with a well-bred pretense of discretion, to remarks imprudently exchanged above her
head. But it would seem that with this needleplay she has
discovered the perfect means of adventuring, stitch by
stitch, point by point, along a road of risks and temptations. Silence . . . The hand armed with the steel dart
moves back and forth. Nothing will stop the unchecked
little explorer. At what moment must I utter the "Stop!"
that will brutally arrest her in full flight? Oh, for those
young embroiderers of bygone days, sitting on a hard little
stool in the shelter of their mother's ample skirts! Maternal
authority kept them there for years and years, never rising except to change the skein of silk or to elope with a
stranger. Think of Philomène de Watteville and her canvas

on which she embroidered the loss and the despair of
Albert Savarus. . . .

"What are you thinking about, Bel-Gazou?"

"Nothing, Mother. I'm counting the stitches."

Silence. The needle pierces the material. A coarse trail
of chainstitches follows very unevenly in its wake. Silence. . . .

"Mother?"

"Darling?"

"Is it only when people are married that a man can put
his arm around a lady's waist?"

"Yes. . . . No. . . . It depends. If they are very good
friends and have known each other a long time, you
understand . . . As I said before: it depends. Why do
you want to know?"

"For no particular reason, Mother."

Two stitches, ten misshapen chainstitches.

"Mother? Is Madame X married?"

"She has been. She is divorced."

"I see. And Monsieur F, is he married?"

"Why, of course he is; you know that."

"Oh! Yes. . . . Then it's all right if one of the two is
married?"

"What is all right?"

"To depend."

"One doesn't say 'To depend.' "

"But you said just now that it depended."

"But what has it got to do with you? Is it any concern of yours?"

"No, Mother."

I let it drop. I feel inadequate, self-conscious, displeased
with myself. I should have answered differently and I
could not think what to say.

Bel-Gazou also drops the subject; she sews. But she
pays little attention to her sewing, overlaying it with
pictures, associations of names and people, all the re-
sults of patient observation. A little later will come other
curiosities, other questions, and especially other silences.
Would to God that Bel-Gazou were the bewildered and
simple child who questions crudely, open-eyed! But she is
too near the truth, and too natural not to know as a birth-

right that all nature hesitates before that most majestic and most disturbing of instincts, and that it is right to tremble, to be silent and to lie when one draws near to it.

[TRANSLATED BY UNA TROUBRIDGE AND ENID MCLEOD]

The Savages, from Sido

"Savages, that's what they are," my mother used to say, "just savages. What can one do with such savages?" And she would shake her head.

Her discouragement was in part due to a deliberate and considered refusal to interfere and in part perhaps to an awareness of her own responsibility. She gazed at her two boys, the half brothers, and found them beautiful, especially the elder, the seventeen-year-old, with his chestnut hair and clear blue eyes and that crimson mouth that smiled only at us and a few pretty girls. But the dark one, at thirteen, was not bad either, with his hair that needed a cutting falling into his lead-blue eyes, which were like our father's.

Two light-footed savages, lean and bony, frugal like their parents; instead of meat preferring brown bread, hard cheese, salads, fresh eggs, and leek or pumpkin pies. Temperate and pure they were—true savages indeed.

"What shall I do with them?" sighed my mother. By their very gentleness they evaded all attempts to interfere with them or separate them. The elder was the leader, while the younger mingled with his enthusiasm a sense of fantasy that cut him off from the world. But the elder knew he was soon to begin his medical studies, whereas the younger silently hoped that for him nothing ever would begin, except the next day, except the hour when he could escape from civilized constraint, except complete freedom to dream and remain silent. He is hoping still.

They rarely played, unless indeed it was a kind of game to spurn all but the flower, the cream of that radiant village world and choose only the most solitary, the untrodden ways, all that renews its youth and springs afresh far from the haunts of men. One never saw them dressed up like Robinson Crusoe or disguised as warriors or acting plays they had made up themselves. On one occasion when the younger joined a group of stagestruck boys, the only part he would accept was a silent one: the part of the "idiot boy."

I have to go back to my mother's stories when, like all of us as we grow older, I am seized with the itch to possess the secrets of a being who has vanished forever: to discover the "key" to his turbulent youth, each hour of it swallowed up by the succeeding hour, yet perpetually renewing itself; to point, thanks to some miraculous guidance, with absolute certainty to that high place whence he allowed himself to fall down to the dead level of mankind; and to spell out the names of his evil stars.

I have said farewell to the dead, to the peerless elder brother; but I turn to my mother's stories and to the memories of my own earlier childhood when I want to find out what went into the making of the sixty-year-old with the gray mustache who glides into my home at nightfall, opens my watch to see the second hand flipping around, cuts a foreign stamp from a crumpled envelope, inhales, as though he had been short of breath all day, a long draft of music from the Gramophone, and disappears without having said a word.

That graying man has grown out of a little boy of six who used to follow mendicant musicians when they passed through our village. Once he followed a one-eyed clarinetist as far as Saints, a distance of almost four miles, and by the time he got back my mother was having all the local wells dragged. He listened good-naturedly to her reproaches and complaints, for he rarely lost his temper. When he had heard the last of his mother's fears, he went to the piano and faithfully reproduced all the clarinetist's tunes, enriching them with simple but perfectly correct little harmonies. He did the same with the tunes of the merry-go-round at the Easter fair on Low Sunday, and indeed with any kind of music, which he would intercept as though it were a flying message.

"He must study technique and harmony," my mother would say. "He's even more gifted than his elder brother. He might become an artist; who can tell?"

When he was six she still believed that she had it in

her power to help or hinder him. He was such an inoffensive little boy, she could find no fault with him, except his tendency to disappear. Small of stature, agile, and very well balanced, by some magic he was suddenly not present. Where to find him? The favorite haunts of the ordinary small boys—the skating rink and the Place du Grand-Jeu pounded flat by childish feet—had not even seen him pass their way. He was more likely to be found in the ancient cold-storage room of the castle, a rough-hewn vault four centuries old, or in the case of the town clock in the Place du Marché, or else dogging the piano tuner who came once a year from the county town to attend to the four "instruments" in our village. "What make is your instrument?" "Madame Vallée's going to exchange her instrument." "Mademoiselle Philippon's instrument is worn out!"

Even now, I confess, the word "instrument" still conjures up in my memory, to the exclusion of all other images, that of a mahogany construction preserved in dim provincial parlors, and brandishing, like an altar, two bronze arms with green candles.

Yes, indeed, an inoffensive little boy who never made any demands except one evening, when he said: "I'd like some dried plums and some hazelnuts."

"The grocery is closed," my mother answered. "Go to sleep now and you shall have some tomorrow."

The next evening the gentle little boy asked again: "I'd like some dried plums and some hazelnuts."

"Why didn't you buy them during the day?" my mother exclaimed impatiently. "Go to bed!"

The next five to ten evenings brought the same teasing, and my mother amply proved what an exceptional mother she was. For she did not spank the persistent child, who was perhaps hoping that she would, or at least counting on a maternal outburst of cries, due to exasperated nerves, and maledictions—an evening uproar that would postpone bedtime. One evening after many such, he assumed his daily expression of childish obstinacy and his reasonable tone of voice: "Mother?"

"Yes," Mother answered.

"Mother, I'd like——"

"Here they are," said she. She got up, fetched for him

from the bottomless cupboard next to the chimney piece two sacks as big as newborn babes, set them down on each side of her little boy, and remarked: "When those are finished, you can buy some more."

He looked up at her, pale and offended beneath his black hair. "It's for you. Take it," my mother insisted. He was the first to lose his composure, and he burst into tears: "But—but—I don't like them!" he sobbed.

Sido bent over him, as attentive as if he were an egg cracking as it began to hatch or an unknown variety of rose or a messenger from the other hemisphere: "You don't like them? Then what was it you wanted?"

Rashly he confessed: "I wanted to ask for them."

Every three months my mother used to go to Auxerre, and when she was setting out in the carriage at two in the morning, she nearly always gave in to the pleadings of the baby of the family. The good fortune of being born last allowed me to keep for a long time this privileged position of being the baby-of-the-family and my place in the back seat of the carriage. But before me it had been occupied for ten years by that agile and elusive little boy. On arrival at the county town he always vanished, evading every attempt to keep an eye on him. He disappeared all over the place, in the cathedral, in the clock tower, and especially in a big grocer's shop while they were packing up the sugar loaf in its oblique wrapping of indigo paper, the ten pounds of chocolate, the vanilla, the cinnamon, the nutmeg, the rum for grog, the black pepper, and the white soap. My mother gave the shrill cry of a vixen: "Hi! Where is he?"

"Who, Madame Colette?"

"My little boy! Did anyone see him go out?"

No one had seen him go out, and since there were no wells, my mother was already peering into the vats of oil and the casks of pickled brine.

This time it did not take them long to find him. He was up near the ceiling, right at the top of one of the cast-iron spiral pillars. Gripping this between his thighs and feet, like a native up a coconut palm, he was fiddling with and listening to the works of a big, hanging clock with a flat, owl face, which was screwed on to the main beam.

When ordinary parents produce exceptional children, they are often so dazzled by them that they push them into careers that they consider superior, even if it takes some lusty kicks on their behinds to achieve this result. My mother found it quite natural, and indeed obligatory, that the children she had produced should be miracles; but it was also her view that "God helps those who help themselves," and to reassure herself she was given to asserting: "Achille will be a doctor. But Léo will never get away from music. As for the little one . . ." At that point she would raise her eyebrows, interrogate the clouds, and postpone me till later.

The strange exception was my elder sister, about whose future there was never any discussion, although she was already of age. But she was a stranger to us, and indeed to everyone, isolated by her own choice in the bosom of her own family.

"Juliette is a different kind of savage," my mother sighed. "A kind that no one can understand, not even I."

She was wrong about us, or rather we disappointed her, more than once. But she never lost heart; she merely supplied us with a fresh halo. All the same she could never admit that her second son had got away, as she put it, from music, for in many a letter dating from the end of her life I read: *"Do you know if Léo has any time to practice his piano? He ought not to neglect such an extraordinary gift; I shall never tire of insisting on that."* At the time when my mother was writing me these letters, my brother was forty-four years old.

Whatever she might say, he did get away from music, then from his pharmaceutical studies, and then successively from everything—from everything except his own elfin past. In my eyes he has not changed; he is an elf of sixty-three. He is attached to nothing but his native place, like an elf to some tutelary mushroom, or a leaf bent like a roof. Elves, we know, live on very little and despise the coarse garments of mortals: mine sometimes wanders about without a tie and with flowing locks. From behind he looks not unlike an empty overcoat, straying bewitched.

He has deliberately chosen his humble, clerical job because it keeps sitting at a table that part of himself that

looks deceptively like a man. All the rest of him is free to
sing, listen to orchestras, compose, and fly back to the
past, to rejoin the small boy of six who opened every
watch, haunted town clocks, collected epitaphs, never
tired of stamping on spongy mosses, and played the piano
from birth. He finds him again without difficulty, slips
into the light and nimble little body that he never leaves
long, and roams through a country of the mind, where
all is to the measure and liking of one who for sixty
years has triumphantly remained a child.

Alas, no child is invulnerable, and this one sometimes
comes back to me badly hurt because he has tried to confront his well-remembered dream with a reality that
betrays it.

One dripping evening, when every arcade of the Palais
Royal was hung with great draperies of water and
shadow, he came to call on me. I had not seen him for
months. He sat down, wet through, beside my fire, absentmindedly took some of his curious nourishment—fon-
dants, very sugary cakes, and syrup—opened my watch,
then my alarm clock, listened to them for a long time,
and said nothing.

I stole an occasional glance at his long face with its
nearly white mustache, my father's blue eyes, and a
coarser version of Sido's nose—inherited features con-
nected by bony modeling and unfamiliar muscles whose
origin I could not trace. A long and gentle face it was, in
the firelight, gentle and distressed. But the habits and
customs of childhood—reserve, discretion, and liberty—
persist so strongly between us that I asked my brother no
questions.

When he had finished drying the sad, rain-sodden wings
that he calls his coat, he smoked with half-shut eyes,
rubbed his hands, which were shriveled and red for lack
of gloves and hot water in all kinds of weather, and
spoke: "Say there!"

"Yes?"

"I've been *back there,* did you know?"

"No! When?"

"I've just returned."

"Oh!" said I with admiration. "You've been to Saint-
Sauveur? How?"

He gave me a conceited little look. "Charles Faroux took me by car."

"My dear! Was it looking lovely at this time of year?"

"Not bad," he said shortly.

His nostrils dilated and he relapsed into silence and gloom. I went back to my writing.

"Say there!"

"Yes?"

"Back there, I went to Roches, you remember?"

A steep path of yellow sand rose in my memory like a serpent against a windowpane. "Oh, how does it look? And the wood at the summit? And the little pavilion? And the foxgloves—the heather—"

My brother whistled. "Gone. Cut down. Nothing left. A clean sweep. You can see the earth. You can see—" He scythed the air with the side of his hand and shrugged derisively, staring into the fire. I respected this derision and did not imitate it. But the old elf, quivering in his pain, could no longer keep silence. Profiting by the half-light of the glowing fire, he whispered: "And that's not all. I went to the Cour du Pâté too."

Back to my mind you rush, childish name for a warm terrace beside a ruined castle, arches of climbing roses spindly with age, shadow and scent of flowering ivy falling from the Saracen tower, and stubborn, rusty gates that close the Cour du Pâté . . .

"And then, my dear, and then?"

My brother gathered himself together.

"Just a moment," he ordered me. "We must begin at the beginning. I arrive at the castle. It's still a home for old people, since that was what Victor Gandrille wished. That's all right, I've nothing against that. I enter the park by the lower entrance, the one near Madame Billette's——"

"Surely not Madame Billette? Why, she must have been dead for at least fifty years!"

"Maybe," said my brother with indifference. "Yes, I suppose that's why they told me another name—an impossible name. If *they* think I'm going to remember names that I don't know! Well then, I enter by the lower entrance and go up the lime avenue. Now that I come to think of it, the dogs didn't bark when I pushed the door open—" he remarked irritably.

"Come now, my dear, they couldn't have been the same dogs. Just think."

"All right, all right—it's a mere detail. I'll say nothing about the potatoes that *they've* planted in place of the bleeding hearts and poppies. I won't even mention," he went on in an intolerant voice, "the wiring around the lawns, a fence of wire netting—you can hardly believe your eyes. It appears it's for the cows. The cows!"

He rocked one of his knees between his clasped hands and whistled with a professional air that suited him about as well as a top hat.

"And was that all, my dear?"

"Just a moment!" he said again, fiercely. "As I said, I go up toward the canal—if indeed," he added, with studied precision, "I dare call canal that filthy pond, that soup of mosquitoes and cow dung. But never mind. So on I go to the Cour du Pâté, and—"

"And?"

He turned toward me, without seeing me, with a vindictive smile.

"I'll admit that at first I wasn't particularly pleased that *they* should have turned the first court—the one before the gate and behind the stables—into a kind of drying ground for the washing. Yes, I'll admit that! But I didn't pay much attention to it because I was waiting for 'the moment of the gate.' "

"What moment of the gate?"

He snapped his fingers impatiently.

"Oh, come now! You see the knob of the gate?"

I could indeed see it—of shiny, black cast iron—as though I were about to grasp it.

"Well, as long as I've known it, when you turn it like that"—he mimicked the gesture—"and let go of the gate, it opens through its own weight and as it swings it says—"

"Ee-ee-ee-ang," we sang in unison, on four notes.

"That's right," said my brother, frantically jiggling his left knee. "I turned it. I let the gate go. I listened. D'you know what *they've* done?"

"No."

"*They've* oiled the gate," he said coldly.

He left almost immediately. He had nothing else to say to me. He folded the damp membranes of his voluminous garment about him and took off, the poorer by four notes. Henceforth his musician's ear would strain in vain to catch that most delicate of offertories, composed by an ancient gate, a grain of sand, and a trace of rust, and dedicated to the one untamed child who was worthy of it.

"What's your score with Mérimée?"

"He owes me a nickel."

"Golly!" exclaimed the elder.

"Yes, but," went on the younger, "I owe a quarter."

"What on?"

"On a Victor Hugo."

"Which one?"

"*Chansons des rues et des bois* and I forget what else. The dirty dog!"

"And what's more I'll bet you skipped," crowed the elder. "Fork over the quarter!"

"Where d'you suppose I'm going to get hold of them? I haven't a cent."

"Ask Mother."

"Oh!"

"Then ask Father. Tell him it's to buy cigarettes and that you're asking him unbeknown to mother, and he'll give them to you."

"But what if he doesn't?"

"Then you'll be fined. Three cents for the delay!"

The two savages, who read as adolescents did read in those days, that is to say, to excess and with frenzy, day and night, in the tops of trees and in haylofts, had put a taboo on the word *mignonne,* which they pronounced "minionne" with a hideous, twisted grimace, followed by a pretense of retching. Every *mignonne,* doomed to execration, discovered in each new book brought a penny into the kitty. On the other hand, an "uncontaminated" book won back a nickel for its reader. The agreement had been in force for two months, and if any money remained at the end of the term it would pay for "feasts," butterfly nets, or a gudgeon trap.

My youth—I was eight—excluded me from the partnership. According to my two brothers, it was too short a time since I had left off scraping the long, tear-shaped drips from the candles, so as to eat them, and the two boys still called me "the Cossack's child." All the same, I knew how to say "minionne" with a twist of my mouth, and make vomiting noises after, and I was learning how to assess novelists according to the new rulings.

"Dickens pays very good dividends," said one savage.

"Dickens shouldn't count," the other objected. "It's a translation, and the translator defrauds us."

"Then Edgar Allan Poe doesn't count either?"

"Mm. If we were sensible we'd exclude history books too. They pay a nickel each, that's for sure. They can't say the Revolution was 'mignonne'—euh! Charlotte Corday isn't 'mignonne'—euh! Mérimée ought to be excluded because he wrote the *Chronique de Charles IX.*"

"Well then, what would you do about *Le Collier de la Reine?*"

"That counts. It's a novel pure and simple."

"And the Balzacs about Catherine de Medici?"

"Don't be silly. Of course they count."

"Oh no they don't, fellow, excuse me!"

"My dear fellow, on your honor now . . . Shut up, there's someone coming."

They never quarreled. Stretched full length along the top of the wall, they would roast in the afternoon sun, arguing hotly but never hurting each other. They would allow me a place on the gently inclined stone coping of the wall. From there we commanded the Rue des Vignes, a deserted lane leading to the kitchen gardens scattered about the valley of Saint-Jean. At the sound of footsteps, no matter how far off, my brothers would fall silent, craftily flatten themselves close against the wall, and thrust out their chins over the primordial foe—their fellow creature.

"It's nothing; only Chebrier going to his kitchen garden," announced the younger.

Forgetting their argument for a moment, they basked in the still-warm air and the slanting light. Other footsteps, quick and distinct, rang out on the flint cobbles. A lilac bodice and a mop of frizzy, copper-red hair lit up the top of the street.

"Yah! The redhead!" whispered the younger. "Yah! Carrots!"

He was only fourteen and he had a grudge against "girls" whom he found altogether too garish and dazzling.

"It's Flore Chebrier going to meet her father," said my elder brother when the gold and lilac had faded out at the end of the street. "She certainly has changed!"

His junior, lying on his stomach, laid his chin on his folded arms. He blinked disdainfully and pouted his lips, already as round and full as those of the little Winds on old nautical maps.

"Carrots, that's what she is! And ginger! Fire! Fire!" he cried rudely, like any jealous schoolboy.

The elder shrugged his shoulders. "You're no judge of blonds," he said. "Personally, I think she's very—yes, really very, very mignonne. . . ."

A shout of boyish laughter, in a cracked voice beginning to break, greeted the accursed word, uttered so caressingly in the dreamy voice of the elder, the charmer with the gray eyes. I heard a scuffle on the wall, the nails of shoes scraping the stone, the soft thud of entwined bodies falling on the yielding, freshly hoed earth at the foot of the apricot trees. But good sense prevailed at once and they let go of each other.

They never had fought or called each other names, and I think they already knew that that mass of red hair and the lilac bodice, wonders to be had for the asking, would never count for a joint wager or find a place among their curious and modest delights. So back they went, their steps well matched, to their cork "display boards," where the swallowtail butterflies were drying, to the fountain they were building, and to a "system" for distilling marsh mint, an unreliable contraption that removed the scent of the mint from the distilled product, but preserved intact the smell of the marsh.

Those wild spirits of theirs were not always harmless. The age we call awkward and the growing pains it inflicts on young bodies exact occasional sacrifices. My brothers had to have a victim. They chose a school friend who used to come to the neighboring district for the holidays. Mathieu M. had no failings and no great merits either. Friendly, nicely dressed, rather towheaded, the mere sight of him roused in my two brothers a willfulness like that of a pregnant woman. And because of that, he attached himself passionately to the two arrogant savages, who, with their canvas shoes and their straw hats, despised his ties. The elder could find nothing harsh enough for this "notary's son," and the younger, following his lead and anxious to go one better, would tear holes in his handkerchief and turn his already too-short trousers up higher still, to welcome Mathieu when, neatly gloved, he got off his tricycle.

"I've brought the score of *Les Noces de Jeannette*," the affectionate victim would call out when he was still some way off, "and the German edition of Beethoven's symphonies, arranged as duets!"

Gloomily, the elder, the fresh-faced, barbarian, would eye the intruder, commonplace child of commonplace parents, whom no dark mood ever touched, who never harbored a longing for solitude and was a stranger to intolerance, and who now became flustered under that look and began to plead: "Wouldn't you like to play duets for a while with me?"

"With you, no; without you, yes."

"Then I'll turn the pages."

The one submissive and the other inexplicably spiteful and threatening, they were hopelessly incompatible; but Mathieu M., patient as an ill-treated wife, never tired of coming back again.

One day the savages took themselves off immediately after lunch and did not return until evening. They seemed tired and excited, and flung themselves down, steaming hot, on the two old sofas covered in green rep.

"Where have you been to get into that state?" my mother asked.

"Miles away," the elder replied pleasantly.

"Mathieu's been here and he seemed surprised not to find you."

"It doesn't take much to surprise that boy."

When they were alone with me, my two brothers began to talk. I never counted, and besides, they had brought me up never to tell tales. I learned that, hidden in a wood overlooking the road from Saint-F., they had not revealed their presence when Mathieu went by. I was not much interested in the details they kept going over and over: "When I heard his tricycle bell . . ." began the younger.

"Go on, I heard it much farther off than you did."

"You can't prove that! D'you remember the moment when he stopped right under our noses to wipe off the sweat?"

They were conversing almost in an undertone, lying on their backs with their eyes on the ceiling. The elder became excited: "And how! That little animal kept looking left and right as though he could smell us."

"You know, that's pretty good, isn't it? Pretty odd, I mean. D'you really think it was we who stopped him by looking at him? He certainly looked very bothered and strange."

The eyes of the elder darkened. "Could be. He had his tartan tie on. I always thought that tie would cause an accident one day."

I flung myself between them, eager for sensation: "Go on. What happened? What accident was there?"

They both gave me the coldest of stares. "Where on earth has this creature sprung from? What's she want with her accident?"

"But it was you who just said—"

They got up and sat down, sniggering in collusion: "Nothing happened," said the elder at last. "What did you expect to happen? We let Mathieu go by and we had a lot of fun."

"Is that all?" I said, disappointed.

The younger leaped to his feet and began to dance up and down, no longer able to contain himself.

"Yes, that's all! You can't understand! We were lying there and we had him on a level with our chins! Him and his tie and his side part, his cuffs and his shiny nose! Oh my, it was amazing!"

He bent over his elder brother and brushed him with his nose like a little animal: "It would have been easy to kill him, wouldn't it?"

His body tense and his eyes closed, the elder made no reply.

"And you didn't kill him?" I asked in astonishment.

No doubt it was my surprise that pulled them out of the dark wood, where, unseen, they had lain in wait, trembling with homicidal pleasure, for they burst out laughing and became childlike once more, at my expense.

"No," said the elder, "we didn't kill him. But I really don't know why."

In high spirits again, he broke into his favorite improvisations, an uncouth medley of words and rhythms, the product of those hours when his student's mind, casting work aside, unconsciously sought relief in divorcing words from their meaning. My small voice echoed his, and I am the only one left now to declare, to the tune of a polka, that:

> A cachet
> Of benzo-naphtol
> Is just the thing
> For a bad headache.
>
> A cachet
> Of benzo-naphtol
> Is just the thing
> For an inflamed neck!

A rash assertion, contrary to all the laws of medicine. I preferred the text, if not the tune, of a familiar serenade:

> The analgesic balm
> Of the pharmacist Bengué
>   Bengué,
> Is very distingué
> It can't do any harm,
> Though it makes you feel more gay,
>   More gay, etc.

That evening, my brother, still overexcited, sang the new version of the *Serenade* by Severo Torelli:

> We didn't kill Mathieu tonight, my dear,
> We thought it was much too soon.

So we're letting him live a bit longer,
Though he's mad as the man in the moon.

The younger boy danced around him, radiant as Lo-
renzaccio after his first crime. He broke off to promise
me kindly: "We'll kill him next time."

My half sister, the eldest of us all—the stranger in our
midst—got engaged just when she seemed about to become an old maid. Plain though she was, with her Tibetan
eyes she was not unpleasing. My mother did not dare to
prevent this unfortunate marriage, but at least she made
no secret of what she thought about it. From the Rue de
la Roche to Gerbaude, and from Bel-Air to Le Grand-
Jeu, the talk was all of my sister's marriage.

"Is Juliette getting married?" a neighbor would ask
my mother. "That's an event!"

"No, an accident," corrected Sido.

A few ventured acidly: "So Juliette's getting married
at last! How unexpected! It almost seemed hopeless!"

"I should rather say desperate," retorted Sido belliger-
ently. "But there's no holding a girl of twenty-five."

"And who is she marrying?"

"Oh, some wretched upstart or other."

At heart she was full of pity for her lonely daughter,
who spent her days in a fever of reading, her head stuffed
with dreams. My brothers considered the "event" entirely
from their own detached point of view. A year of medical
studies in Paris had by no means tamed the elder; magnificent and aloof, he resented the glances of such
women as he did not desire. The words "bridal train,"
"dress clothes," "wedding breakfast," "procession," fell
on the two savages like drops of boiling pitch.

"I won't go to the wedding!" protested the younger,
his eyes pale with indignation under his hair cropped
close as a convict's, as usual. "I won't offer anyone my
arm! I won't wear tails!"

"But you're your sister's best man," my mother pointed
out to him.

"Well then, all she's got to do is not to marry! And
as for what she's marrying! A fellow who stinks of ver-

mouth! Besides, she's always got along without us, so I can't see why she needs us to help her get married!"

Our handsome elder brother was less vocal, but we recognized that look on his face that he always wore when he was planning to leap over a wall and was measuring the obstacles. There were difficult days and recriminations, which my father, full of anxiety himself and eager to avoid the malodorous intruder, was unable to quell. Then all at once the two boys appeared to agree to everything. Better still, they suggested that they themselves should organize a choral mass, and Sido was so delighted that for a few hours she forgot her "upstart" of a son-in-law.

Our Aucher piano was carted along to the church and mingled its sweet but slightly tinny tone with the bleating of the harmonium. Locking themselves in the empty church, the savages rehearsed the "Suite" from *L'Arlésienne,* something of Stradella's, and a piece by Saint-Saens specially arranged for the nuptial ceremony.

Only when it was too late did my mother realize that her sons, each chained to his keyboard as a performer, would not appear for more than a moment at their sister's side. They played, I remember, like angelic musicians, making the village mass and the bare church, which lacked even a belfry, radiant with music. I swaggered about, very proud of my eleven years, my long locks that made me look like a little Eve, and my pink dress, highly delighted with everything except when I looked at my sister. Very small and pale, weighed down with white silk and tulle and trembling with nervous weakness, she was gazing up at that unknown man with a swooning look of such submission on her strange, Mongolian face that the sight filled me with shame.

The violins for dancing put an end to the long meal, and at the mere sound of them the two boys quivered like wild horses. The younger, slightly tipsy, stayed where he was. But the elder, unable to bear any more, disappeared. Jumping over the wall of the Rue des Vignes, he got into our garden, wandered around the closed house, broke a windowpane, and went to bed, where my mother found him when she returned, sad and weary, after hand-ing her bewildered and trembling daughter over to the care of a man.

Long afterward, she described to me that dust-gray, early dawn of summer, her empty house that felt as though it had been pillaged, her joyless fatigue, her dress with its beaded front, and the uneasy cats summoned home by her voice and the night. She told me how she had found her elder boy asleep, his arms folded on his breast, and how his fresh mouth and closed eyes, his whole body, were eloquent of that sternness of his, the sternness of the pure savage.

"Just think of it—it was so that he could be alone, far from those sweating people, and sleep caressed by the night wind, that he broke the windowpane. Was there ever a child so wise?"

I have seen him, that wise one, vault through a window on a hundred occasions, as though by a reflex action, every time there was a ring at the bell that he did not expect. When he was growing gray and prematurely aged by overwork, he could still recover the elasticity of his youth in order to leap into the garden, and his little girls would laugh to see him. Gradually his fits of misanthropy, although he struggled against them, turned his face haggard. Captive as he was, did he perhaps find his prison yard daily more confined and remember those escapes that once upon a time used to lead him to a childish bed where he slept half naked, chaste, and voluptuously alone?

[TRANSLATED BY ENID McLEOD]

From *The Last of Chéri*

Without hurrying, he climbed the single flight of stairs up to Léa's apartment. At six in the evening, after the rain, the Rue Raynouard reechoed, like the garden of a boarding school, with the chirrup of birds and the cries of small children. He glanced quickly, coldly, at everything, refusing to be surprised by the heavy looking glasses in the entrance hall, the polished steps, the blue carpet, or the elevator lavishly splashed with as much lacquer and gold as a sedan chair. On the landing he experienced for a moment the deceptive sense of detachment and freedom from pain felt by a sufferer on the dentist's doorstep. He nearly turned away, but, fearful that he might feel compelled to return later, he pressed the bell with a determined finger. The maid, who had taken her time in coming to the door, was young and dark, with a butterfly cap of fine linen on her bobbed hair: her unfamiliar face took from Chéri his last chance to feel moved.

"Is madame at home?"

The young servant, apparently lost in admiration of him, could not make up her mind.

"I do not know, monsieur. Is monsieur expected?"

"Of course," he said, with a return of his old harshness.

She left him standing there, and disappeared. In the half-light he was quick to take in his surroundings, with eyes blurred by the gloom, and alert sensitive nostrils. There was nowhere a vestige of that light golden scent, and some ordinary pine essence sputtered in an electric scent burner. Chéri felt annoyed, like someone who discovers that he is on the wrong floor. But a great peal of girlish laughter rang out, its notes running down a deep descending scale. It was muffled by some curtain

79

or other, but at once the intruder was cast into a whirl-pool of memories.

"Will monsieur please come to the drawing room."

He followed the white butterfly, saying over to himself as he went: "Léa's not alone. She's laughing. She can't be alone. So long as it's not my mother." Beyond an open door, he was welcomed by rosy pink daylight, and he waited, standing there, for the rebirth of the world heralded by this dawn.

A woman was writing at a small table, facing away from him. Chéri was able to distinguish a broad back and the padded cushion of a fat neck beneath a head of thick, gray, vigorous hair, cut short like his mother's. "So I was right, she's not alone. But who on earth can this good woman be?"

"And, at the same time, write down your masseur's address for me, Léa, and his name. You know what I'm like about names. . . ."

These words came from a woman dressed in black, also seated, and Chéri felt a preliminary tremor of expectation running through him: "Then—where is Léa?"

The gray-haired lady turned around, and Chéri received the full impact of her blue eyes.

"Oh, good heavens, child—it's you!"

He went forward as if in a dream, and kissed an outstretched hand.

"Monsieur Frédéric Peloux—Princess Cheniaguine."

Chéri kissed another hand, then took a seat.

"Is he—?" queried the lady in black, referring to him with as much freedom as if he had been a deaf-mute.

Once again the great peal of girlish laughter rang out, and Chéri sought for the source of this laugh here, there, and everywhere—anywhere but in the throat of the gray-haired woman.

"No, no, he isn't! Or rather, he isn't any longer, I should say. Valérie, come now, what are you thinking about?"

She was not monstrous, but huge, and loaded with exuberant buttresses of fat in every part of her body. Her arms, like rounded thighs, stood out from her hips on plump cushions of flesh just below her armpits. The plain skirt and the nondescript long jacket, opening on a linen blouse with a jabot, proclaimed that the wearer had abdicated, was no longer concerned to be a woman, and had acquired a kind of sexless dignity.

Léa was now standing between Chéri and the window, and he was not dismayed at first by her firm, massive, almost cubic, bulk. When she moved to reach a chair, her features were revealed, and he began to implore her with silent entreaties, as though faced with an armed lunatic. Her cheeks were red and looked overripe, for she now disdained the use of powder, and when she laughed her mouth was packed with gold. A healthy old woman, in short, with sagging cheeks and a double chin, well able to carry her burden of flesh and freed from restraining stays.

"Tell me, child, where have you sprung from? I can't say I think you're looking particularly well."

She held out a box of cigarettes to Chéri, smiling at him from blue eyes that had grown smaller, and he was frightened to find her so direct in her approach and as jovial as an old gentleman. She called him "child," and he turned away his eyes, as though she had let slip an improper word. But he exhorted himself to be patient, in the vague hope that this first picture would give place to a shining transfiguration.

The two women looked him over calmly, sparing him neither good will nor curiosity.

"He looks a little like Hernandez. . . ." said Valérie Cheniaguine.

"Oh, I don't see that at all," Léa protested. "Ten years ago perhaps—and, anyhow, Hernandez had a much more pronounced jaw!"

"Who's that?" Chéri asked, with something of an effort.

"A Peruvian who was killed in a car accident about six months ago," said Léa. "He was living with Maximilienne. It made her very unhappy."

"Didn't prevent her finding consolation," said Valérie.

"Like anyone else," Léa said. "Surely you wouldn't have wished her to die of it?"

She laughed again, and her merry blue eyes disappeared, lost behind wide cheeks bulging with laughter. Chéri turned away his head and looked at the woman in black. She had brown hair and an ample figure, vulgar

and feline like thousands and thousands of women from
the south. She seemed in disguise, so very carefully was she dressed as a woman in good society. Valérie was wearing what had long been the uniform of
foreign princesses and their ladies—a black tailor-made
suit of undistinguished cut, tight in the sleeves, with a
blouse of extremely fine white batiste, a little tight at the
breast. The pearl buttons, the famous necklace, the high
stiff whalebone collar, everything about Valérie was as
royal as the name she legitimately bore. Like royalty, too,
she wore stockings of medium quality, flat-heeled walking
shoes, and expensive gloves embroidered in black and
white.

From the cool and disinterested way she looked him
over, Chéri might have been a piece of furniture. She
went on aloud with her criticisms and comparisons.

"Yes, yes, there is something of Hernandez, I tell
you. But, to hear Maximilienne today, Hernandez might
never have existed—now that she has made quite certain
of her famous Amerigo. And yet! And yet! I know
what I'm talking about. I've seen him, her precious Amerigo. I've just got back from Deauville. I saw the pair of
them!"

"No! Tell us!"

Léa sat down, overflowing the whole armchair. She
had acquired a new trick of tossing back her thick gray
hair; and at each shake of the head, Chéri saw a quivering of the lower part of her face, which looked like Louis
XVI's. Ostensibly, she was giving Valérie her full attention, but several times Chéri noticed a mischievous lowering of one of the little shrunken blue eyes as they sought
to catch those of the unexpected visitor.

"Well, then," Valérie started on her story, "she had
hidden him in a villa miles outside Deauville, at the back
of beyond. But that did not suit Amerigo at all—as you
will readily understand, monsieur!—and he grumbled at
Maximilienne. She was piqued and said: 'Ah, that's what
the matter is—you want to be on view to the world and
his wife, and so you shall be!' So she telephoned to reserve a table at the Normandy for the following evening.
Everyone knew this an hour later, and so I booked a table
as well, with Becq d'Ambez and Zahita. And we said to

ourselves: 'We're going to be allowed to see this marvel at last!' On the stroke of nine there was Maximilienne, all in white and pearls, and Amerigo. . . . Oh, my dear, what a disappointment! Tall, yes, that goes without saying—as a matter of fact, rather too tall. You know what I always say about men who are too tall. I'm still waiting to be shown one, just one, who is well put together. Eyes, yes, eyes, I've got nothing to say against his eyes. But—from here to there, don't you see" (she was pointing to her own face), "from here to there, something about the cheeks that is too rounded, too soft, and the ears set too low. . . . Oh, a very great disappointment. And holding himself as stiff as a poker."

"You're exaggerating," said Léa. "The cheeks—well, what about cheeks?—they aren't so very important. And, from here to there, well really it's beautiful, it's noble; the eyelashes, the bridge of the nose, the eyes—the whole thing is really too beautiful! I'll grant you the chin: that will quickly run to flesh. And the feet are too small, which is ridiculous in a boy of that height."

"No, there I don't agree with you. But I certainly noticed that the thigh was far too long in proportion to the leg, from here to there."

They went on to thrash out the question, sizing up, with a wealth of detail and point by point, every portion of the fore- and hind-quarters of this expensive animal.

"Judges of pedigreed fat cattle," Chéri thought. "The right place for them is the Commissariats."

"Speaking of proportions," Léa continued, "you'll never come across anything to touch Chéri. . . . You see, Chéri, you've come at just the right moment. You ought to blush. Valérie, if you can remember what Chéri was like only six, or say seven, years ago . . ."

"Of course I remember clearly. And monsieur has not changed so very much after all. . . . And you were so proud of him!"

"No," said Léa.

"You weren't proud of him?"

"No," said Léa with perfect calm, "I was in love with him."

She maneuvered the whole of her considerable body in his direction, and let her gay glance rest upon Chéri,

quite innocently. "It's true I was in love with you, very
much in love, too."

He lowered his eyes, stupidly abashed before these
two women, the stouter of whom had just proclaimed so
serenely that she and he had been lovers. Yet at the same
time the voluptuous and almost masculine tone of Léa's
voice besieged his memory, torturing him unbearably.

"You see, Valérie, how foolish a man can look when
reminded of a love that no longer exists? Silly boy, it
doesn't upset me in the least to think about it. I love my
past. I love my present. I'm not ashamed of what I've
had, and I'm not sad because I have it no longer. Am I
wrong, child?"

He uttered a cry, almost as if someone had stepped
on his big toe. "No, no, of course not! The very reverse!"

"It's charming to think you have remained such good
friends," said Valérie.

Chéri waited for Léa to explain that this was his first
visit to her in five years, but she just gave a good-
humored laugh and winked with a knowing air. He felt
more and more upset. He did not know how to protest,
how to shout out loud that he laid no claim to the friendship of this colossal woman with the cropped hair of an
elderly cellist—that, had he but known, he would never
have come upstairs, never crossed her threshold, set foot
on her carpet, never collapsed in the cushioned armchair, in the depths of which he now lay defenseless and
dumb.

"Well, I must be going," Valérie said. "I don't mean
to wait for rush hour in the Métro, you can be certain."

She rose to face the strong light, and it was kind to her
Roman features. They were so solidly constructed that
the approach of her sixtieth year had left them unharmed:
the cheeks were touched up in the old-fashioned way,
with an even layer of white powder, and the lips with a
red that was almost black and looked oily.

"Are you going home?" Léa asked.

"Of course I am. What d'you suppose my little jade
would be up to if left to herself!"

"Are you still pleased with your new apartment?"

"It's a dream! Especially since the iron bars were put
across the windows. And I've had a steel grid fixed over

the pantry fanlight, which I had forgotten about. With my electric bells and my burglar alarms— Ouf! It's been long enough before I could feel at all safe!"

"And your old house?"

"Bolted and barred. Up for sale. And the pictures in storage. My little mezzanine apartment is a gem for the eighteen hundred francs it costs me. And no more servants looking like hired assassins. You remember those two footmen? The thought of them still gives me the creeps!"

"You took much too black a view, my dear."

"You can't realize, my poor friend, without having been through it all. Monsieur, delighted to have met you. . . . No, don't you move, Léa."

She enfolded them both in her velvety, barbaric gaze and was gone. Chéri followed her with his eyes until she reached the door; yet he lacked the courage to follow her example. He remained where he was, all but crushed by the conversation of these two women who had been speaking of him in the past tense, as though he were dead. But now Léa was coming back into the room, bursting with laughter. "Princess Cheniaguine! Sixty million! And a widow! And she's not in the least bit happy. If that can be called enjoying life, it's not my idea of it, I can tell you."

She slapped her hand on her thigh as if it were a horse's rump.

"What's the matter with her?"

"Scared. Scared, that's all. She's not the sort of woman who knows how to carry such wealth. Cheniaguine left her everything. But one might say that it would have done her less harm if he'd taken her money instead of leaving her his. You heard what she said?"

She subsided into the depths of a well-upholstered armchair, and Chéri hated to hear the gentle sigh of its cushions as they took the weight of her vast bulk. She ran the tip of her finger along the grooved molding of the chair, blew away the few specks of dust, and her face grew somber.

"Ah, things are not at all what they were, not even servants. Eh?"

He felt that he had lost color, and that the skin around

his mouth was growing tighter, as during a severe frost. He fought back an overwhelming impulse to burst out into rancor mingled with entreaties. He longed to cry out loud: "Stop! Show me your real self! Throw off your disguise! You must be somewhere behind it, since it's your voice I hear. Appear in your true colors! Arise as a creature reborn, with your hair newly hennaed this morning, your face freshly powdered: put on your long stays again, the blue dress with its delicate jabot, the scent like a meadow that was so much a part of you. In these new surroundings I search for it in vain! Leave all this behind and come away to Passy—never mind the showers—Passy with its dogs and its birds, and in the Avenue Bugeaud we'll be sure to find Ernest polishing the brass bars on your front door." He shut his eyes, utterly worn out.

"And now, my child, I'm going to tell you something for your own good. What you need is to have your urine tested. Your color's shocking and you've got that pinched look around your lips—sure signs, both of them: you're not taking proper care of your kidneys."

Chéri opened his eyes again, and they took their fill of this placid epitome of disaster seated in front of him. Heroically, he said: "D'you really think so? It's quite possible."

"You mean, it's certain. And also, you don't have enough flesh on you. . . . It's no use telling me that the best fighting cocks are lean. You could do with a good ten pounds more on you."

"Give them to me," he said with a smile. But he found his cheeks singularly recalcitrant and opposed to smiling, almost as though his skin had stiffened with age.

Léa burst into a peal of happy laughter, and Chéri tasted a pleasure that he could not have borne for long; he listened again to its full and rounded tones, the very laugh that in the old days used to greet some outrageous impertinence on the part of the "naughty little boy."

"That I could well afford! I've certainly been putting on weight, haven't I? Eh? Look—here—would you believe it? And again here!"

She lit a cigarette, exhaled a double jet of smoke

through her nostrils, and shrugged her shoulders. "It's age!"

The word flew out of her mouth so lightly that it gave Chéri a sort of extravagant hope. "Yes: she's only joking. In a flash she'll reappear as her real self." For an instant she seemed to take in the meaning of the look he gave her.

"I've changed a lot, haven't I, child? Fortunately, it doesn't much matter. As for you, I don't like the look of you at all. . . . You've been fluttering your wings too much, as we used to say in the old days. Eh?"

He detested this new "Eh?" with which she peppered her sentences so freely. But he stiffened at each interrogation and each time mastered his rising excitement, preferring to remain in ignorance of both its reason and its aim.

"I don't ask whether you have any troubles at home. In the first place, it's none of my business; and besides, I know your wife as if I were her mother."

He listened to the sound of her voice without paying much attention. He noticed, above all, that when she stopped smiling or laughing, she ceased to belong to any assignable sex. Despite her enormous breasts and crushing backside, she seemed by virtue of age altogether virile and happy in that state.

"And I know your wife to be thoroughly capable of making a man happy."

He was powerless to hide his inward laughter, and Léa quickly went on to say, "What I said was 'a man,' and not 'any man.' Here you are in my house, without a word of warning. You haven't come, I take it, just to gaze into my beautiful eyes, eh?"

She turned on Chéri those once "beautiful blue eyes," now so diminished, marbled with tiny red veins, quizzical, neither kind nor unkind, alert and bright certainly, but —but where was now the limpid freshness that had washed their whites in palest blue? Where the contour of their orbs, with the roundness of fruit or breast or hemisphere, and blue as a land watered by many a river?

Jestingly, he said, "Pooh! Aren't you sharp! A real detective!" And it amazed him to find that he had fallen into such a carefree posture, with his legs crossed, like a handsome young man with bad manners. For inwardly he was watching his other self, hopelessly distracted and on his knees, waving his arms, baring his breast, and shrieking incoherently.

"I'm not a particularly stupid woman. But you must admit that you don't present me today with a very difficult problem!"

She drew in her chin and its lower folds spread over her neck: the kneeling ghost of his other self bowed its head like a man who has received a deathblow.

"You show every known sign of suffering from the disease of your generation. No, no, let me go on. Like all your soldier friends, you're looking everywhere for your paradise, eh! the paradise they owe you as a war hero: your own special Victory Parade, *your* youth, *your* lovely women. . . . They owe you all that and more, for they promised you everything, and, dear God, you deserved it. And what do you find? A decent, ordinary life. So you go in for nostalgia, listlessness, disillusion, and neurasthenia. Am I wrong?"

"No," said Chéri, for he was thinking that he would give his little finger to stop her talking.

Léa clapped him on the shoulder, letting her hand with its large rings rest there. As he bent his head down toward it he could feel on his cheek the heat of this heavy hand.

"Oh!" Léa continued, raising her voice. "You're not the only one! I've come across dozens of boys, since the war ended, exactly in your state of——"

"Where?" Chéri interrupted.

The suddenness of the interruption and its aggressive character put an end to Léa's mealy-mouthed eloquence. She withdrew her hand.

"They're to be met with everywhere, my child. Is it possible to be so vain? You seem to think you're unique because you find the postwar world tasteless. Don't flatter yourself."

She gave a low chuckle, and a toss to her sportive gray hair, and then a self-important smile like a judge who has a nice taste in wine. "And you do flatter yourself, you know, always imagining that you're the only one of your kind."

She took a step back and narrowed her gaze, adding, perhaps a little vindictively: "You were unique only for—for a time."

Behind this veiled but carefully chosen insult, Chéri discovered something of her femininity at last. He sat bolt upright, delighted to find himself suffering less acutely. But by this time Léa had reverted to her milk and honey.

"But you didn't come here to have that said about you. Did you make up your mind on the spur of the moment?"

"Yes," said Chéri.

He could have wished that this monosyllable might have been the last word between the two of them. Shyly, he let his gaze wander to all the things that surrounded Léa. From the nearest plate he took a dry cake shaped like a curved tile, and then put it back, convinced that it would turn to brick-red grit in his mouth were he to take a bite out of it. Léa noticed this action, and the painful way he swallowed his saliva.

"Tut, tut, so we're suffering from nerves, are we? A sharp chin, and dark lines under the eyes. That's a fine state of affairs!"

He closed his eyes and, like a coward, decided to listen and not look.

"Listen to me, child, I know a little restaurant in the Avenue des Gobelins. . . ."

He looked up at her, filled with the hope that she was going mad, that in this way he would be able to forgive her for both looking and behaving like an old woman.

"Yes, I know a little restaurant . . . Let me speak! Only, you must be quick, before the smart set and the newspapers take it into their heads to make it fashionable, and the good woman herself is replaced by a chef. She does all the cooking at present, and, my dear . . ." She brought thumb and forefinger together on the tip of her lips, and blew an imitation kiss. Chéri turned away to look out of the window, where the shadow, thrown by a branch, flicked at the steady shaft of sunlight, impatiently but at regular intervals, much as a bent reed or river plant appears to strike at the ripples of a regularly flowing current.

"What an odd sort of conversation . . ." he ventured in strained tones.

"No more odd than your presence in my house," Léa snapped back at him.

With a wave of the hand he made it clear that he wanted peace, only peace, with as few words spoken as possible, and preferably none at all. He felt defeated in the face of this elderly woman's boundless reserves of energy and appetite. Léa's quick blood was now rising and turning her bulging neck and her ears to purple. "She's got a crop like an old hen," he thought, with something of his old enjoyment of cruelty.

"And that's the truth!" she hurled at him excitedly. "You drag yourself around here like an apparition, and when I do my best to find some way of setting things straight, I who, when all's said and done, do happen to know you rather well . . ."

He smiled at her despondently. "And how in the world should she know me? When far shrewder people than she, and even than I myself . . ."

"A certain kind of sickness of the soul, my child, of disillusion, is just a question of stomach. Yes, yes, you may laugh!" He was not laughing, but she might well think he was. "Romanticism, nerves, distaste for life: stomach. The whole lot, simply stomach. Love itself! If one wished to be perfectly sincere, one would have to admit there are two kinds of love—well-fed and ill-fed. The rest is pure fiction. If only I knew how to write or to make speeches, my child, what things I could say about that! Oh, of course it wouldn't be anything new, but I would at least know what I was talking about, and that would be a change from our present-day writers."

Something worse than this obsession with the kitchen was upsetting Chéri: the affectation, the false tone of voice, the almost studied joviality. He suspected Léa of putting on an act of hearty and sybaritic geniality, just as a fat actor, on the stage, plays "jovial" characters because he has developed a paunch.

As though defiantly, she rubbed her shiny, almost blotchy, red nose with the back of her first finger and fanned the upper part of her body with the aid of the two

panels of her long jacket. In so doing, she was altogether
too cheerfully inviting Chéri to sit in judgment on her
appearance, and she even ran her hand through her thick
gray locks as she shook them free of her head.

"Do you like my hair short?"

He deigned to reply only by a silent shake of the head,
just like someone brushing aside an idle argument.

"Weren't you saying something just now about a little
restaurant in the Avenue des Gobelins . . . ?"

It was now her turn to brush aside an irrelevance. She
was beginning to understand, and he could see from the
quivering of her nostrils that at last she was piqued.
His animal instincts, which had been shocked into dull-
ness, were now on the alert, and it was as though a
weight had been lifted from his mind. He intended somehow to find a way past this shameless flesh, the graying
curls and "merry friar" joviality, and reach the being
concealed behind them, to whom he was coming back,
as to the scene of a crime. He remained close to this
buried treasure, burrowing toward it spontaneously. "How
in the world did old age come upon her? All of a sudden,
on waking up one morning? Or little by little? And this
surplus fat, this extra avoirdupois, under the weight of
which armchairs groan? Was it some sudden shock that
brought about this change and unsexed her? Could it,
perhaps, have been grief on my account?" But he asked
these questions of no one but himself, and without voic-
ing them. "She is piqued. She's on the way to understanding me. She's just going to tell me. . . ."

He watched her rise to her feet, walk over to the bureau, and start to tidy the papers lying on the open
hinged flap. He noticed that she was holding herself more
upright than when he had first entered the room, and
that, under his following eye, she straightened her back
still more. He accepted the fact that she was really colossal, her body seeming to run absolutely straight from
armpit to hip. Before turning around again to face Chéri,
she arranged a white silk scarf tightly around her neck,
despite the heat of the room. He heard her take a deep
breath before she came toward him with the slow rolling
gait of a ponderous animal.

She smiled at him. "I am not doing my duty as a

hostess, it would seem. It's not very polite to welcome someone by giving them advice, especially useless advice."

From under a fold of her white scarf peeped insinuatingly a twisting, coiling, resplendent string of pearls, which Chéri at once recognized.

Held captive beneath the translucent skin, the seven colors of the rainbow flickered with some secret fire of their own all over the surface of each precious sphere. Chéri recognized the pearl with a dimple, the slightly egg-shaped pearl, and the biggest pearl of the string, distinguishable by its unique pink. "These pearls, these, at least, are unchanged! They and I remain unchanged."

"So you've still got your pearls," he said.

She was astonished by the foolish phrase and looked as though she wanted to interpret it. "Yes, in spite of the war. Are you thinking that I could, or should, have sold them? Why should I have sold them?"

"Or 'for whom'?" he answered jokingly, in a tired voice.

She could not restrain a rapid glance toward the bureau and its scattered papers; and Chéri, in his turn, felt he knew the thought behind it, guessing that it was aimed at some yellowed, postcard photograph, probably the frightened features of a beardless boy in uniform. Disdainfully, he considered this imaginary face and said to himself, "That's none of my concern," adding a moment later, "But what is there here that does concern me?"

The agitation that he had brought in his heart was now excited by everything around him; everything added to it—the setting sun, the cries of insect-chasing swallows, and the ember-glowing shafts of light stabbing through the curtains. He remembered that Léa carried with her wherever she went this incandescent rose pink, as the sea, on its ebbtide, carries with it far out from shore the earthy smells of pastures and new-mown hay.

No word passed between them for a while, and they were rescued by pretending to listen to the clear, fresh notes of a child singing. Léa had not sat down again. Standing massively in front of him, she carried her irretrievable chin higher than before and betrayed some vague distress by the frequent fluttering of her eyelids.

"Am I making you late? Do you have to go out this evening? Do you want to dress?" The questions were abrupt, and made Léa look at Chéri.

"Dress? Good Lord, and in what do you wish me to dress? I *am* dressed—irrevocably—once and for all."

She laughed her incomparable laugh, starting on a high note and descending the scale by leaps of equal interval till she got to the deep musical reaches reserved for sobs and amorous moans. Chéri unconsciously raised a hand in supplication.

"Dressed for life, I tell you! And how convenient that is! Blouses, fine linen, and this uniform on top, and here I am all dressed up. Equally ready for dinner either at Montagné's or somewhere modest, ready for the cinema, for bridge, or for a stroll in the Bois."

"And what about love—which you're forgetting to mention?"

"Oh, child!"

She blushed, and though her face was dark with the chronic red of sufferers from arthritis, the blush could not be concealed. Chéri, after the first mean satisfaction at having said something outrageous, was seized with shame and remorse at the sight of this maidenly reaction.

"I was only joking," he said, in some confusion. "Have I gone too far?"

"Of course not. But you know very well I have never cared for certain kinds of impropriety or for jokes that are not really funny."

She strove to control her voice, but her face revealed that she was hurt, and every coarsened feature gave signs of a distress that could perhaps be outraged modesty.

"Dear God, if she takes it into her head to cry!" and he imagined the catastrophic effect of tears coursing down each cheek into the single deep ravine near the mouth, and of her eyelids reddened by the salt of tears.

He hastened to intercept: "No, no, you mustn't think that! How could you! I never meant— Please, Léa. . . ."

From her quick reaction he realized suddenly that this was the first time he had spoken her name. Proud, as in the old days, of her self-control, she gently stopped him.

"Don't worry, child. I'm not offended. But I've only

got you here for a few minutes, so don't spoil them by saying anything I shouldn't care to remember."

Her gentle tone left him cold, and her actual words seemed offensively tactful to him. "Either she's lying or she really has become the sort of person she pretends. Peace, purity, and the Lord knows what! She might as well wear a ring in her nose! Peace of heart, eating well, and the cinema. . . . Lies, lies, all lies! She wants to make me think that women find growing old comfortable, positively enjoyable. How can she expect *me* to swallow that? Let her fool anyone else she likes with her fine talk about how cozy life is, and the little restaurants with the most delicious country dishes. But not me! Before I could toddle, I knew all there is to know about reducing. I was *born* among aging beauties! All my life I've watched them, my painted pixies, squabbling about their wrinkles and, well into their fifties, scratching each other's eyes out over some wretched gigolo!"

"You sit there saying nothing, and I'm not used to it any more. I keep on thinking that there's something you want to say to me."

On her feet, separated from Chéri by a small table with a decanter and port glasses, she made no effort to defend herself against the severe inspection to which she was being subjected; but from the almost invisible tremors that pressed over her body, Chéri noted the muscular effort required to keep in her spreading stomach. "How many times must she have put on her full-length corset again, left it off, then valiantly put it on again, before abandoning it forever . . . ? How often of a morning must she have varied the shades of her face powder, rubbed a new rouge on her cheeks, massaged her neck with cold cream and a small lump of ice tied up in a handkerchief, before becoming resigned to the varnished hide that now shines on her cheeks!" Impatience alone, perhaps, had made her tremble, yet this faint tremor led him to expect—so stubbornly blind was he to reality— some miraculous new blossoming, some complete metamorphosis.

"Why don't you say something?" Léa persisted.

Little by little she was losing her poise, though she was careful not to move. She was playing with her rope of large pearls, knotting and unknotting, around her big well-manicured and wrinkled fingers, their luminous, indescribably bedewed and everlasting luster.

"Perhaps it's simply because she's frightened of me," Chéri mused. "A man who says nothing must always seem a little mad. She's thinking of Valérie Cheniaguine's terrors. If I put my hand out, would she scream for help? My poor Nounoune!" He lacked the courage to pronounce this name out loud, and to protect himself from even a moment's sincerity, he spoke: "What are you going to think of me?"

"It all depends," Léa answered guardedly. "At the moment you remind me of people who bring along a little box of cakes and leave it in the hall, saying to themselves: 'There'll be plenty of time to present these later,' and then pick them up again when they go out."

Reassured by the sound of their voices, she had begun to reason like the Léa of old, quick on the uptake and as wily as a sharp-witted peasant. Chéri rose to his feet, walked around the table that separated him from Léa, and the daylight streaming through the pink curtains struck him full in the face. This made it easy for her to compute the passage of days and years from his features, which were all of them in danger, though still intact. There was something about so secret a falling away to tempt her pity and trouble her memory, and perhaps extract from her the word or gesture that would precipitate Chéri into a frenzy of humiliation. As he stood there, a sacrifice to the light, with eyes lowered as if he were asleep, it seemed to him this was his last chance of extorting from her one last affront, one last prayer, one final act of respect.

Nothing happened, so he opened his eyes. Once more he had to accept the true picture—in the shape of his stalwart old friend, who, prudently keeping her distance, was bestowing on him a certain degree of benevolence from small and slightly suspicious blue eyes.

Disillusioned and bewildered, he looked all over the room for her, except in the very spot where she stood. 'Where is she? Where is she? This old woman is hiding her from me. She's bored by me, and she's waiting for me to go, thinking it all an infernal nuisance, these crowding memories and this returning ghost. . . . But if by any chance I did ask for her help, if I beg her to give me back Léa . . ." Deep inside him, his kneeling double was still palpitating, like a body from which the lifeblood is being drained. With an effort of which he would never have deemed himself capable, Chéri tore himself away from this tortured image.

"I must be going," he said out loud, and he added on a note of rather cheap wit, "and I'm taking my box of cakes with me."

Léa's exuberant bosom heaved with a sigh of relief. "As you like, my child. But I'm always here, you know, if you're in any trouble."

Though she seemed so obliging, Chéri could sense an underlying resentment. Within that vast edifice of flesh crowned with silvery thatch, femininity had for a moment reasserted itself in tones resounding with an intelligent harmony. But like a ghost he had come, and with the shyness of a ghost he must vanish, in spite of himself.

"Of course," Chéri replied, "and I thank you."

From that moment on, he knew, unerringly and spontaneously, exactly how to manage his exit. All the right words sprang to his lips, fluently, mechanically.

"You do understand, don't you, I came here today— why not sooner, you may ask? I know I ought to have come a long time ago. . . . But you will forgive me. . . ."

"Of course," Léa said.

"I'm even more harebrained than before the war, you know, so that—"

"I understand, I understand."

And because of this interruption, he thought that she must be impatient to see the last of him. A few words were exchanged during Chéri's retreat, in the intervals of bumping into some piece of furniture, crossing a strip of sunshine from the courtyard window—after the pink light in the drawing room it seemed by comparison almost blue—kissing a puffy hand bulging with rings when it was raised to his lips. Another of Léa's laughs, which broke off abruptly halfway down its usual scale, just like a fountain when the jet is turned off and the

crest of the plume, suddenly bereft of its stem, falls
back to earth in myriad separate pearls. . . . The staircase seemed to glide away under Chéri's feet like a
bridge connecting two dreams, and once more he was
in the Rue Raynouard. Even the street was unfamiliar.

He noticed that the rosy tints of the sky were wonderfully reflected in the rain-filled gutters and on the blue
backs of the low-skimming swallows. And now, because
the evening was fresh, and because the recollection he
was bringing away with him was slipping back into the
recesses of his mind—there to assume its final shape and
intensity—he came to believe that he had forgotten everything, and he felt happy.

[TRANSLATED BY ROGER SENHOUSE]

From *Break of Day*

"Sir,

"*You ask me to come spend a week with you, which means I would be near my daughter, whom I adore. You who live with her know how rarely I see her, how much her presence delights me, and I'm touched that you should ask me to come see her. All the same, I'm not going to accept your kind invitation, for the time being at any rate. The reason is that my pink cactus is probably going to flower. It's a very rare plant I've been given, and I'm told that in our climate it flowers only once every four years. Now, I am already a very old woman, and if I went away when my pink cactus is about to flower, I am certain I shouldn't see it flower again.*

"*So I beg you, sir, to accept my sincere thanks and my regrets, together with my kind regards.*"

This note, signed "*Sidonie Colette, née Landoy,*" was written by my mother to one of my husbands, the second. A year later she died, at the age of seventy-seven.

Whenever I feel myself inferior to everything about me, threatened by my own mediocrity, frightened by the discovery that a muscle is losing its strength, a desire its power, or a pain the keen edge of its bite, I can still hold up my head and say to myself: "I am the daughter of the woman who wrote that letter—that letter and so many more that I have kept. This one tells me in ten lines that at the age of seventy-six she was planning journeys and undertaking them, but that waiting for the possible bursting into bloom of a tropical flower held everything up and silenced even her heart, made for love. I am the daughter of a woman who, in a mean, close-fisted, confined little place, opened her village home to stray cats, tramps, and pregnant servant girls. I am the daughter of

a woman who many a time, when she was in despair at
not having enough money for others, ran through the
wind-whipped snow to cry from door to door, at the
houses of the rich, that a child had just been born in a
poverty-stricken home to parents whose feeble, empty
hands had no swaddling clothes for it. Let me not forget
that I am the daughter of a woman who bent her head,
trembling, between the blades of a cactus, her wrinkled
face full of ecstasy over the promise of a flower, a woman
who herself never ceased to flower, untiringly, during
three-quarters of a century."

Now that little by little I am beginning to age, and
little by little taking on her likeness in the mirror, I
wonder whether, if she were to return, she would recognize me for her daughter, in spite of the resemblance of
our features. She might if she came back at break of day
and found me up and alert in a sleeping world, awake as
she used to be, and as I often am, before everyone.

Before almost everyone, O my chaste, serene ghost!
But you wouldn't find me in a blue apron with pockets
full of grain for the fowls, nor with pruning shears or a
wooden pail. Up before almost everyone, but half naked
in a fluttering wrap hastily slipped on, standing at my
door, which had admitted a nightly visitor, my arms
trembling with passion and shielding—let me hide myself
for shame!—the shadow, the thin shadow of a man.

"Stand aside and let me see," my beloved ghost would
say. "Why, isn't what you're embracing my pink cactus,
which has survived me? How amazingly it's grown and
changed! But now that I look into your face, my child, I
recognize it. I recognize it by your agitation, by your air
of waiting, by the devotion in your outspread hands,
by the beating of your heart and your suppressed cry, by
the growing daylight all about you, yes, I recognize, I lay
claim to all of that. Stay where you are, don't hide, and
may you both be left in peace, you and the man you're
embracing, for I see that he is in truth my pink cactus,
which has at last consented to flower."

Is this house going to be my last? I size it up and
listen to it during that short private night that enwraps
us, here in the Midi, immediately after the hour of noon.

The cicadas creak and so does the new wattle fencing that shelters the terrace, a nameless insect is crushing tiny grits between its shards, the reddish bird in the pine tree calls every ten seconds, and the west wind, circling watchfully around my walls, leaves unruffled the flat, dense, hard sea, whose harsh blue will soften toward nightfall.

Is this house going to be my last, the one that will find me faithful, the one I shall never leave again? It is so ordinary that it could have no rivals.

I hear the clink of the bottles being carried to the well from which they will be pulled up, cooled, for dinner tonight. One of them, red-currant pink, will accompany the green melon; the other, a sand-grown wine, amber colored and overgenerous, goes with the salad of tomatoes, pimentos, and onions soaked in oil, and with the ripe fruit. After dinner I mustn't forget to irrigate the little runnels that surround the melons, and to water by hand the balsams, phlox, and dahlias, and the young tangerine trees, which haven't yet got roots long enough to drink unaided in the depths of the earth, nor strength to break into leaf without help, under the steady scorching of the heavens. The young tangerine trees, planted— for whom? I don't know. Perhaps for me. The cats will spring sideways at the moths when by ten the air is as blue as a morning glory. The pair of Japanese hens, perching drowsily on the arm of a rustic armchair, will chirp like birds in a nest. The dogs, already far away from this world, will be thinking of the coming dawn, and I shall have the choice of a book, bed, or the coast road studded with fluting toads.

Tomorrow I shall surprise the red dawn on the tamarisks wet with salty dew, and on the mock bamboos where a pearl hangs at the tip of each blue lance. The coast road that leads up from the night, the mist, and the sea; then a bath, work, and rest. How simple everything could be! Can it be that I have attained here what one never starts a second time? Everything is much as it was in the first years of my life, and little by little I recognize the road back. The way my country house has grown smaller, the cats, the aged bitch, my sense of wonder, and a serenity whose breath I can feel from far off—a merciful moisture, a promise of healing rain hanging over my still-stormy life—all these help me to recognize it. Many stretches of the road have been completed and left behind. A castle inhabited for a moment has melted into the distance, replaced by this little house. Properties scattered over France have dwindled little by little in response to a wish that in times past I never dared to put into words. How wonderfully confident and vital must that past have been to inspire even the lowly guardian angels of the present: the servitors who have once again become humble and competent. The housemaid adores digging, and the cook soaps the linen in the washhouse. Does there then exist here on earth a kitchen-garden path where I can retrace my own footsteps, a path I thought I should never follow again except on the other side of life? Is that maternal ghost, in the old-fashioned dress of blue sateen, filling the watering cans at the edge of the well? This coolness of spray, this sweet enticement, this provincial spirit, in short, this innocence —isn't all this the charm of declining years? How simple everything has become! Everything, even to the second place that I sometimes lay opposite my own on the shady table.

A second place doesn't take much room now: a green plate, a thick antique glass, slightly cloudy. If I say that it is to be taken away for good, no pernicious blast will blow suddenly from the horizon to make my hair stand on end and alter the direction of my life as once it did. If that place is removed from my table, I shall still eat with appetite. There is no longer any mystery, no longer a serpent coiled under the napkin that is ringed to distinguish it from mine with a brass lyre that once held in place, at the top of a music stand of the last century, the loose pages of a score where only the downbeats were marked, spaced at intervals as regular as tears. This place belongs to the friend who comes and goes, and no longer to a master of the house given to treading the resounding boards of a bedroom up above during the night. On days when the plate, the glass, and the lyre are not in front of me, I am merely alone, and not abandoned. Now that my friends are reassured about that, they trust me.

Very few, only two or three, remain of those friends who in former days thought they saw me going under in my first shipwreck: for I honestly thought so myself and said as much to them. To these, one by one, death is bringing rest. I have friends who are younger, and in particular younger than I. I instinctively like to acquire and store up what promises to outlast me. I have not caused such great torments to these, at most a few cares: "There now, *He's* going to spoil her for us again. . . . How long is *He* going to remain so important?" They would speculate on the outcome of the disease, its crises, and its temperature chart: "A dangerous typhoid or a mild rash? Confound the woman, why does she always manage to catch such serious complaints!" My true friends have always given me that supreme proof of devotion, a spontaneous aversion for the man I loved. "And what if this one disappears too, what a lot of trouble it will give us, what a job to help her recover her balance!"

But at bottom they never grumbled greatly—very much the other way—when they saw me coming back to them, overheated by the struggle, licking my wounds, counting my tactical errors, reveling in being biased, heaping crimes on the enemy who defies me, then whitewashing him out of all measure, then secretly hugging his letters and pictures: "He was charming. . . . I ought to have . . . I ought not to have . . ." Then reason would return, bringing with it the calm that I do not like and my belatedly courteous, belatedly reserved silence, which is, I really believe, the worst moment of all. Such is the routine of suffering, like the habitual clumsiness of those in love, and the compulsion that makes every couple innocently poison their homelife.

Then is that militant life, which I thought I should never see the last of, over and done with? I have nothing left now but my dreams with which to revive from time to time a dead love, by which I mean love purged of its brief and localized pleasures. Sometimes it happens that in a dream one of my loves begins again with an indescribable noise, a tumult of words, of looks that can be interpreted in two or three contradictory ways, of demands. Without any break or transition, the same dream ends in an exam in decimal fractions for the

elementary diploma. And if when I wake the pillow
under the nape of my neck is a bit damp, it is because of
the elementary diploma. "A second longer and I
should have failed in the orals," stammers memory, still
caught in the toils. "Ah, that look he had in my dream!
Who? The highest common factor? No, of course not,
He, He when he used to spy on me through the window to
see if I had deceived him. But it wasn't He, it was. . . .
Was it?" The light mounts, forcibly enlarging the gilded
green field of vision between my eyelids. "Was it He, or
else . . . ? I'm sure it's at least seven o'clock—if it's
seven it's too late to water the eggplants: the sun is on
them. And why, before I woke, didn't I brandish under
his nose that letter in which he promised me peace,
friendship, a better mutual knowledge of ourselves and
—it's the first time I've got up so late this whole season."
For to dream and then to return to reality only means
that our qualms suffer a change of place and significance.

A little wing of light is beating between the two
shutters, touching with irregular pulsations the wall or
the long heavy table where we write or read or play,
that eternal table that has come back from Brittany,
as I have come back. Sometimes the wing of light is
pink on the pink-washed wall, and sometimes blue on
the blue cotton Moroccan rug. Dressers stacked with
books, armchairs, and chests of drawers have made a
roundabout journey with me over fifteen years, through
two or three French provinces. Elegant armchairs with
tapering arms, countrified like peasant girls with delicate
limbs, yellow plates that sing like bells when you rub
them with your finger, dishes of thick white glaze—we
are all astonished to find ourselves back in a country
that is our own. For isn't the house of my father and my
grandparents on the Mourillon, fifty miles from here?
It is true that other regions have cradled me, and some
of them roughly. A woman lays claim to as many native
lands as she has had happy loves. She is born, too,
under every sky where she has recovered from the pain
of loving. By that reckoning this blue salt shore, bright
with tomatoes and pimentos, is doubly mine. How rich
it is, and what a lot of time I've spent not knowing about

it! The air is light, the grapes ripen so quickly that they are dried and wrinkled on the vine by the sun, the garlic is highly flavored. That noble bareness that thirst sometimes confers on the soil, the refined idleness that one learns from a frugal people—for me these are recently discovered riches. But let me not complain. My maturity is the right time for them. My angular youth would have bled at the touch of the striated, mica-spangled rocks; the forked pine needles; the aloe; the spines of the sea urchin; the bitter, sticky cistus and the fig tree, the underside of whose every leaf is a wild beast's tongue. What a country! The invader endows it with villas and garages, with motorcars and dance halls built to look like cottages. The barbarians from the north parcel out the land, speculate, and deforest, and that is certainly a great pity. But during the course of the centuries, how many ravishers have not fallen in love with such a captive? They arrive plotting to ruin her, stop suddenly and listen to her breathing in her sleep, and then, turning silent and respectful, they softly shut the gate in the fence. Submissive to your wishes, Provence, they fasten on your vine-leaf crown again, replant the pine tree and the fig, sow the variegated melon and have no other desire, Beauty, than to serve you and enjoy it.

The others will inevitably abandon you. Once upon a time they would have dishonored you. But one horde more or less doesn't matter to you. Those who have come on the strength of a casino, a hotel, or a postcard will leave you. They will flee, burned and bitten by your wind white with dust. Keep your lovers, who drink water from the pitcher and the dry wine that ripens in the sand; keep those who pour oil religiously and turn away their heads when they pass in front of dead animals; keep those who rise early and lull themselves asleep in bed in the evening to the faint chugging of the pleasure boats in the bay. Keep me. . . .

The ripening color of the half-light marks the end of my siesta. The prostrate cat will now certainly stretch herself to a phenomenal length, produce from her body a front paw whose exact length no one knows, and say, with a yawn like a flower: "It's long past four o'clock."

The first motorcar is not far off, rolling on its little cloud of dust toward the shore; others will follow it. One of them will stop for a moment at the gate, and out of it there will pour onto the path, amid the feathery shade of the mimosas, menfriends without their wives and womenfriends with their lovers. I haven't yet got to the point of shutting my gate in their faces and baring my teeth behind it. But the tone of my cordiality, familiar but cold, does not deceive them and keeps them in check. The men like my dwelling without a master; they like its smell, its doors with no locks. Some of the women say, with an air of sudden ecstasy: "Oh, what a paradise!" and secretly add up all it lacks. But both the women and the men appreciate the patience with which I, who have no projects of my own, listen to theirs. They are "mad about this country," they want "a very simple little farm" or to build "a cottage on this headland above the sea—good Lord, what a view!" At that point I become charming because I listen and say: "Yes, yes." For I do not covet the field alongside, I am not buying my neighbor's vineyard, and I'm not "adding a wing." There's always one of my comrades who eyes my vines, walks from the house to the sea without going up or down a step, returns, and concludes: "The long and the short of it is that this property, just as it is, suits you perfectly."

And I say "Yes, yes," as I do when he or someone else assures me: "You don't change!"—which means: "We've made up our minds that you never will change any more."

I'd very much like to try once again.

The door leading to the vines from the enclosure walled with openwork bricks is straining slightly on its hinges; the wind must be rising. It will swiftly sweep a quarter of the horizon and fasten on the wintry purity of the greenish north. Thereupon the whole hollow of the bay will rumble like a shell. Good-bye to my night in the open on the raffia mattress! If I had persisted in sleeping out of doors, that powerful mouth that breathes coldness and drought, deadens all scents and anesthetizes the earth, the enemy of work, voluptuousness and sleep, would have torn off me the sheets and blankets that it knows how to twist into long rolls. What a strange tormentor, as intent on man as any wild beast! Those who are highly strung know more about it than I do. When the wind strikes her near the well, my Provençal cook puts down her buckets, holds her head, and cries: "It's killing me!" On nights when the mistral blows she groans under it in her little hut among the vines, and perhaps she sees it.

Having retired to my bedroom, I wait with controlled impatience for the departure of this visitor for whom no sanctum is private, and who is already pushing under my door a strange tribute of withered petals, finely sifted seeds, sand, and battered butterflies. Go, go, I've discouraged other tokens before now; and I'm no longer forty, to avert my eyes at the sight of a fading rose. Is that militant life over and done with, then? There are three good times for thinking of it: the siesta, a short hour after dinner when the rustling of the newspaper, just arrived from Paris, seems oddly to fill the room, and then the irregular insomnia of the small hours, before dawn. Yes, it will soon be three o'clock. But even during these precarious small hours, which merge so quickly into day, where can I find that great cavern of bitterness promised me by my past griefs and joys, as well as my own books and those of others? Humble as I always am when I'm faced with anything I don't understand, I'm afraid of being mistaken when I imagine that this is the beginning of a long rest between myself and men. Come, Man, my friend, let us simply exist side by side! I have always liked your company. Just now you're looking at me so gently. What you see emerging from a confused heap of feminine castoffs, still weighed down like a drowned woman by seaweed (for even if my head is saved, I cannot be sure that my struggling body will be), is your sister, your comrade: a woman who is escaping from the age when she is a woman. She has, like you, rather a thick neck, bodily strength that becomes less graceful as it weakens, and that authority which shows you that you can no longer make her despair, or only dispassionately. Let us remain together; you no longer have any reasons now for saying good-bye to me forever.

Love, one of the great commonplaces of existence, is slowly leaving mine. The maternal instinct is another great commonplace. Once we've left these behind, we find that all the rest is gay and varied, and that there is plenty of it. But one doesn't leave all that behind when or as one pleases. How wise one of my husbands was when he remonstrated: "But is it impossible for you to write a book that isn't about love, adultery, semi-incestuous relations, and a final separation? Aren't there other things in life?" If he had not been in such a hurry to get to his amorous rendezvous—for he was handsome and charming—he might perhaps have taught me what can take the place of love, in a novel or out of it. But he went and I continued obstinately covering that same bluish paper, gleaming at this moment from the dark table to guide my hand, with chapters dedicated to love or regret for love, chapters blind with love. In them I called myself Renée Néré, or else, prophetically, I introduced a Léa. So it came about that both legally and familiarly, as well as in my books, I now have only one name, which is my own. Did it take only thirty years of my life to reach that point, or rather to get back to it? I shall end by thinking that it wasn't too high a price to pay. Can it be that chance has made me one of those women so immersed in one man that, whether they are barren or not, they carry with them to the grave the shriveled innocence of an old maid? At the thought of such a fate my plump double that I see in the sloping mirror, tanned by sun and sea, would tremble if it could still tremble at a past danger.

A hawkmoth from the oleanders is banging against the fine wire netting in front of the French window, returning to the charge again and again until the taut netting reverberates like the skin of a drum. It is cool. The generous dew trickles, the mistral has put off its offensive. The stars, magnified by the damp and salty air, twinkle broadly. Once again the most beautiful of all nights precedes the most beautiful of all days, and not being asleep, I can enjoy it. Let us hope tomorrow will find me equally sweet-tempered! In all sincerity I no longer ask for anything except what I can't have. Has someone broken my spirit, that I should be so gentle? Not at all: it's a very long time since I knew anyone really wicked—knew them face to face, bosom to bosom, and limb to limb. As for an authentic villain, the real thing, the absolute, the artist, one rarely meets him even once in a lifetime. The ordinary "bad sort" is always in part a decent fellow. It's true that the third hour of the morning encourages indulgence in those who enjoy it in the open and have an assignation with no one but themselves beneath the deepening blue of their window. The crystalline emptiness of the sky, the already conscious sleep of the animals, the chilly contraction that closes the calyxes up again, are so many antidotes to passion and iniquity. But I don't need to be feeling indulgent in order to say that in my past no one has broken my spirit. I have suffered, oh yes, certainly I learned how to suffer. But is suffering so very serious? I have come to doubt it. It may be quite childish, a sort of undignified pastime—I'm referring to the kind of suffering a man inflicts on a woman or a woman on a man. It's extremely painful. I agree that it's hardly bearable. But I very much fear that this sort of pain deserves no consideration at all. It's no more worthy of respect than old age or illness, for both of which I'm acquiring a great repulsion: both of them are anxious to get me in their clutches before long, and I'm holding my nose in advance. The love-sick, the betrayed, and the jealous all smell alike.

I remember very definitely that when I was wretched because I had been disappointed in love, my animals loved me less. They scented my grief, that great admission of failure. I have seen an unforgettable look in the eyes of a beautiful well-bred bitch, a look still generous but restrained and politely bored, because she no longer loved as much all that I stood for—a man's look, the look of a certain man. Shall we never have done with that cliché, so stupid that it could only be human, about the sympathy of animals for man when he is unhappy? Animals love happiness almost as much as we do. A fit of crying disturbs them: they'll sometimes imitate sobbing, and for a moment they'll reflect our sadness. But they flee unhappiness as they flee fever, and I believe that in the long run they are capable of boycotting it.

What a good use the two tomcats fighting outside are making of the July night! Those unearthly songs of the male cat have accompanied so many nocturnal hours in my life that they have become a symbol of wakefulness, of ritual insomnia. Yes, I know it is three o'clock and that I'm going to fall asleep again, and that when I wake I shall be sorry to have thrown away the moment when the milky blueness begins to rise up from the sea, reaches the sky, and flows over it until it stops at a red rift flush with the horizon.

The great baritone voice of a wild beast, long drawn out, persists through the sharp sounds of a tenor cat, clever at tremolos and at shrill chromatic scales interrupted by furious innuendos growing more nasal the more insulting they become. The two tomcats do not hate each other, but the clear nights suggest battle and declamatory dialogues. Why sleep? They make their choice and in summer take only the best parts of the night and the day. They choose. All animals who are well treated choose whatever is best in us and in their surroundings. It was the realization of that that helped me to emerge from the period when their comparative coldness revealed to me my own lack of dignity. I choose the phrase "lack of dignity" advisedly. Surely I ought to have thrown off that sordid domination? It was all in such deplorable taste, those half-dried tears, those eloquent looks, those stands taken in front of half-lifted curtains, that melodrama. What opinion of a woman like that could one expect from an animal, a bitch, for instance, herself compact of hidden fire and secrets, a bitch who had never groaned under the whip or wept in public? She despised me, that goes without saying. And though I didn't hide my hurt from the eyes of my fellows, I blushed for it in her presence. It is true that she and I loved the same man. But for all that it was in her eyes that I read a thought that I've since read in one of my mother's last letters: "Love is not a sentiment worthy of respect."

One of my husbands used to suggest to me: "When you're about fifty you ought to write a sort of handbook to teach women how to live in peace with the man they love, a code for life as a couple." Perhaps I am writing it now. O Man, my former loves, how one gains and learns in your company! Yet the best of friends must part; but I pledge myself here to take my leave courteously. No, you have not broken me, perhaps you never meant me any harm. Farewell, dear Man, and welcome to you too. Across my bed, which since I am in good health is better arranged for writing than a sickbed, a blue light creeps until it reaches the blue paper, my hand, and my bronze-colored arm; the smell of the sea warns me that the hour when air is colder than water is at hand. Shall I get up? To sleep is sweet.

[TRANSLATED BY ENID MCLEOD]

"Look!"

"To look is to learn," they say, and we all agree that is true. But in our concern for that wild, unknown being, the child, who is both bottomless pit and impregnable fortress, we are apt to accuse him of not looking often enough or carefully enough. We show him things that he seems not to see, and we nag at him without noticing that he is busy taking in—how? By hearing, feeling, the pores of his skin, or an ephemeral sixth sense?—some marvel that he keeps to himself.

"Look! Look quickly!"

"I *am* looking," he says, with a rather bewildered air, and we lower our voice to complain to one of our fellows, meaning of course another grown-up: "It's odd, but there are times when that child is unaccountably stupid."

"Look at that splendid horse going by! You won't see splendid horses like that much longer, little one!"

He looked and saw, close to the ear of the gaily decorated horse, a red artificial carnation, three little varnished green leaves which surrounded it, the rib running down the middle of each leaf, the serrated edge of the petals, two little stalks rolled in the form of a crozier to imitate the stamens of the flower. He did not see the horse.

"Look at that pretty flower in the grass, darling! No, stupid, not there, here!"

But at that very moment a cloud passed over the sun, and the child scampered after its huge blue shadow on the green field, a shadow of a dragon, an elephant, a giant of a man, with three arms, who dissolved in smoke. Number, color, form, kind, movement—the whole vast world opens before him. The child seeks, loses his way, thrills with a hundred hidden poems, becomes frightened and discouraged. "Look!"

But look at what? Should he rather gaze at what is near, intent on detail, indifferent to anything beyond the limits of his own room, his own garden? Or should be boldly turn his eyes to the far-off things, drawn by the mountain, the cloud, the distant ship? "Look, look!" we say, pointing out to him the very thing he did not want to see. It tires him to have to obey to no purpose, and so he shuts himself up and shrinks into himself, and irritates us. He takes refuge in his picture books, unless he is one of those privileged creatures who surrender themselves absolutely to the greatest masters of all: the forest, the fields, and the sea.

I have watched and respected the solitude of a child sent to spend the whole summer by the sea and the autumn and winter in a country of hills and chestnut woods. Both so entirely satisfied her that I was a little jealous of them, especially of the sea, which captivates all new creatures, who take to her as though they had known her before.

For a long time the child depended on me alone to contrive the necklace of chestnuts, the whistle of grass or bark, the pipe made out of an acorn cup, and the rattle that needs half a walnut shell, an elastic thread, and a match, which I then put into her childish, still clumsy hands. But how could I compete with the first sea horse? And what, when it really came to it, did I know of the crab, and the turtle, and the seaweed with floats? How could any treasure of knowledge that we might bring equal those that the wave casts at the feet of our child? He is already on familiar terms with the sea while we are still uneasy with her. He christens the eggs of the cuttlefish "grapes," calls the barbels of the sea dace "front paws," and laughs at the flounder's tricks of mimicry: "There's another sole pretending to be sand and thinking I don't see him!" Before long it will be he who teaches us to look. If our aim is to guide his eyes and widen their field of vision, it is important not to be in a hurry and to make as few mistakes as possible. There are miracles enough, but we are not always worthy of introducing them to a child.

I have not forgotten how I used to take a child every

year to the sea, as to a maternal element better fitted than I to teach, ripen, and perfect the mind and body that I had merely roughhewn.

[TRANSLATED BY ENID MCLEOD]

From *The Cat*

Toward ten o'clock, the family poker players began to show signs of weariness. Camille was fighting against sleepiness, as one does at nineteen. By starts she would become fresh and clear-eyed again; then she would yawn behind her clasped hands and reappear pale, her chin white and her cheeks a little black under their ocher-tinted powder, with two tiny tears in the corners of her eyes.

"Camille, you ought to go to bed!"

"At ten o'clock, Mummy, at ten o'clock! Who on earth goes to bed at ten o'clock?"

Her eyes appealed to her fiancé, who lay back, overcome, in the depths of an armchair.

"Leave them alone," said another maternal voice. "They still have seven days to wait for each other. They're a bit dazed at the moment. It's very natural."

"Exactly. One hour more or less . . . Camille, you should go home to bed. So should we."

"Seven days!" cried Camille. "But it's Monday today! And I hadn't given it a thought! Alain! Wake up, Alain!"

She threw her cigarette into the garden and lit a fresh one. Then she sorted out the scattered cards, shuffled them, and laid them out as fortune-tellers do.

"To know whether we'll get the car, that marvelous baby roadster, before the ceremony! Look, Alain! I'm not cheating! It's coming out with a journey and an important piece of news!"

"What's that?"

"The roadster, of course!"

Without raising the nape of his neck from the chair, Alain turned his head toward the open French window, through which came the sweet smell of fresh spinach and new-mown hay. The grass had been cut during the day, and the honeysuckle, which draped a tall dead tree, added the nectar of its first flowers. A crystalline tinkle announced the entrance of the ten o'clock tray of soft drinks and iced water, carried by old Émile's tremulous hands, and Camille got up to fill the glasses.

She served her fiancé last, offering him the misted tumbler with a smile of secret understanding. She watched him drink and felt a sudden pang of desire at the sight of his mouth pressing against the rim of the glass. But he felt so weary that he refused to share that pang and merely touched the white fingers with the red nails as they removed his empty tumbler.

"Are you coming to lunch tomorrow?" she asked him under her breath.

"Ask the cards."

Camille drew back quickly, and began to clown a little over her fortune-telling.

"Never, never joke about Twenty-four Hours! Doesn't matter so much about crossed knives, or pennies with holes in them, or the talkies, or God the Father——"

"Camille!"

"Sorry, Mummy. But one mustn't joke about Twenty-four Hours! He's a good little fellow, the knave of spades. A nice black express messenger, always in a hurry."

"In a hurry to do what?"

"Why, to talk, of course! Just think, he brings news of the next twenty-four hours, even of the next two days. If you put two more cards on his right and left, he fore-tells the coming week."

She was talking fast, scratching at two little smudges of lipstick at the corners of her mouth with a pointed nail. Alain listened to her, not bored, but not indulgent either. He had known her for several years and classified her by her own standard, as a typical modern girl. He knew the way she drove a car, a little too fast and a little too well; her eye alert and her scarlet mouth always ready to swear violently at a taxi driver. He knew that she lied unblushingly, as children and adolescents do; that she was capable of deceiving her parents so as to get out after dinner and meet him at a nightclub. There they danced together, but they drank only orange juice because Alain disliked alcohol.

Before their official engagement, she had yielded her

discreetly wiped lips to him both by daylight and in the dark. She has also yielded her impersonal breasts, always imprisoned in a lace brassiere, and her very lovely legs in the flawless stockings she bought in secret; stockings "like Mistinguett's, you know. Watch out for the stockings, Alain!" Her stockings and her legs were the best things about her.

"She's pretty," Alain thought dispassionately, "because not one of her features is ugly, because she's an out-and-out brunet. Those lustrous eyes perfectly match that sleek, glossy, frequently washed hair that's the color of a new piano." He was also perfectly aware that she could be as violent and capricious as a mountain stream.

She was still talking about the roadster.

"No, Daddy, *no*! Absolutely no question of my letting Alain take the wheel while we're driving through Switzerland! He's too absentminded. And besides, he doesn't really like driving. I know him!"

"She knows me," Alain echoed in his own mind. "Perhaps she really thinks she does. Over and over again, I've said to her too: 'I know you, my girl.' Saha knows her too. Where is that Saha?"

His eyes searched around for the cat. Then, starting limb by limb, first one shoulder, then the other, he pulled himself from the armchair and went lazily down the five steps.

The garden was very large and surrounded by other gardens. It breathed out into the night the heavy smell of well-manured earth given over to flowers and constantly forced into fertility. Since Alain's birth, the house had hardly changed at all. "An only son's house," Camille said. She did not hide her contempt for the high-pitched roof with the top-story windows set in the slates and for certain modest moldings that framed the French windows on the ground floor, like certain pastries.

The garden, like Camille, also seemed to despise the house. Huge trees, which showered down the black, calcined twigs that fall from elms in their old age, protected it from neighbors and passersby. A little farther on, in a property for sale and in the playground of a school, stood isolated pairs of similar old elms, relics of a princely avenue, which had formed part of a park that the new Neuilly was fast destroying.

"Where are you, Alain?"

Camille was calling him from the top of the steps, but, on an impulse, he held back from answering. Deliberately, he made for the safer refuge of the shadows, feeling his way along the edge of the shaven lawn with his foot. High in the sky a hazy moon held court, looking larger than usual through the mist of the first warm days. A single tree—a poplar with newly opened glossy leaves— caught the moonlight and trickled with as many sparkles as a waterfall. A silver shadow leaped out of a clump of bushes and glided like a fish against Alain's ankles.

"Ah! There you are, Saha! I was looking for you. Why didn't you appear at table tonight?"

"Me-rrou-wa," answered the cat, "me-rrou-wa."

"What, me-rrou-wa? And why me-rrou-wa? Do you really mean it?"

"Me-rrou-wa," insisted the cat, "me-rrou-wa."

He stroked her, tenderly groping his way down the long spine, which was softer than a hare's fur. Then he felt under his hand the small, cold nostrils dilated by her violent purring. "She's my cat. My very own cat."

"Me-rrou-wa," said the cat very softly. "R . . . rrou-wa."

Camille called once more from the house, and Saha vanished under a clipped euonymus hedge, black-green like the night.

"Alain! We're going!"

He ran to the steps while Camille watched him with a welcoming smile.

"I can see your hair running," she called out. "It's crazy to be as fair as all that!"

He ran quicker still, strode up the five steps in one bound, and found Camille alone in the drawing room.

"Where are the others?" he asked under his breath.

"Cloakroom," she whispered back. "Cloakroom and visit to 'work in progress.' General gloom. 'It's not getting on! It'll never be finished.' What the devil do we care! If one were smart, one could hold on to Patrick's studio for keeps. Patrick could find himself another. I'll fix it if you like."

"But Patrick would leave the 'Wedge' only as a special favor to please *you*."

"Of course. One will take advantage of that."

Her face sparkled with that peculiarly feminine unscrupulousness, which Alain could not bring himself to accept as a matter of course. But he remonstrated only about her habit of saying "one" for "we," and she took this as a reproach.

"I'll soon get into the habit of saying 'we.' "

So that he should want to kiss her, she turned out the ceiling light as if by accident. The one lamp left alight on a table threw a tall, sharply defined shadow behind the girl.

With her arms raised and her hands clasped on the nape of her neck, Camille gave him an inviting look. But he had eyes only for the shadow. "How beautiful she is on the wall! Just fine-drawn enough, just as I should like her to be."

He sat down to compare the one with the other. Flattered, Camille arched herself, thrusting out her breasts and her hips like a nautch girl, but the shadow was better at the game than she was. Unclasping her hands, the girl walked across the room, preceded by the ideal shadow. Arrived at the open French window, the shadow leaped to one side and fled out into the garden along the pink gravel of a path, embracing the moon-spangled poplar between its two long arms as it went. "What a pity!" sighed Alain. Then he weakly reproached himself for his inclination to love in Camille herself some perfected or motionless image of Camille. This shadow, for example, or a portrait or the vivid memory she left him of certain moments, certain dresses.

"What's the matter with you tonight? Come and help me put on my cape, at least."

He was shocked by what that "at least" secretly implied and also because Camille, as she passed before him through the door leading to the cloakroom and pantry, had almost imperceptibly shrugged her shoulders. "She doesn't need to shrug her shoulders. Nature and habit do that for her anyway. When she's not careful, her neck makes her look dumpy. Ever, ever so slightly dumpy."

In the cloakroom they found Alain's mother and Ca-

mille's parents stamping as if with cold and leaving foot-
marks the color of dirty snow on the matting. The cat,
seated on the windowsill outside, watched them inhos-
pitably but with no animosity. Alain imitated her patience and endured the ritual of pessimistic lamentations.

"It's the same old thing."

"It's hardly any further on than it was a week ago."

"My dear, if you want to know what *I* think, it won't
be another two weeks, it'll be a month. What am I talking about, a month? More likely *two* months before their
nest . . ."

At the word "nest" Camille flung herself into the
peaceful fray so shrilly that Alain and Saha closed their
eyes.

"But since we've already decided what to do! And
since we're actually *pleased* at having Patrick's place!
And since it suits Patrick down to the ground because
he has no dough—hasn't any money—sorry, Mummy.
We'll just take our suitcases and—Alley Oop!—straight
up to heaven on the ninth floor! Won't we, Alain?"

He opened his eyes again, smiled into the void, and
put her light cape around her shoulders. In the mirror
opposite them he met Camille's black, reproachful look,
but it did not soften his heart. "I didn't kiss her on the
lips when we were alone. All right, very well then, I
didn't kiss her on the lips. She hasn't had her full ration
of kisses-on-the-lips today. She had the quarter-to-
twelve one in the Bois, she had the two o'clock one after
coffee, she had the half-past-six one in the garden, but
she's missed tonight's. Well, if she's not satisfied, she'll
have to put it down on the account . . . What's the matter with me? I'm dying for sleep. This life's idiotic: we're
seeing far too much of each other and yet we never see
each other properly. On Monday I'll definitely go down
to the shop and . . ."

In imagination, the chemical acidity of the bales of
new silk assailed his nostrils. But the inscrutable smile
of M. Veuillet appeared to him as in a dream, and, as in
a dream, he heard words that at twenty-four he had still
not learned to hear without dread. "No, no, my young
friend. Will a new adding machine that costs seventeen
thousand francs pay back its initial outlay within the

year? It all depends on that. Allow your poor father's oldest partner . . ." Catching sight again in the looking glass of the vindictive image and handsome dark eyes that were watching him, he folded Camille in both his arms.

"Well, Alain?"

"Oh, my dear, let him alone! These poor infants . . ."

Camille blushed and disengaged herself. Then she held up her cheek to Alain with such a boyish, brotherly grace that he nearly put his head on her shoulder. "Oh, to lie down and go to sleep! Oh, good Lord! Just to lie down and sleep!"

From the garden came the voice of the cat.

"Me-rrou-wa . . . Rrr-rrouwa."

"Listen to that cat! She must be hunting," said Camille calmly. "Saha! Saha!"

The cat was silent.

"Hunting?" protested Alain. "Whatever makes you think that? To begin with, it's May. And then she's saying: 'Me-rrou-wa!' "

"So what?"

"She wouldn't be saying 'Me-rrou-wa' if she were hunting! What she's saying there—and it's really rather strange—means a warning. It's almost a cry calling her little ones together."

"Good Lord!" cried Camille, flinging up her arms. "If Alain's going to start interpreting the cat, we shall be here all night!"

She ran down the steps, and at the touch of old Émile's shaking hand, two old-fashioned gas globes, like huge mauve planets, illuminated the garden.

Alain walked ahead with Camille. At the entrance gate, he kissed her under her ear, breathed in, under a perfume too old for her, a good smell of bread and dark hair, and squeezed the girl's bare elbows under her cape. When she seated herself at the steering wheel, with her parents in the back, he felt suddenly wide awake and gay.

"Saha! Saha!"

The cat sprang out of the shadow, almost under his feet. When he began to run, she ran too, leaping ahead of him with long bounds. He guessed she was there with-

out seeing her; she burst before him into the hall and
came back to wait for him at the top of the steps. With
her frill standing out and her ears low, she watched him
running toward her, urging him on with her yellow eyes.
Those deep-set eyes were proud and suspicious, completely masters of themselves.

"Saha! Saha!"

Pronounced in a certain way, under his breath, with
the "h" strongly aspirated, her name made her wild. She
lashed her tail, bounded into the middle of the poker
table and with her two cat's hands spread wide open,
she scattered the playing cards.

"That cat, that cat!" said his mother's voice. "She
hasn't the faintest notion of hospitality. Look how delighted she is that our friends have gone!"

Alain let out a spurt of childish laughter, the laugh he
kept for home and the close intimacy that did not ex-
tend beyond the screen of elms or the black, wrought-
iron gate. Then he gave a frantic yawn.

"Good heavens, how tired you look! Is it possible to
look as tired as that when one's happy? There's still some
orangeade. No? We can go up then. Don't bother, Émile
will turn out the lights."

"Mother's talking to me as if I were getting over an
illness or as if I were starting up a fever again."

"Saha! Saha! What a demon! Alain, couldn't you per-
suade that cat . . . ?"

By a vertical path known to herself, marked on the
worn brocade, the cat had almost reached the ceiling.
One moment she imitated a gray lizard, flattening against
the wall with her paws spread out; then she pretended to
be giddy and tried an affected little cry of appeal. Alain
obediently came and stood below, and Saha slid down,
glued to the wall like a raindrop sliding down a pane.
She came to rest on Alain's shoulder and the two of
them went up together to their bedroom.

A long hanging cluster of laburnum, black outside the
open window, became a long, pale-yellow cluster when
Alain turned on the ceiling light and the bedside lamp.
He poured the cat off onto the bed by inclining his shoulder, then wandered aimlessly to and fro between his

room and the bathroom like a man who is too tired to go to bed.

He leaned out over the garden, looked with a hostile eye for the white mass of the uncompleted "alterations." Then he opened and shut several drawers and boxes in which reposed his real secrets: a gold dollar, a signet ring, an agate charm attached to his father's watch chain, some red and black seeds from an exotic canna plant, a First Communicant's mother-of-pearl rosary, and a thin broken bracelet, the souvenir of a tempestuous young mistress who had passed swiftly and noisily out of his life. The rest of his worldly goods consisted merely of some paper-covered books he had had rebound and some letters and photographs.

Dreamily, he turned over these little scraps of wreckage, bright and worthless as the colored stones one finds in the nests of pilfering birds. "Should I throw all this away . . . or leave it here? It means nothing to me. Or does it mean something?" Being an only child, he was attached to everything that he had never shared with anyone else and for whose possession he had never had to fight.

He saw his face in the glass and became suddenly irritated with himself. "Why can't you go to bed? You look a wreck. Positively disgraceful!" he said to the handsome fair young man. "People only think me handsome because I'm fair. If I were dark, I'd be hideous." For the hundredth time, he criticized his long cheeks and his slightly equine nose. But, for the hundredth time, he smiled so as to display his teeth to himself and admiringly touched the natural wave in his fair, over-thick hair. Once again he was pleased with the color of his eyes, greenish-gray between dark lashes. Two wrinkles hollowed his cheeks on either side of the smile, the eyes receded, circled with mauve shadows. He had shaved that morning, but already a pale, stubbly bristle coarsened his upper lip. "What a mug! I pity myself. No, I repel myself. Is *that* a face for a wedding night?" In the depths of the mirror, Saha gravely watched him from the distance.

"I'm coming, I'm coming."

He flung himself on the cool expanse of the sheets, humoring the cat. Rapidly, he went through certain ritual litanies dedicated to the particular graces and virtues of a small, perfect, pure-bred Russian Blue.

"My little bear with the big cheeks. Exquisite, exquisite, exquisite cat. My blue pigeon. Pearl-colored demon."

As soon as he turned out the light, the cat began to trample delicately on her friend's chest. Each time she pressed down her feet, one single claw pierced the silk of the pajamas, catching the skin just enough for Alain to feel an uneasy pleasure.

"Seven more days, Saha," he sighed.

In seven days and seven nights he would begin a new life in new surroundings with an amorous and untamed young woman. He stroked the cat's fur, warm and cool at the same time and smelling of clipped box, thuya, and lush grass. She was purring full-throatedly, and in the darkness, she gave him a cat's kiss, laying her damp nose for a second under Alain's nose between his nostrils and his lip. A swift, immaterial kiss, which she rarely accorded him.

"Ah, Saha! Our nights . . ."

The headlights of a car in the nearest avenue pierced the leaves with two revolving white beams. Over the wall of the room passed the enlarged shadow of the laburnum and of a tulip tree that stood alone in the middle of a lawn. Above his own face Alain saw Saha's face illuminated for a moment. Before it was eclipsed again, he had seen that her eyes were hard.

"Don't frighten me!" he implored.

For when Alain was sleepy, he became once more weak and fanciful, caught in the mesh of a sweet and interminable adolescence.

He shut his eyes while Saha kept vigil, watching all the invisible signs that hover over sleeping human beings when the light is put out.

He always dreamed a great deal and descended into his dreams by definite stages. When he woke up, he did not talk about his adventures of the night. He was jealous of a realm that had been enlarged by a delicate and ill-governed childhood; by long sojourns in bed during his swift growth into a tall, frail, slender boy.

He loved his dreams and cultivated them. Not for anything in the world would he have revealed the successive stages that awaited him. At the first stopping place, while he could still hear the car horns on the avenue, he met an eddy of faces, familiar yet distorted, which he passed through as he might have passed through a friendly crowd, greeting one here and there. Eddying, bulbous, the faces approached Alain, growing larger and larger. Light against a dark background, they became lighter still as if they received their illumination from the sleeper himself. Each was furnished with one great eye and they circled around in an effortless gyration. But a submerged electric current shot them far away as soon as they touched an invisible barrier. In the humid gaze of a circular monster, in the eye of a plump moon or that of a wild archangel with rays of light for hair, Alain could recognize the same expression, the same intention that none of them had put into words and that the Alain of the dream noted with a sense of security: "They'll tell it to me tomorrow."

Sometimes they disappeared by exploding into scattered, faintly luminous fragments. At other times they continued only as a hand, an arm, a forehead, an eyeball full of thoughts, or as a starry dust of chins and noses. But always there remained that prominent, convex eye that just at the moment of making itself clear turned around and exposed only its other, black, surface.

The sleeping Alain pursued, under Saha's watchful care, his nightly shipwreck. He passed beyond the world of convex faces and eyes and descended through a zone of darkness, where he was conscious of nothing but a powerful, positive blackness, indescribably varied and, as it were, composed of submerged colors. On the confines of this, he launched into the real, complete, fully formed dream.

He came up violently against a barrier, which gave a great clang like the prolonged, splintering clash of a cymbal. And then he found himself in the dream city, among the passersby, the inhabitants standing in their doorways, the gold-crowned guardians of the square and the stage crowd posted along the path of an Alain who was completely naked and armed with a walking stick.

This Alain was extremely lucid and sagacious: "If I walk rather fast, after tying my tie in a special way, and particularly if I whistle, there's every chance that no one will notice I am naked." So he tied his tie in a heart-shaped knot and whistled. "That's not whistling, what I'm doing. It's purring. Whistling's like this . . ." But he still continued to purr. "I'm not at the end of my tether yet. All I've got to do—it's perfectly simple—is to cross this sun-drenched open space and go around the bandstand, where the military band is playing. Child's play. I run, making perilous jumps to distract attention, and I come out in the zone of shadow . . ."

But he was paralyzed by the warm, dangerous look of a dark man in the stage crowd; a young man with a Greek profile perforated by a great eye like a carp's. "The zone of shadow . . . the zone of *the* shadow . . ." Two long shadowy arms, graceful and rustling with poplar leaves, appeared at the word "shadow" and carried Alain away, so that, during the most ambiguous hour of the short night, he might rest in that provisional tomb where the living exile sighs, weeps, fights, and succumbs, and from which he rises, remembering nothing, with the day.

[TRANSLATED BY ANTONIA WHITE]

Gigi

"Don't forget you are going to Aunt Alicia's. Do you hear me, Gilberte? Come here and let me do your curls. Gilberte, do you hear me?"

"Couldn't I go there without having my hair curled, Grandmama?"

"I should think not," said Madame Alvarez quietly. She took an old pair of curling irons, with prongs ending in little round metal knobs, and put them to heat over the blue flame of a spirit lamp while she prepared the tissue papers.

"Grandmama, couldn't you do my hair in waves down the side of my head for a change?"

"Out of the question. Ringlets at the very ends—that's as far as a girl of your age can possibly go. Now sit down on the footstool."

To do so, Gilberte folded up under her the heronlike legs of a girl of fifteen. Below her tartan skirt, she revealed ribbed cotton stockings to just above the knees, unconscious of the perfect oval shape of her kneecaps. Slender calf and high arched instep—Madame Alvarez never let her eyes run over these fine points without regretting that her granddaughter had not studied dancing professionally. At the moment, she was thinking only of the girl's hair. She had corkscrewed the ends and fixed them in tissue paper, and was now compressing the ash-blond ringlets between the heated knobs. With patient, soft-fingered skill she gathered up the full magnificent weight of finely kept hair into sleek ripples that fell to just below Gilberte's shoulders. The girl sat quite still. The smell of the heated tongs and the whiff of vanilla in the curling papers made her feel drowsy. Besides, Gilberte knew that resistance would be useless.

She hardly ever tried to elude the restraints exercised by her family.

"Is Mama singing Frasquita today?"

"Yes. And this evening in *Si j'étais Roi*. I have told you before, when you're sitting on a low seat you must keep your knees close to each other and lean both of them together, either to the right or to the left, for the sake of decorum."

"But, Grandmama, I've got on my drawers and my petticoat."

"Drawers are one thing, decorum is another," said Madame Alvarez. "Everything depends on the attitude."

"Yes, I know. Aunt Alicia has told me often enough," Gilberte murmured from under her tent of hair.

"I do not require the help of my sister," said Madame Alvarez testily, "to instruct you in the elements of propriety. On that subject, thank goodness, I know rather more than she does."

"Supposing you let me stay here with you today, Grandmama, couldn't I go see Aunt Alicia next Sunday?"

"What next!" said Madame Alvarez haughtily. "Have you any other *purposal* to make to me?"

"Yes, I have," said Gilberte. "Have my skirts made a little longer, so I don't have to fold myself up in a Z every time I sit down. You see, Grandmama, with my skirts too short, I have to keep thinking of my you-know-what."

"Silence! Aren't you ashamed to call it your you-know-what?"

"I don't mind calling it by any other name, only—"

Madame Alvarez blew out the spirit lamp, looked at the reflection of her heavy Spanish face in the looking glass above the mantelpiece, and then laid down the law: "There is no other name."

A skeptical look passed across the girl's eyes. Beneath the cockleshells of fair hair they showed a lovely dark blue, the color of glistening slate. Gilberte unfolded with a bound.

"But, Grandmama, all the same, look! If only my skirts were just that much longer! Or if a small frill could be added!"

"That *would* be nice for your mother, to be seen with a great mare who looks at least eighteen! In her profession! Where are your brains!"

"In my head," said Gilberte. "Since I hardly ever go out with Mama, what would it matter?"

She pulled down her skirt, which had climbed up toward her slim waist, and asked, "Can I go in my everyday coat? It's good enough."

"That wouldn't show that it's Sunday! Put on your serge coat and blue sailor hat. When will you learn what's what?"

On her feet, Gilberte was as tall as her grandmother. Madame Alvarez had taken the name of a Spanish lover now dead and, accordingly, had acquired a creamy complexion, an ample bust, and hair lustrous with brilliantine. She used too white a powder, and her heavy cheeks had begun to draw down her lower eyelids a little, so that eventually she took to calling herself Inez. Her family pursued their fixed orbit around her. Her unmarried daughter Andrée, forsaken by Gilberte's father, now preferred the sober life of a second-lead singer in a state-controlled theater to the fitful opulence of a life of gallantry. Aunt Alicia—none of her admirers, it seemed, had ever mentioned marriage—lived alone, on an income she pretended was modest. The family had a high opinion of Alicia's judgment and of her jewels.

Madame Alvarez looked her granddaughter up and down, from the felt sailor hat trimmed with a quill to the ready-made cavalier shoes.

"Can't you ever manage to keep your legs together? When you stand like that, the Seine could flow between them. You haven't the shadow of a stomach, and yet you somehow contrive to stick it out. And don't forget your gloves, I beg of you."

Gilberte's every posture was still governed by the unconcern of childish innocence. At times she looked like Robin Hood, at others like a stone angel, or again like a boy in skirts; but she seldom resembled a nearly grown-up girl. "How can you expect to be put into long skirts when you haven't the sense of a child of eight?" Madame Alvarez would ask. And Andrée would sigh, "I find Gilberte so discouraging." To which Gilberte would answer quietly, "If you didn't find *me* discouraging, then you'd find something else." For she was sweet and gentle, resigned to a stay-at-home life and to seeing few people outside the family. As for her features, no one could yet predict their final mold. A large mouth, which showed beautiful strong white teeth when she laughed, no chin to speak of, and, between high cheekbones, a nose—"Heavens, where did she get that button?" whispered her mother under her breath. "If you can't answer that question, my girl, who can?" retorted Madame Alvarez. Whereupon Andrée, who had become prudish too late in life and disgruntled too soon, relapsed into silence, automatically stroking her sensitive larynx. "Gigi is just a bundle of raw material," Aunt Alicia affirmed. "It may turn out very well—and, just as easily, all wrong."

"Grandmama, there's the bell! I'll open the door on my way out. Grandmama," Gigi shouted from the passage, "it's Uncle Gaston!"

She came back into the room with a tall, youngish-looking man, her arm linked through his, chattering to him with the childish pomposity of a schoolgirl out of class.

"What a pity it is, Tonton, that I've got to desert you so soon! Grandmama wishes me to pay a call on Aunt Alicia. Which motorcar are you using today? Did you come in the new four-seater-de-Dion-Boutan-with-the-collapsible-hood? I hear it can be driven simply with one hand! Goodness, Tonton, those are smart gloves, and no mistake! So you've had a fight with Liane, Tonton?"

"Gilberte," scolded Madame Alvarez, "what business of yours can that be?"

"But, Grandmama, everybody knows about it. The whole story was in the *Gil Blas*. It began: 'A secret bitterness is seeping into the sweetened product of the sugarbeet. . . .' At school all the girls were asking me about it, for of course they know I know you. And I can tell you, Tonton, there's not a soul at school who takes Liane's side! They all agree that she's behaved disgracefully!"

"Gilberte," repeated Madame Alvarez, "say good-bye to Monsieur Lachaille and run along!"

"Leave her alone, poor child," Gaston Lachaille sighed. "She, at any rate, intends no harm. And it's perfectly true that all's over between Liane and me. You're off to Aunt Alicia's, Gigi? Take my motorcar and send it back for me."

Gilberte gave a little cry, a jump of joy, and hugged Lachaille.

"Thank you, Tonton! Just think of Aunt Alicia's face! The concierge's eyes will be popping from her head!"

Off she went, with the clatter of a young filly not yet shod.

"You spoil her, Gaston," said Madame Alvarez.

But in this she was not altogether speaking the truth. Gaston Lachaille did not know how to "spoil" anyone —even himself. His luxuries were cut and dried: motor-cars, a dreary mansion on the Parc Monceau, Liane's monthly "allowance" and birthday jewels, champagne and baccarat at Deauville in the summer, at Monte Carlo in the winter. From time to time he would drop a fat check into some charity fund, or finance a new daily paper, or buy a yacht only to resell it almost at once to some Central European monarch—yet from none of this did he get any fun. He would say as he looked at himself in the glass, "That's the face of a man who's been rooked." Because of his rather long nose and large dark eyes, he was regarded on all sides as easy game. His commercial instinct and rich man's caution stood him in good stead, however; no one had succeeded in robbing him of his pearl studs, of his massive gold or silver cigarette cases encrusted with precious stones, of his dark sable-lined greatcoat.

From the window he watched his motorcar start up. That year fashionable automobiles were being built with a slightly higher body and a rather wider top to accommodate the exaggerated hats affected by Caroline Otero, Liane de Pougy, and other conspicuous figures of 1899 —and in consequence they would sway gently at every turn of the wheel.

"Mamita," said Gaston Lachaille, "you wouldn't make me a cup of camomile?"

"Two rather than one," answered Madame Alvarez. "Sit down, my poor Gaston."

From the depths of a dilapidated armchair she removed some crumpled illustrated papers, a stocking waiting to be darned, and a box of licorice candies known as *agents de change*. The jilted man settled down into the chair luxuriously while his hostess put out the tray and two cups.

"Why does the camomile they brew at home always smell of faded chrysanthemums?" sighed Gaston.

"It's simply a matter of taking pains. You may not believe it, Gaston, but I often pick my best camomile flowers in Paris, growing on waste ground, insignificant little flowers you would hardly notice. But they have a taste that is *esquisite*. My goodness, what beautiful cloth your suit is made of! That deep-woven stripe is as smart as can be. Just the sort of material your poor father liked! But, I must confess, he would never have carried it so elegantly."

Never more than once during the course of a conversation did Madame Alvarez evoke the memory of an elder Lachaille, whom she claimed to have known intimately. From her former relationship, real or invented, she drew no advantage other than the close relationship of Gaston Lachaille and the pleasure to be derived from watching a rich man enjoying the comforts of the poor when he made himself at home in her old armchair. Under their gas-blackened ceiling, these three feminine creatures never asked him for pearls, chinchillas, or solitaire diamonds, and they knew how to converse with tact and due solemnity on scandalous topics traditional and recondite. From the age of twelve, Gigi had known that Madame Otero's string of large black pearls were "dipped," that is to say, artificially tinted, whereas the three strings of her matchlessly graded pearl necklace were worth "a king's ransom"; that Madame de Pougy's seven rows lacked "life"; that Eugénie Fougère's famous diamond bolero was quite worthless; and that no self-respecting woman gadded about, like Madame Antokolski, in a coupé upholstered in mauve satin. She had obediently broken her friendship with a school friend,

Lydia Poret, after the girl had shown her a solitaire, set as a ring, presented by the Baron Ephraim.

"A solitaire!" Madame Alvarez had exclaimed. "For a girl of fifteen! Her mother must be mad!"

"But, Grandmama," pleaded Gigi, "it's not Lydia's fault if the Baron gave it to her!"

"Silence! I'm not blaming the Baron. The Baron knows what is expected of him. But plain common sense should have told the mother to put the ring in a safe at the bank, while waiting."

"While waiting for what, Grandmama?"

"To see how things turn out."

"Why not in her jewel box?"

"Because one never knows. Especially since the Baron is the sort of man who might change his mind. If on the other hand he has declared himself openly, Madame Poret has only to withdraw her daughter from her studies. Until the matter has been properly cleared up, you will oblige me by not walking home with that little Poret. Who ever heard of such a thing!"

"But supposing she marries, Grandmama?"

"Marries? Marries whom, pray?"

"Why, the Baron!"

Madame Alvarez and her daughter exchanged glances of stupefaction. "I find the child so discouraging," Andrée had murmured. "She comes from another planet."

"My poor Gaston," said Madame Alvarez, "is it really true, then, that you have broken with her? In some ways, it may be the best thing for you; but in others, I'm sure you must find it most upsetting. Whom can one trust, I ask you!"

Poor Gaston listened while he drank the scalding camomile. The taste of it gave him as much comfort as the sight of the plaster rose on the ceiling, still black from the hanging lamp now "converted to electricity," still faithfully retaining its shader—vast frilly bell of palest green. Half the contents of a workbasket lay strewn over the dining-room table, from which Gilberte had forgotten to remove her notebook. Above the upright piano hung an enlarged photograph of Gilberte at eight months, as a pendant to a portrait in oil of Andrée, dressed

for her part in *Si j'etais Roi*. The completely inoffensive
untidiness, the ray of spring sunshine coming through
the lace curtains, the warmth given out by a little stove
kept at a low heat—all these homely things were like
so many soothing potions to the nerves of a jilted and
lonely millionaire.

"Are you positively in torment, my poor Gaston?"

"To be exact, I'm not in torment. I'm just very upset,
as you say."

"I have no wish to appear inquisitive," said Madame
Alvarez, "but how did it all happen? I've read the papers,
of course; but can one believe what they say?"

Lachaille tugged at his small, waxed mustache and
ran his fingers over his thick, cropped hair.

"Oh, much the same as on previous occasions. She
waited for the birthday present, then off she trotted.
And, into the bargain, she had to go bury herself in
such a wretched little hole in Normandy—so stupid of
her! Any fool could have discovered that there were
only two rooms at the inn, one occupied by Liane, the
other by Sandomir, a skating instructor from the *Palais
de Glace*."

"He's Polaire's teatime waltzing partner, isn't he? Oh,
women don't know where to draw the line nowadays!
And just after her birthday, too! Oh, it's so tactless!
What could be more unladylike!"

Madame Alvarez stirred the teaspoon around and
around in her cup, her little finger in the air. When she
lowered her gaze, her lids did not quite cover her pro-
tuberant eyeballs, and her resemblance to George Sand
became marked.

"I'd given her a 'rope,'" said Gaston Lachaille.
"What you might call a rope—thirty-seven pearls. The
middle one as big as the ball of my thumb."

He held out his white, beautifully manicured thumb,
to which Madame Alvarez accorded the admiration due
to a middle pearl.

"You certainly know how to do things in style," she
said. "You came out of it extremely well, Gaston."

"I came out of it with a pair of horns, certainly."

Madame Alvarez did not seem to have heard him.

"If I were you, Gaston, I would try to get even with her. I would take up with some society lady."

"That's a nice pill to offer me," said Lachaille, who was absentmindedly helping himself to the *agents de change*.

"Yes, indeed, I might even say that sometimes the cure may prove worse than the disease," Madame Alvarez continued, tactfully agreeing with him. "Out of the frying pan into the fire." After which she respected Gaston Lachaille's silence.

The muffled sounds of a piano penetrated through the ceiling. Without a word, the visitor held out his empty cup, and Madame Alvarez refilled it.

"Is the family all right? What's new with Aunt Alicia?"

"Oh, my sister, you know, is always the same. She's smart enough to keep herself to herself. She says she would rather live in a splendid past than in an ugly present. Her King of Spain, her Milan of Serbia, her Khedive, her rajahs by the half dozen—or so she would have you believe! She is very considerate to Gigi. She finds her a trifle backward for her age, as indeed she is, and puts her through her paces. Last week, for instance, she taught her how to eat *homard a l'américaine* in faultless style."

"Whatever for?"

"Alicia says it will be extremely useful. The three great stumbling blocks in a girl's education, she maintains, are *homard a l'américaine,* a boiled egg, and asparagus. Bad table manners, she says, have broken up many a happy home."

"That can happen," said Lachaille dreamily.

"Oh, Alicia is no fool! And it's just what Gigi requires—she is so greedy! If only her brain worked as well as her jaws! But she might well be a child of ten! And what breathtaking scheme have you got for the Battle of Flowers? Are you going to dazzle us again this year?"

"Oh Lord no!" groaned Gaston. "I shall take advantage of my misfortune and save on the red roses."

Madame Alvarez clasped her hands.

"Oh, Gaston, you mustn't do that! If you're not there, the procession will look like a funeral!"

"I don't care what it looks like," said Gaston gloomily.

"You're never going to leave the prize banner to people like Valérie Cheniaguine? Oh, Gaston, we can't allow that!"

"You will have to. Valérie can very well afford it."

"Especially since she does it so cheaply! Gaston, do you know where she went for the ten thousand bunches thrown last year? She had three women tying them up for two days and two nights, and the flowers were bought in the flower market! In the market! Only the four wheels, and the coachman's whip, and the harness trappings bore the label of Lachaume."

"That's a trick worth remembering!" said Lachaille, cheering up. "Good Lord! I've finished the licorice!"

The tap-tap of Gilberte's marching footsteps could be heard crossing the outer room.

"Back already!" said Madame Alvarez. "What's the meaning of this?"

"The meaning," said the girl, "is that Aunt Alicia wasn't in good form. But I've been out in Tonton's 'tuf-tuf.' "

Her lips parted in a bright smile.

"You know, Tonton, all the time I was in your automobile, I put on a martyred expression—like this—as if I was bored to death with every luxury under the sun. I had the time of my life."

She sent her hat flying across the room, and her hair fell tumbling over her forehead and cheeks. She perched herself on a rather high stool and tucked her knees up under her chin.

"Well, Tonton? You look as if you were dying of boredom. What about a game of piquet? It's Sunday, and Mama doesn't come back between the two performances. Who's been eating all my licorice? Oh, Tonton, you can't get away with that! The least you can do is to send me some more to make up for it."

"Gilberte, your manners!" scolded Madame Alvarez. "Lower your knees! Gaston hasn't the time to bother about your licorice. Pull down your skirts. Gaston, would you like me to send her to her room?"

Young Lachaille, with one eye on the dirty pack of cards in Gilberte's hand, was longing simultaneously to give way to tears, to confide his sorrows, to go to sleep in the old armchair, and to play piquet.

"Let the child stay! In this room I can relax. It's restful. Gigi, I'll play you for twenty pounds of sugar."

"Your sugar's not very tempting. I much prefer sweets."

"It's the same thing. And sugar is better for you than sweets."

"You only say that because you make it."

"Gilberte, you forget yourself!"

A smile enlivened the mournful eyes of Gaston Lachaille.

"Let her say what she likes, Mamita. And if I lose, Gigi, what would you like? A pair of silk stockings?"

The corners of Gilberte's big childish mouth fell.

"Silk stockings make my legs itch. I would rather—"

She raised the snub-nosed face of an angel toward the ceiling, put her head on one side, and tossed her curls from one cheek to the other.

"I would rather have a Nile-green Persephone corset, with rococo roses embroidered on the garters. No, I'd rather have a music case."

"Are you studying music now?"

"No, but my older friends at school carry their notebooks in music cases because it makes them look like students at the Conservatoire."

"Gilberte, you're becoming indiscreet!" said Madame Alvarez.

"You shall have your case and your licorice. Cut, Gigi."

The next moment, the heir of Lachaille-Sugar was deep in the game. His prominent nose, large enough to appear false, and his slightly black eyes did not in the least intimidate his opponent. With her elbows on the table, her shoulders on a level with her ears, and her blue eyes and red cheeks at their most vivid, she looked like a tipsy page. They both played passionately, almost in silence, exchanging occasional insults under their breath. "You spindly spider! You sorrel run to seed!" Lachaille muttered. "You old crow's beak!" the girl countered. The March twilight deepened over the narrow street.

"Please don't think I want you to go, Gaston," said

Madame Alvarez, "but it's half-past seven. Will you excuse me while I just see about our dinner?"

"Half-past seven!" cried Lachaille. "And I'm supposed to be dining at Larue's with De Dion, Feydeau, and one of the Barthous! This must be the last hand, Gigi."

"Why one of the Barthous?" asked Gilberte. "Are there several of them?"

"Two. One handsome and the other less so. The best known is the least handsome."

"That's not fair," said Gilberte. "And Feydeau, who's he?"

Lachaille plopped down his cards in amazement.

"Well, I must say! She doesn't know who Feydeau is! Don't you ever go to a play?"

"Hardly ever, Tonton."

"Don't you like the theater?"

"I'm not mad about it. And Grandmama and Aunt Alicia both say that going to plays prevents one from thinking about the serious side of life. Don't tell Grandmama I told you."

She lifted the weight of her hair away from her ears and let it fall forward again. "Phew!" she sighed. "This mane does make me hot!"

"And what do they mean by the serious side of life?"

"Oh, I don't know it all by heart, Uncle Gaston. And what's more, they don't always agree about it. Grandmama says: 'Don't read novels, they only depress you. Don't put on powder, it ruins the complexion. Don't wear a corset, it spoils the figure. Don't dawdle and gaze at shop windows when you're by yourself. Don't get to know the families of your school friends, especially not the fathers who wait at the gates to fetch their daughters home from school.'"

She spoke very rapidly, panting between words like a child who has been running.

"And on top of that, Aunt Alicia goes off on another tack! I've reached the age when I can wear a corset, and I should take lessons in dancing and deportment, and I should be aware of what's going on, and know the meaning of 'carat,' and not be taken in by the clothes that actresses wear. 'It's quite simple,' she tells me. 'Of all the dresses you see on the stage, nineteen out of twenty would look ridiculous in the paddock.' In fact, my head is ready to split with it all! What will you be eating at Larue's this evening, Tonton?"

"How should I know! *Filets de sole aux moules,* for a change. And of course, saddle of lamb with truffles. Get on with the game, Gigi! I've got a point of five."

"That won't get you anywhere. I've got all the cards in the pack. Here at home we're having the warmed-up remains of the *cassoulet*. I'm very fond of *cassoulet*."

"A plain dish of *cassoulet* with bacon rind," said Inez Alvarez modestly as she came in. "Goose was exorbitant this week."

"I'll have one sent to you from Bon-Abri," said Gaston.

"Thank you very much, Gaston. Gigi, help Monsieur Lachaille on with his overcoat. Fetch him his hat and stick!"

When Lachaille had gone, rather sulky after a regretful sniff at the warmed-up *cassoulet,* Madame Alvarez turned to her granddaughter.

"Will you please inform me, Gilberte, why it was you returned so early from Aunt Alicia's? I didn't ask you in front of Gaston. Family matters must never be discussed in front of a third person, remember that!"

"There's no mystery about it, Grandmama. Aunt Alicia was wearing her little lace cap to show me she had a headache. She said to me, 'I'm not very well.' I said to her, 'Oh! Then I mustn't tire you out. I'll go home again.' She said to me, 'Sit down and rest for five minutes.' 'Oh,' I said to her, 'I'm not tired. I drove here.' 'You drove here!' she said to me, raising her hands like this. As you may imagine, I had kept the motor car waiting a few minutes, to show Aunt Alicia. 'Yes,' I said to her, 'the four-seater-De-Dion-Bouton-with-the-collapsible-hood, which Tonton lent me while he was paying a call on us. He has had a fight with Liane.' 'Who do you think you're talking to?' she says to me. 'I don't have one foot in the grave yet! I'm still kept informed about public events when they're important. I know that he has had a fight with that great lampstand of a woman. Well, you'd better run along home

and not bother about a poor sick old woman like me.'
She waved to me from the window as I got into the
motor car."

Madame Alvarez pursed her lips.

"A poor sick old woman! She has never suffered so
much as a cold in her life! I like that! What . . ."

"Grandmama, do you think he'll remember my licorice and the music case?"

Madame Alvarez slowly lifted her heavy eyes toward
the ceiling.

"Perhaps, my child, perhaps."

"But, since he lost, he owes them to me, doesn't he?"

"Yes, yes, he owes them to you. Perhaps you'll get
them after all. Slip on your smock and set the table.
Put away your cards."

"Yes, Grandmama. Grandmama, what did he tell you
about Madame Liane? Is it true she ran out on him
with Sandomir and the rope of pearls?"

"In the first place, one doesn't say 'ran out on' anyone. In the second, come here and let me tighten your
ribbon, so that your curls won't get soaked in the soup.
And finally, the sayings and doings of a person who has
broken the rules of etiquette are not for your ears.
These happen to be Gaston's private affairs."

"But, Grandmama, they are no longer private since
everyone's talking about them, and the whole thing came
out in *Gil Blas*."

"Quiet! All you need to know is that the conduct of
Madame Liane d'Exelmans has been the reverse of sensible. The ham for your mother is between two plates:
you will put it in a cool place."

Gilberte was asleep when her mother—Andrée Alvar,
in small type on the Opéra-Comique playbills—returned
home. Madame Alvarez, the elder, seated at a game of
patience, inquired from force of habit whether she was
not too tired. Following polite family custom, Andrée
reproached her mother for having waited up, and Madame Alvarez made her ritual reply: "I shouldn't sleep
in peace unless I knew you were in. There is some ham
and a little bowl of warm *cassoulet*. And some stewed
prunes. The beer is on the windowsill."

"The child is in bed?"

"Of course."

Andrée Alvar ate a solid meal—pessimists have good appetites. She still looked pretty in theatrical make-up. Without it, the rims of her eyes were pink and her lips colorless. For this reason, Aunt Alicia declared, Andrée never met with the admiration in real life that she gained on the stage.

"Did you sing well, my child?"

"Yes, I sang well. But where does it get me? All the applause goes to Tiphaine, as you may well imagine. Oh dear, oh dear, I really don't think I can bear to go on with this sort of life."

"It was your own choice. But you would bear it much better," said Madame Alvarez sententiously, "if you had someone! It's your loneliness that gets on your nerves and makes you take such black views. You're behaving contrary to nature."

"Oh, Mother, don't start that all over again. I'm tired enough as it is. What news is there?"

"None. Everyone's talking of Gaston's break with Liane."

"Yes, they certainly are! Even in the green room at the Opéra-Comique, which can hardly be called up-to-date."

"It's an event of worldwide interest," said Madame Alvarez.

"Is there talk of who's in the running?"

"I should think not! It's far too recent. He is in full mourning, so to speak. Can you believe it, at a quarter to eight he was sitting exactly where you are now, playing a game of piquet with Gigi? He says he has no wish to attend the Battle of Flowers."

"Not really!"

"Yes. If he doesn't go, it will cause a great deal of talk. I advised him to think twice before making such a decision."

"They were saying at the *Théâtre* that a certain music-hall artiste might stand a chance," said Andrée. "The one billed as the Cobra at the Olympia. It seems she does an acrobatic turn, and is brought on in a

basket hardly big enough for a fox terrier, and from
this she uncurls like a snake."

Madame Alvarez protruded her heavy lower lip in contempt.

"What an idea! Gaston Lachaille has not sunk to that
level! A music-hall performer! Do him the justice to
admit that, as befits a bachelor of his standing, he has
always confined himself to the great ladies of the profession."

"A fine pack of bitches!" murmured Andrée.

"Be more careful how you express yourself, my child.
Calling people and things by their names has never done
anyone any good. Gaston's mistresses have all had an air
about them. A liaison with a great professional lady is
the only suitable way for him to wait for a great marriage, always supposing that some day he does marry.
Whatever may happen, we're in the front row when anything fresh turns up. Gaston has such confidence in me!
I wish you had seen him asking me for camomile! A boy,
a regular boy! Indeed, he is only thirty-three. And all
that wealth weighs so heavily on his shoulders."

Andrée's pink eyelids blinked ironically.

"Pity him, Mother, if you like. I'm not complaining, but
all the time we've known Gaston, he has never given you
anything except his confidence."

"He owes us nothing. And thanks to him we've always
had sugar for our jams and, from time to time, for my
curaçao; and birds from his farm, and odds and ends
for the child."

"If you're satisfied with that!"

Madame Alvarez held high her majestic head.

"Perfectly satisfied. And even if I was not, what difference would it make?"

"In fact, as far as we're concerned, Gaston Lachaille,
rich as he is, behaves as if he wasn't rich at all. Supposing we were in real straits! Would he come to our
rescue, do you suppose?"

Madame Alvarez placed her hand on her heart.

"I'm convinced that he would," she said. And after a
pause, she added, "But I would rather not have to ask
him."

Andrée picked up the *Journal* again, in which there

was a photograph of Liane, the ex-mistress. "When you take a good look at her, she's not so extraordinary."

"You're wrong," retorted Madame Alvarez, "she is extraordinary. Otherwise she would not be so famous. Success and fame are not a matter of luck. You talk like those scatterbrains who say, 'Seven rows of pearls would look every bit as well on me as on Madame de Pougy. She certainly cuts a fine figure—but so could I.' Such nonsense makes me laugh. Take what's left of the camomile to bathe your eyes."

"Thank you, Mother. Did the child go to Aunt Alicia's?"

"She did indeed, and in Gaston's motorcar, what's more! He lent it to her. It can go forty miles an hour, I believe! She was in seventh heaven."

"Poor lamb, I wonder what she'll make of her life. She's quite capable of ending up as a mannequin or a salesgirl. She's so backward. At her age I—"

There was no indulgence in the glance Madame Alvarez gave her daughter.

"Don't boast too much about what you were doing when you were her age. If I remember rightly, at her age you were snapping your fingers at Monsieur Mennesson and all his flour mills, though he was perfectly ready to make you your fortune. Instead, you had to run off with a wretched music master."

Andrée Alvar kissed her mother's lustrous braids.

"My darling mother, don't curse me at this hour. I'm so sleepy. Good night, Mother. I've a rehearsal tomorrow at a quarter to one. I'll eat at the dairy during the entr'acte; don't bother about me."

She yawned and walked in the dark through the little room where her daughter was asleep. All she could see of Gilberte in the obscurity was a bush of hair and the Russian braid of her nightdress. She locked herself into the diminutive bathroom and, late though it was, lit the gas under a kettle. Madame Alvarez had instilled into her progeny, among other virtues, a respect for certain rites. One of her maxims was, "You can, at a pinch, leave the face till the morning when traveling or pressed for time. For a woman, attention to the lower parts is the first law of self-respect."

The last to go to bed, Madame Alvarez was the first to
rise, and allowed the daily cleaning woman no hand in
preparing the breakfast coffee. She slept in the dining-
sitting room on a sofa bed, and at the stroke of half-
past seven she opened the door to the papers, the quart
of milk, and the daily maid—who was carrying the others.
By eight o'clock she had taken out her curling pins, and
her beautiful coils of hair were brushed and smooth. At
ten minutes to nine, Gilberte left for school, clean and
tidy, her hair well brushed. At ten o'clock Madame
Alvarez was "thinking about" the midday meal, that is,
she got into her waterproof, slipped her arm through the
handle of her shopping bag, and set off to market.

Today, as on all other days, she made sure that her
granddaughter would not be late; she placed the coffee
pot and the jug of milk piping hot on the table and unfolded the newspaper while waiting for her. Gilberte came
in fresh as a flower, smelling of lavender water, with some
vestiges of sleep still clinging to her. A cry from Madame
Alvarez made her fully wide awake.

"Call your mother, Gigi! Liane d'Exelmans has committed suicide."

The child replied with a long drawn-out "Oooh!" and
asked, "Is she dead?"

"Of course not. She knows how to do things."

"How did she do it, Grandmama? A revolver?"

Madame Alvarez looked pityingly at her granddaughter.

"The idea! Laudanum, as usual. 'Doctors Morèze and
Pelledoux, who have never left the heartbroken beauty's
bedside, cannot yet answer for her life, but their
diagnosis is reassuring. . . .' My own diagnosis is that if
Madame d'Exelmans goes on playing that game, she'll
wind up ruining her stomach."

"The last time she killed herself, Grandmama, was for
the sake of Prince Georgevitch, wasn't it?"

"Where are your brains, my darling? It was for Count
Berthou de Sauveterre."

"Oh, so it was. And what will Tonton do now, do you
think?"

A dreamy look passed across the huge eyes of Madame
Alvarez.

"It's a toss-up, my child. We'll know everything in good time, even if he starts by refusing to give an interview to anybody. You must always start by refusing to give an interview to anybody. Then later you can fill the front page. Tell the concierge, by the way, to get us the evening papers. Have you had enough to eat? Did you have your second cup of milk and your two pieces of bread and butter? Put on your gloves before you go out. Don't dawdle on the way. I'm going to call your mother. What a story! Andrée, are you asleep? Oh, so you're out of bed! Andrée, Liane has committed suicide!"

"That's a nice change," muttered Andrée. "She has only one idea in her head, that woman, but she sticks to it."

"You haven't take out your curlers yet, Andrée?"

"And have my hair go limp in the middle of rehearsal? No thank you!"

Madame Alvarez ran her eyes over her daughter, from the spiky tips of her curlers to the felt slippers. "It's plain that there's no man here for you to bother about, my child! A man in the house soon cures a woman of traipsing about in dressing gown and slippers. What excitement, this suicide! Unsuccessful, of course."

Andrée's pallid lips parted in a contemptuous smile: "It's getting too boring—the way she takes laudanum as if it was castor oil!"

"Anyhow, who cares about her? It's the Lachaille heir who matters. This is the first time such a thing has happened to him. He's already had—let me see. He's had Gentiane, who stole his private papers; then that foreigner, who tried to force him into marriage; but Liane is his first suicide. In such circumstances a man so much in the public eye has to be extremely careful about what sort of thing he says."

"Hm! He'll be bursting with pride, you may be sure."

"And with good reason, too," said Madame Alvarez. "We shall be seeing great things before very long. I wonder what Alicia will have to say about the situation."

"She'll do her best to make a mountain of a molehill."

"Alicia is no angel. But I must confess that she is farsighted. And that without ever leaving her room!"

"She's no need to, since she has the telephone. Mother, won't you have one put in here?"

"It's expensive," said Madame Alvarez thoughtfully. "We only just manage to make both ends meet as it is. The telephone is of real use only to important business-men or to women who have something to hide. Now, if you were to change your mode of life—and I'm only putting it forward as a supposition—and if Gigi were to start on a life of her own, I would be the first to say, 'We'll have the telephone put in.' But we haven't reached that point yet, unfortunately."

She allowed herself a single sigh, pulled on her rubber gloves, and coolly set about her household chores. Thanks to her care, the modest flat was growing old without too many signs of deterioration. She retained, from her past life, the honorable habits of women who have lost their honor, and these she taught to her daughter and her daughter's daughter. Sheets never stayed on the beds longer than ten days, and the combination cleaning- and washer-woman told everyone that the chemises and draw-ers of the ladies of Madame Alvarez' were changed more often than she could count, and so were the table napkins. At any moment, at the cry of "Gigi, take off your shoes!" Gilberte had to remove shoes and stockings, exhibit white feet to the closest inspection, and announce the least suspicion of a corn.

During the week following Madame d'Exelmans' suicide, Lachaille's reactions were somewhat incoherent. He en-gaged the stars of the National Musical Academy to dance at a midnight fete held at his own house, and, wishing to give a supper party at the Pré-Catalan, he arranged for that restaurant to open a fortnight earlier than was their custom. The clowns Footit and Chocolat did a turn: Rita del Erido caracoled on horseback between the sup-per tables, wearing a divided skirt of white lace flounces, a white hat on her black hair with white ostrich feathers frothing around the relentless beauty of her face. Indeed, Paris mistakenly proclaimed, such was her beauty, that Gaston Lachaille was hoisting her astride a throne of sugar. Twenty-four hours later, Paris was undeceived. For in the false prophecies it had published, *Gil Blas* nearly lost the subsidy it received from Gaston Lachaille. A specialized weekly, *Paris en amour,* provided another red herring, under the headline: "Young Yankee millionairess makes no secret of weakness for French sugar."

Madame Alvarez' ample bust shook with incredulous laughter when she read the daily papers: she had received her information from none other than Gaston Lachaille in person. Twice in ten days he had found time to drop in for a cup of camomile, to sink into the depths of the now-sagging, conch-shaped armchair, and there forget his business worries and his dislike of being unattached. He even brought Gigi an absurd Russian leather music case with a silver-gilt clasp, and twenty boxes of licorice. Madame Alvarez was given a *pâté de foie gras* and six bottles of champagne, and of these bounties Tonton Lachaille partook by inviting himself to dinner. Throughout the meal Gilberte regaled them rather tipsily with tittle-tattle about her school, and later won Gaston's gold pencil at piquet. He lost with good grace, recovered his spirits, laughed, and, pointing to the child, said to Madame Alvarez, "There's my best pal!" Madame Alvarez' Spanish eyes moved with slow watchfulness from Gigi's reddened cheeks and white teeth to Lachaille, who was pulling her hair by the fistful. "You little devil, you had the fourth king up your sleeve all the time!"

It was at this moment that Andrée, coming back from the Opéra-Comique, looked at Gigi's disheveled head rolling against Lachaille's sleeve and saw the tears of excited laughter in her lovely slate-blue eyes. She said nothing and accepted a glass of champagne, then another, and yet another. After her third glass, Gaston Lachaille was threatened with the Bell Song from *Lakmé,* at which point Andrée's mother led her away to bed.

The following day, no one spoke of this family party except Gilberte, who exclaimed, "Never, never in all my life, have I laughed so much! And the pencil is real gold!" Her unreserved chatter met with a strange silence, or rather with "Now then, Gigi, try to be a little more serious!" thrown out almost absentmindedly.

After that, Gaston Lachaille let two weeks go by without showing a sign of life, and the Alvarez family gathered its information from the papers only.

"Did you see, Andrée? In the gossip column it says that Monsieur Gaston Lachaille has left for Monte Carlo. 'The reason for this seems to be of a sentimental nature —a secret that we respect.' What next!"

"Would you believe it, Grandmama, Lydia Poret was saying at the dancing class that Liane traveled on the same train as Tonton, but in another compartment! Grandmama, do you think it can be true?"

Madame Alvarez shrugged her shoulders.

"If it was true, how on earth would those Porets know? Have they become friends with Monsieur Lachaille all of a sudden?"

"No, but Lydia Poret heard the story in her aunt's dressing room at the Comédie Française."

Madame Alvarez exchanged looks with her daughter.

"In her dressing room! That explains everything!" she exclaimed, for she held the theatrical profession in contempt, although Andrée worked so hard. When Madame Emilienne d' Alençon had decided to present performing rabbits, and Madame de Pougy—shyer on the stage than any young girl—had amused herself by pantomiming the part of Columbine in spangled black tulle, Madame Alvarez had stigmatized them both in a single phrase: "What! Have they sunk to that?"

"Grandmama, tell me, Grandmama, do you know him, this Prince Radziwill?" Gilberte went on again.

"What's come over the child today? Has she been bitten by a flea? Which Prince Radziwill, to begin with? There's more than one."

"I don't know," said Gigi. "The one who's getting married. Among the list of presents, it says here, '. . . are three writing sets in malachite.' What is malachite?"

"Oh, you're being tiresome, child. If he's getting married, he's no longer interesting."

"But if Tonton got married, wouldn't he be interesting either?"

"It all depends. It would be interesting if he were to marry his mistress. When Prince Cheniaguine married Valérie d'Aigreville, it was obvious that the life she had led him for the past fifteen years was all he wanted; scenes, plates flung across the room, and reconciliations in the middle of the restaurant Durand, Place de la

Madeleine. Clearly, she was a woman who knew how to make herself valued. But all that is too complicated for you, my poor Gigi."

"And do you think it's to marry Liane that he's gone away with her?"

Madame Alvarez pressed her forehead against the windowpane and seemed to be consulting the spring sunshine, which bestowed upon the street a sunny side and one with shade.

"No," she said, "not if I know anything about anything. I must have a word with Alicia. Gigi, come with me as far as her house; you can leave me there and find your way back along the quais. It will give you some fresh air, since, it would seem, one must have fresh air nowadays. I have never been in the habit of taking the air more than twice a year myself, at Cabourg and at Monte Carlo. And I am none the worse for that."

That evening Madame Alvarez came in so late that the family dined off tepid soup, cold meat, and some cakes sent by Aunt Alicia. To Gilberte's "Well, what did she have to say?" she presented an icy front and answered in clarion tones: "She says that she is going to teach you how to eat ortolans."

"Lovely!" cried Gilberte. "And what did she say about the summer frock she promised me?"

"She said she would see. And that there's no reason why you should be displeased with the result."

"Oh!" said Gilberte gloomily.

"She also wants you to go to luncheon with her on Thursday, at twelve sharp."

"With you, too, Grandmama?"

Madame Alvarez looked at the willowy slip of a girl facing her across the table, at her high, rosy cheekbones beneath eyes as blue as an evening sky, at her strong, even teeth biting a fresh-colored but slightly chapped lip, and at the primitive splendor of her ash-gold hair.

"No," she said at last. "Without me."

Gilberte got up and wound an arm about her grandmother's neck.

"The way you said that, Grandmama, surely doesn't mean that you're going to send me to live with Aunt Alicia? I don't want to leave here, Grandmama!"

Madame Alvarez cleared her throat, gave a little cough, and smiled.

"Goodness gracious, what a foolish creature you are! Leave here! Why, my poor Gigi, I'm not scolding you, but you haven't reached the first stage toward leaving."

For a bellpull, Aunt Alicia had hung from her front door a length of bead-embroidered braid on a background of twining green vine leaves and purple grapes. The door itself, varnished and revarnished till it glistened, shone with the glow of a dark brown caramel. From the very threshold, where she was admitted by a "manservant," Gilberte enjoyed in her undiscriminating way an atmosphere of discreet luxury. The carpet, spread with Persian rugs, seemed to lend her wings. After hearing Madame Alvarez pronounce her sister's Louis XV little drawing room to be "boredom itself," Gilberte echoed her words by saying: "Aunt Alicia's drawing room is very pretty, but it's boredom itself!" reserving her admiration for the dining room, furnished in pale, almost golden, lemonwood dating from the Directoire, quite plain but for the grain of a wood as transparent as wax. "I shall buy myself a set like that one day," Gigi had once said in all innocence.

"In the Faubourg Antoine, I dare say," Aunt Alicia had answered teasingly, with a smile of her cupid's bow mouth and a flash of small teeth.

She was seventy years old. Her fastidious taste was everywhere apparent: in her silver-gray bedroom with its red Chinese vases, in her narrow white bathroom as warm as a hothouse, and in her robust health, concealed by a pretense of delicacy. The men of her generation, when trying to describe Alicia de Saint-Efflam, fumbled for words and could only exclaim, "Ah, my dear fellow!" or "Nothing could give you the faintest idea . . ." Those who had known her intimately produced photographs that younger men found ordinary enough. "Was she really so lovely? You wouldn't think so from her photographs!" Looking at portraits of her, old admirers would pause for an instant, recollecting the turn of a wrist like a swan's neck, the tiny ear, the profile revealing a delicious kinship between the heart-shaped mouth and the wide-cut eyelids with their long lashes.

Gilberte kissed the pretty old lady, who was wearing a peak of black Chantilly lace on her white hair and, on her slightly dumpy figure, a tea gown of shot taffeta.

"You have one of your headaches, Aunt Alicia?"

"I'm not sure yet," replied Aunt Alicia. "It depends on the luncheon. Come quickly, the eggs are ready! Take off your coat! What on earth is that dress?"

"One of Mama's, altered to fit me. Are they difficult eggs today?"

"Not at all. *Oeufs brouilles aux croutons.* The ortolans are not difficult, either. And you shall have chocolate cream. So shall I."

With her young voice, a touch of pink on her amiable wrinkles, and lace on her white hair, Aunt Alicia was the perfect stage marquise. Gilberte had the greatest reverence for her aunt. In sitting down at the table in her presence, she would pull her skirt up behind, join her knees, hold her elbows close to her sides, straighten her shoulder blades, and to all appearances become the perfect young lady. She would remember what she had been taught, break her bread quickly, eat with her mouth shut, and take care when cutting her meat not to let her forefinger reach the blade of her knife.

Today her hair, severely tied back in a heavy knot at the nape of her neck, disclosed the fresh line of her forehead and ears, and a very powerful throat, rising from the rather ill-cut opening of her altered dress. This was a dingy blue, the bodice pleated about a let-in piece, and to cheer up this patchwork, three rows of mohair braid had been sewn around the hem of the skirt, and three times three rows of mohair braid around the sleeves, between the wrist and the elbow.

Aunt Alicia, sitting opposite her niece and examining her through fine dark eyes, could find no fault.

"How old are you?" she asked suddenly.

"The same as I was the other day, Aunt. Fifteen and a half. Aunt, what do you really think of this business of Tonton Gaston?"

"Why? Does it interest you?"

"Of course, Aunt. It worries me. If Tonton takes up with another lady, he won't come and play piquet with us any more or drink camomile tea—at least not for some time. That would be a shame."

"That's one way of looking at it, certainly."

Aunt Alicia examined her niece critically, through narrowed eyelids.

"Do you work hard, in class? Who are your friends? Ortolans should be cut in two, with one quick stroke of the knife, and no grating of the blade on the plate. Bite up each half. The bones don't matter. Go on eating while you answer my question, but don't talk with your mouth full. You must manage it. If I can, you can. What friends have you made?"

"None, Aunt. Grandmama won't even let me have tea with the families of my school friends."

"She is quite right. Apart from that, there is no one who follows you, no little clerk hanging around your skirts? No schoolboy? No older man? I warn you, I shall know at once if you lie to me."

Gilberte gazed at the bright face of the imperious old lady who was questioning her so sharply.

"Why, no, Aunt, no one. Has somebody been telling you tales about me? I am always by myself. And why does Grandmama stop me from accepting invitations?"

"She is right, for once. You would be invited only by ordinary people, that is to say, useless people."

"And what about us? Aren't we ordinary people ourselves?"

"No."

"What makes these ordinary people inferior to us?"

"They have weak heads and dissolute bodies. Besides, they are married. But I don't think you understand."

"Yes, Aunt, I understand that we don't marry."

"Marriage is not forbidden to us. Instead of marrying 'at once,' it sometimes happens that we marry 'at last.' "

"But does that prevent me from seeing girls of my own age?"

"Yes. Are you bored at home? Well, be a little bored. It's not a bad thing. Boredom helps one to make decisions. What is the matter? Tears? The tears of a silly child who is backward for her age. Have another ortolan."

Aunt Alicia, with three glittering fingers, grasped the stem of her glass and raised it in a toast.

"To you and me, Gigi! You shall have an Egyptian cigarette with your coffee. On condition that you do not wet the end of your cigarette, and that you don't spit out specks of tobacco—going *ptu, ptu.* I shall also give you a note to the *première vendeuse* at Béchoff-David, an old friend of mine who was not a success. Your wardrobe is going to be changed. Nothing ventured, nothing gained."

The dark blue eyes gleamed. Gilberte stammered with joy.

"Aunt! Aunt! I'm going to—to Bé—"

"—choff-David. But I thought you weren't interested in clothes?"

Gilberte blushed.

"Aunt, I'm not interested in homemade clothes."

"I sympathize with you. Can it be that you have taste? When you think of looking your best, how do you see yourself dressed?"

"Oh, but I know just what would suit me, Aunt! I've seen——"

"Explain yourself without gestures. The moment you gesticulate you look common."

"I've seen a dress—oh, a dress created for Madame Lucy Gérard! Hundreds of tiny ruffles of pearl-gray silk muslin from top to bottom. And then a dress of lavender-blue cloth cut out on a black velvet foundation, the cutout design making a sort of peacock's tail on the train."

The small hand with its precious stones flashed through the air.

"Enough! Enough! I see your fancy is to be dressed like a leading *comédienne* at the Théâtre Français—and don't take that as a compliment! Come and pour out the coffee. And without jerking up the lip of the coffee pot to cut off the last drop. I'd rather have a footbath in my saucer than see you juggling like a waiter in a café."

The next hour passed very quickly for Gilberte: Aunt Alicia had unlocked a casket of jewels to use for a lesson that dazzled her.

"What is that, Gigi?"

"A marquise diamond."

"We say, a marquise-shaped brilliant. And that?"

"A topaz."

Aunt Alicia threw up her hands and the sunlight, glancing off her rings, set off a myriad scintillations.

"A topaz! I have suffered many humiliations, but this surpasses them all. A topaz among my jewels! Why not an aquamarine or a chrysolite? It's a yellow diamond, little goose, and you won't often see it's like. And this?"

Gilberte half opened her mouth, as if in a dream.

"Oh! That's an emerald. Oh, how beautiful it is!"

Aunt Alicia slipped the large square-cut emerald on one of her thin fingers and was lost in silence.

"Do you see," she said in a hushed voice, "that almost blue flame darting about in the depths of the green light? Only the most beautiful emeralds contain that miracle of elusive blue."

"Who gave it to you, Aunt?" Gilberte dared to ask.

"A king," said Aunt Alicia simply.

"A great king?"

"No. A little one. Great kings do not give very fine stones."

"Why not?"

For a fleeting moment, Aunt Alicia proffered a glimpse of her tiny white teeth.

"If you want my opinion, it's because they don't want to. Between ourselves, the little ones don't either."

"Then who does give great big stones?"

"Who? The shy. The proud, too. And the boors, because they think that to give a monster jewel is a sign of good breeding. Sometimes a woman does, to humiliate a man. Never wear second-rate jewels. Wait till the really good ones come to you."

"And if they don't?"

"Well, then it can't be helped. Rather than a wretched little diamond full of flaws, wear a simple, plainly inexpensive ring. In that case you can say, 'It's a memento. I never part with it, day or night.' Don't ever wear artistic jewelry, it wrecks a woman's reputation."

"What is an artistic jewel?"

"It all depends. A mermaid in gold with eyes of chrysoprase. An Egyptian scarab. A large engraved amethyst. A not-very-heavy bracelet said to have been chased by a master-hand. A lyre or star mounted as a brooch. A

studded tortoise. In a word, all of them, frightful. Never
wear baroque pearls, not even as hatpins. Beware, above
all things, of family jewels!"

"But Grandmama has a beautiful cameo, set as a
medallion."

"There are no beautiful cameos," said Alicia with a
toss of the head. "There are precious stones and pearls.
There are white, yellow, blue, blue-white, or pink diamonds. We won't speak of black diamonds; they're not
worth mentioning. Then there are rubies—when you can
be sure of them; sapphires, when they come from Kashmir;
emeralds, provided they have no fatal flaw or are not
too light in color or have a yellowish tint."

"Aunt, I'm very fond of opals, too."

"I am very sorry, but you are not to wear them. I
won't allow it."

Dumbfounded, Gilbert remained for a moment open-
mouthed.

"Oh! Do you too, Aunt, really believe that they bring
bad luck?"

"Why in the world not? You silly little creature," Alicia
went bubbling on, "you must pretend to believe in such
things. Believe in opals, believe—let's see, what can I
suggest—in turquoises that die, in the evil eye . . ."

"But," said Gigi, haltingly, "those are—are supersti-
tions!"

"Of course they are, child. They also go by the name
of weaknesses. A pretty little collection of weaknesses
and a terror of spiders are indispensable stock-in-trade
with men."

"Why, Aunt?"

The old lady closed the casket and kept Gilberte kneeling before her.

"Because nine men out of ten are superstitious, nineteen out of twenty believe in the evil eye, and ninety-
eight out of a hundred are afraid of spiders. They forgive us—oh, for many things, but not for the absence in
us of their own failings," she said. "What makes you
sigh?"

"I shall never remember all that!"

"The important thing is not for *you* to remember, but
for me to know it."

"Aunt, what is a writing set in—in malachite?"

"Always a calamity. But where on earth did you pick up such terms?"

"From the list of presents at grand weddings, Aunt, printed in the papers."

"Nice reading! But at least you can gather from it what kind of presents you should never give or accept."

While speaking she began to touch here and there the young face on a level with her own, with the sharp pointed nail of her index finger. She lifted one slightly chapped lip, inspected the spotless enamel of the teeth.

"A fine jaw, my girl! With such teeth I should have gobbled up Paris and the rest of the world into the bargain. As it was, I had a good bite out of it. What's this you've got here? A small pimple? You shouldn't have a small pimple near your nose. And this? You've pinched a blackhead. You've no business to have such things or to pinch them. I'll give you some of my astringent lotion. You mustn't eat anything from the pork butcher's except cooked ham. You don't put on powder?"

"Grandmama won't let me."

"I should hope not. Do you go you-know-where regularly? Let me smell your breath. Not that it means anything at this hour. You've just had luncheon."

She laid her hands on Gigi's shoulders.

"Pay attention to what I'm going to say. You have it in your power to please. You have an impossible little nose, a nondescript mouth, cheeks rather like the wife of a muzhik—"

"Oh, Aunt!" sighed Gilberte.

"But, with your eyes and eyelashes, your teeth, and your hair, you can get away with it if you're not a perfect fool. As for the rest—"

She cupped her hands like conch shells over Gigi's bosom and smiled.

"A promise, but a pretty promise, neatly molded. Don't eat too many almonds, they add weight to the breasts. Ah, remind me to teach you how to choose cigars."

Gilberte opened her eyes so wide that the tips of her lashes touched her eyebrows.

"Why?"

She received a little tap on the cheek.

"Because—because I do nothing without good reason. If I take you in hand at all, I must do it thoroughly. Once a woman understands the tastes of a man, cigars included, and once a man knows what pleases a woman, they may be said to be well matched."

"And then they fight," concluded Gigi with a knowing air.

"What do you mean, they fight?"

The old lady looked at Gigi in consternation.

"Ah," she added, "you certainly never invented the triple mirror! Come, you little psychologist! Let me give you a note for Madame Henriette at Béchoff."

While her aunt was writing at a miniature rose-pink writing table Gilberte breathed in the scent of the fastidiously furnished room. Without wanting them for herself, she examined the objects she knew so well but hardly appreciated: Cupid, the Archer, pointing to the hours on the mantelpiece; two rather daring pictures; a bed like the basin of a fountain and its chinchilla coverlet; a rosary of small seed pearls and the New Testament on the bedside table; two red Chinese vases fitted as lamps —a happy note against the gray of the walls.

"Run along, my little one. I shall send for you again quite soon. Don't forget to ask Victor for the cake you're to take home. Gently—don't disarrange my hair! And remember, I shall have my eye on you as you leave the house. Woe betide you if you march like a guardsman or drag your feet behind you!"

The month of May fetched Gaston Lachaille back to Paris and brought to Gilberte two well-cut dresses and a lightweight coat—"a sack coat like Cléo de Mérode's," she called it—as well as hats and boots and shoes. To these she added, on her own account, a few curls over the forehead, which cheapened her appearance. She paraded in front of Gaston in a blue and white dress reaching almost to the ground. "A full seven and a half yards around, Tonton, my skirt measures!" She was more than proud of her slender waist, held in by a grosgrain sash with a silver buckle; but she tried every dodge to free her lovely strong neck from its whalebone collar of "imitation Venetian point," which matched the tucks of the bodice. The full sleeves and wide flounced skirt of blue and white striped silk rustled deliciously, and Gilberte delighted in picking at the sleeves, to puff them out just below the shoulder.

"You remind me of a performing monkey," Lachaille said to her. "I liked you much better in your old tartan dress. In that uncomfortable collar you look just like a hen with a full gullet. Take a look at yourself!"

Feeling a little ruffled, Gilberte turned around to face the looking glass. She had a lump in one of her cheeks caused by a large caramel, out of a box sent all the way from Nice at Gaston's order.

"I've heard a good deal about you, Tonton," she retorted, "but I've never heard it said that you had any taste in clothes."

He stared, almost choking, at this newly fledged young woman, then turned to Madame Alvarez. "Charming manners you've taught her! I congratulate you!"

Whereupon he left the house without drinking his camomile tea, and Madame Alvarez wrung her hands.

"Look what you've done to us now, my poor Gigi!"

"I know," said Gigi, "but then why does he fly at me? He must know by now, I should think, that I can give as good as I get!"

Her grandmother shook her by the arm.

"But think what you've done, you wretched child! Good heavens! When will you learn to think? You've mortally offended the man, as likely as not. Just when we are doing our utmost to—"

"To do what, Grandmama?"

"Why, to do everything, to make an elegant young lady of you, to show you off to advantage."

"For whose benefit, Grandmama? You must admit that one doesn't have to turn oneself inside out for an old friend like Tonton!"

But Madame Alvarez admitted nothing; not even to her astonishment, when, the following day, Gaston Lachaille arrived in the best of spirits, wearing a light-colored suit.

"Put on your hat, Gigi! I'm taking you out to tea."

"Where?" cried Gigi.

"To the *Réservoirs,* at Versailles!"

"Hurrah! Hurrah! Hurrah!" chanted Gilberte.

She turned toward the kitchen.

"Grandmama, I'm having tea at the *Réservoirs* with Tonton!"

Madame Alvarez appeared and, without stopping to untie the flowered satinette apron across her stomach, interposed her soft hand between Gilberte's arm and that of Gaston Lachaille.

"No, Gaston," she said simply.

"What do you mean, No?"

"Oh, Grandmama!" wailed Gigi.

Madame Alvarez seemed not to hear her.

"Go to your room a minute, Gigi. I should like to talk to Monsieur Lachaille in private."

She watched Gilberte leave the room and close the door behind her; then, returning to Gaston, she met his dark, rather brutal, stare without flinching.

"What is the meaning of all this, Mamita? Ever since yesterday, I find quite a change here. What's going on?"

"I shall be glad if you will sit down, Gaston. I'm tired," said Madame Alvarez. "Oh, my poor legs!"

She sighed, waited for a response that did not come, and then untied her apron, under which she was wearing a black dress with a large cameo pinned upon it. She motioned her guest to a high-backed chair, keeping the armchair for herself. Then she sat down heavily, smoothed her graying black coils, and folded her hands on her lap. The unhurried movement of her large, dark, lambent eyes and the ease with which she remained motionless were sure signs of her self-control.

"Gaston, you cannot doubt my friendship for you!" Lachaille emitted a short, businesslike laugh and tugged at his mustache. "My friendship and my gratitude. Nevertheless, I must never forget that I have a soul entrusted to my care. Andrée, as you know, has neither the time nor the inclination to look after the girl. Our Gilberte doesn't have the gumption to make her own way in the world, like so many. She is just a child."

"Of sixteen," said Lachaille.

"Of nearly sixteen," consented Madame Alvarez. "For years you have been giving her sweets and playthings. She swears by Tonton, and by him alone. And now you want to take her out to tea, in your automobile, to the *Réservoirs*!"

Madame Alvarez placed a hand on her heart.

"Upon my soul and conscience, Gaston, if there were only you and me, I should say to you, 'Take Gilberte anywhere you like, I entrust her to you blindly.' But there are always the others. The eyes of the world are on you. To be seen tête-à-tête with you is, for a woman—"

Gaston Lachaille lost patience.

"All right, all right, I understand. You want me to believe that once she is seen having tea with me, Gilberte is compromised! A slip of a girl, a fledgling, a kid whom no one knows, whom no one notices!"

"Let us say, rather," interrupted Madame Alvarez gently, "that she will be labeled. No matter where you put in an appearance, Gaston, your presence is commented on. A young girl who goes out alone with you is no longer and ordinary girl, or even—to put it bluntly—a respectable girl. Now our little Gilberte must not, above all things, cease to be an ordinary young girl, at least not by that method. So far as it concerns you, it will simply end in one more story to be added to the long list already in existence, but personally, when I read of it in *Gil Blas,* I shall not be amused."

Gaston Lachaille rose, paced from the table to the door, then from the door to the window, before replying.

"Very good, Mamita, I have no wish to vex you. I won't argue," he said coldly. "Keep your precious child."

He turned around again to face Madame Alvarez, his chin held high.

"I can't help wondering, as a matter of interest, whom you are keeping her for! A clerk earning a hundred a year, who'll marry her and give her four children in three years?"

"I know the duty of a mother better than that," said Madame Alvarez composedly. "I shall do my best to entrust Gigi only to the care of a man capable of saying, 'I take charge of her and answer for her future.' May I have the pleasure of brewing you some camomile tea, Gaston?"

"No, thank you. I'm late already."

"Would you like Gigi to come and say good-bye?"

"Don't bother, I'll see her another time. I can't say when, I'm sure. I'm very much taken up these days."

"Never mind, Gaston, don't worry about her. Have a good time, Gaston."

Once alone, Madame Alvarez mopped her forehead and went to open the door of Gilberte's room.

"You were listening at the door, Gigi!"

"No, Grandmama."

"Yes, you had your ear to the keyhole. You must never listen at keyholes. You don't hear properly and so you get things all wrong. Monsieur Lachaille has gone."

"So I can see," said Gilberte.

"Now you must rub the new potatoes in a cloth. I'll sauté them when I come in."

"Are you going out, Grandmama?"

"I'm going around to see Alicia."

"Again?"

"Is it your place to object?" said Madame Alvarez severely. "You had better bathe your eyes in cold water, since you have been silly enough to cry."

"Grandmama!"

"What?"

"What difference could it make to you if you'd let me go out with Tonton Gaston in my new dress?"

"Silence! If you can't understand anything about anything, at least let those who are capable of using their reason do so for you. And put on my rubber gloves before you touch the potatoes!"

Throughout the whole of the following week, silence reigned over the Alvarez household, except for a surprise visit, one day, from Aunt Alicia. She arrived in a hired brougham, all black lace and dull silk with a rose at her shoulder, and carried on an anxious conversation, strictly between themselves, with her younger sister. As she was leaving she bestowed only a moment's attention on Gilberte, pecked at her cheek with a fleeting kiss, and was gone.

"What did she want?" Gilberte asked Madame Alvarez.

"Oh, nothing—the address of the heart specialist who treated Madame Buffetery."

Gilberte reflected for a moment.

"It was a long one," she said.

"What was long?"

"The address of the heart specialist. Grandmama, I should like a *cachet*. I have a headache."

"But you had one yesterday. A headache doesn't last forty-eight hours!"

"Presumably my headaches are different from other people's," said Gilberte, offended.

She was losing some of her sweetness and, on her return from school, would make some such remark as "My teacher has it in for me!" or complain of not being able to sleep. She was gradually slipping into a state of idleness, which her grandmother noticed but did nothing to overcome.

One day Gigi was busy applying liquid chalk to her white canvas button boots when Gaston Lachaille put in an appearance without ringing the bell. His hair was too long, his complexion suntanned, and he was wearing a broad check summer suit. He stopped short in front of Gilberte, who was perched high on a kitchen stool, her left hand shod with a boot.

"Oh! Grandmama left the key in the door. That's just like her!"

As Gaston Lachaille looked at her without saying a word she began to blush, put down the boot on the table, and pulled her skirt down over her knees.

"So, Tonton, you slip in like a burglar! I believe you're thinner. Aren't you fed properly by that famous chef of yours who used to be with the Prince of Wales? Being thinner makes your eyes look larger and at the same time makes your nose longer and——"

"I have something to say to your grandmother," interrupted Gaston Lachaille. "Run into your room, Gigi."

For a moment she remained open-mouthed; then she jumped off her stool. The strong column of her neck, like an archangel's, swelled with anger as she advanced on Lachaille.

"Run into your room! Run into your room! And suppose I said the same to you? Who do you think you are here, ordering me to run into my room? All right, I'm

going to my room! And I can tell you one thing: as long
as you're in the house, I won't come out of it!"

She slammed the door behind her, and there was a
dramatic click of the bolt.

"Gaston," breathed Madame Alvarez, "I shall insist on
the child's apologizing; yes, I shall insist; if necessary,
I'll—"

Gaston was not listening to her, and stood staring at
the closed door.

"Now, Mamita," said he, "let us talk briefly and to the
point."

"Let us go over it all once again," said Aunt Alicia.
"To begin with, you are quite sure he said, 'She will be
spoiled, more than——' "

"Than any woman before her!"

"Yes, but that's the sort of vague phrase that every
man comes out with. I like things cut and dried."

"Just what they were, Alicia, for he said that he would
guarantee Gigi against every imaginable mishap, even
against himself, by an insurance policy; and that he regarded himself more or less as her godfather."

"Yes, hmm . . . Not bad, not bad. But vague, vague as
ever."

She was still in bed, her white hair arranged in curls
against the pink pillow. She was absentmindedly tying
and untying the ribbon of her nightdress. Madame Alvarez, as pale and wan under her morning hat as the
moon behind passing clouds, was leaning cross-armed
against the bedside.

"And he added, 'I don't wish to rush anything. Above
all, I am Gigi's best pal. I shall give her all the time she
wants to get used to me.' There were tears in his eyes.
And he also said, 'After all, she won't have to deal with
a savage.' A gentleman, in fact. A perfect gentleman."

"Yes, yes. Rather a vague gentleman. And the child,
have you spoken frankly to her?"

"As was my duty, Alicia. This is no time for us to be
treating her like a child from whom the cakes have to be
hidden. Yes, I spoke frankly. I referred to Gaston as a
miracle, as a god, as——"

"Tut, tut, tut," criticized Alicia, "I should have

stressed the difficulties rather: the cards to be played, the fury of all those ladies, the conquest represented by so conspicuous a man."

Madame Alvarez wrung her hands.

"The difficulties! The cards to be played! Do you imagine she's like you? Don't you know her at all? She's very far from calculating, she's——"

"Thank you."

"I mean she has no ambition. I was even struck by the fact that she did not react either one way or the other. No cries of joy, no tears of emotion! All I got from her was, 'Oh, yes! Oh, it's very considerate of him.' Then, only at the very end, did she lay down, as her conditions——"

"Conditions, indeed!" murmured Alicia.

"——that she would answer Monsieur Lachaille's proposals herself and discuss the matter alone with him. In other words, it was her business, and hers only."

"Let us be prepared for the worst! You've brought a nitwit into the world. She will ask for the moon and, if I know him, she won't get it. He is coming at four o'clock?"

"Yes."

"Hasn't he sent anything? No flowers? No little present?"

"Nothing. Do you think that's a bad sign?"

"No. It's what one would expect. See that the child is nicely dressed. How is she looking?"

"Not too well, today. Poor little lamb——"

"Come, come!" said Alicia heartlessly. "You'll have time for tears another day—when she's succeeded in ruining the whole affair."

"You've eaten scarcely anything, Gigi."

"I wasn't too hungry, Grandmama. May I have a little more coffee?"

"Of course."

"And a drop of Combier?"

"Why, yes. There's nothing in the world better than Combier for settling the stomach."

Through the open window rose the noise and heat

from the street below. Gigi let the tip of her tongue lick
around the bottom of her liqueur glass.

"If Aunt Alicia could see you, Gigi!" said Madame
Alvarez lightheartedly.

Gigi's only reply was a disillusioned little smile. Her
old plaid dress was too tight across the breast, and under
the table she stretched out her long legs well beyond the
limits of her skirt.

"What can Mama be rehearsing today that's kept her
from coming back to eat with us, Grandmama? Do you
think there really is a rehearsal going on at her Opéra-
Comique?"

"She said so, didn't she?"

"Personally, I don't think she wanted to eat here."

"What makes you think that?"

Without taking her eyes off the sunny window, Gigi
simply shrugged her shoulders.

"Oh, nothing, Grandmama."

When she had drained the last drop of her Combier,
she rose and began to clear the table.

"Leave all that, Gigi. I'll do it."

"Why, Grandmama? I do it as a rule."

She looked Madame Alvarez straight in the face with
an expression the old lady could not meet.

"We began our meal late. It's almost three o'clock and
you're not dressed yet; do pull yourself together, Gigi."

"It's never before taken me a whole hour to change
my clothes."

"Won't you need my help? Are you satisfied your
hair's all right?"

"It will do, Grandmama. When the doorbell rings,
don't bother. I'll go and open it."

On the stroke of four, Gaston Lachaille rang three
times. A childish, wistful face looked out from the bedroom door, listening. After three more impatient rings,
Gilberte advanced as far as the middle of the hall. She
still had on her old plaid dress and cotton stockings. She
rubbed her cheeks with both fists, then ran to open the
door.

"Good afternoon, Uncle Gaston."

"Didn't you want to let me in, you bad girl?"

They bumped shoulders in passing through the door,

said "Oh, sorry!" a little too self-consciously, then
laughed awkwardly.

"Please sit down, Tonton. D'you know, I didn't have
time to change. Not like you! That navy blue serge
couldn't look better!"

"You don't know what you're talking about! It's
tweed."

"Of course. How silly of me!"

She sat down facing him, pulled her skirt over her
knees, and they stared at each other. Gilberte's tomboy
assurance deserted her; a strange woebegone look made
her blue eyes seem twice their natural size.

"What's the matter with you, Gigi?" asked Lachaille
softly. "Tell me something! Do you know why I'm here?"

She assented with an exaggerated nod.

"Do you want to or don't you?" he asked, lowering his
voice.

She pushed a curl behind her ear and swallowed
bravely.

"I don't want to."

Lachaille twirled the tips of his mustache between two
fingers and for a moment looked away from a pair of
darkened blue eyes, a pink cheek with a single freckle,
curved lashes, a mouth unaware of its power, a heavy
mass of ash-gold hair, and a neck as straight as a column, strong, hardly feminine, all of a piece, innocent of
jewelry.

"I don't want what you want," Gilberte began again.
"You said to Grandmama——"

He put out his hand to stop her. His mouth was slightly twisted to one side, as if he had a toothache.

"I know what I said to your grandmother. It's not
worth repeating. Just tell me what it is you don't want.
You can then tell me what you do want. I shall give it
to you."

"You mean that?" cried Gilberte.

He nodded, letting his shoulders droop, as if tired out.
She watched, with surprise, these signs of exhaustion
and torment.

"Tonton, you told Grandmama you wanted to make
me my fortune."

"A very fine one," said Lachaille firmly.

"It will be fine if I like it," said Gilberte, no less firmly. "They've drummed into my ears that I am backward for my age, but all the same I know the meaning of words. 'Make me my fortune,' that means I should go away from here with you and that I should sleep in your bed."

"Gigi, I beg of you!"

She stopped because of the strong note of appeal in his voice.

"But, Tonton, why should I mind speaking of it to you? You didn't mind speaking of it to Grandmama. Neither did Grandmama mind speaking of it to me. Grandmama wanted me to see nothing but the bright side. But I know more than she told me. I know very well that if you make me my fortune, then I must have my photograph in the papers, go to the Battle of Flowers and to the races at Deauville. When we quarrel, *Gil Blas* and *Paris en amour* will tell the whole story. When you throw me over once and for all, as you did Gentiane des Cevennes when you'd had enough of her——"

"What! You've heard about that? They've bothered you with all those old stories?"

She gave a solemn little nod.

"Grandmama and Aunt Alicia. They've taught me that you're world famous. I know too that Maryse Chuquet stole your letters, and you brought a lawsuit against her. I know that Countess Pariewsky was angry with you because you didn't want to marry a *divorcée*, and she tried to shoot you. I know what all the world knows."

Lachaille put his hand on Gilberte's knee.

"Those are not the things we have to talk about together, Gigi. All that's in the past. All that's over and done with."

"Of course, Tonton, until it begins again. It's not your fault if you're world famous. But I haven't got a world-famous sort of nature. So it won't do for me."

In pulling at the hem of her skirt, she caused Lachaille's hand to slip off her knee.

"Aunt Alicia and Grandmama are on your side. But as it concerns me a little, after all, I think you must allow me to say a word on the subject. And my word is, that it won't do for me."

She got up and walked about the room. Gaston

Lachaille's silence seemed to embarrass her. She punctuated her wanderings with, "After all, it's true, I suppose! No, it really won't do!"

"I would like to know," said Gaston at last, "whether you're not just trying to hide from me the fact that you dislike me. If you dislike me, you had better say so at once."

"Oh no, Tonton, I don't dislike you at all! I'm always delighted to see you! I'll prove it by making a suggestion in my turn. You could go on coming here as usual, even more often. No one would see any harm in it since you're a friend of the family. You could go on bringing me licorice, champagne on my birthdays, and on Sunday we could have an extra-special game of piquet. Wouldn't that be a pleasant little life? A life without all this business of sleeping in your bed and everybody knowing about it, losing strings of pearls, being photographed all the time, and having to be so careful."

She was absentmindedly twisting a strand of hair around her nose and pulled it so tight that she snuffled, and the tip of her nose turned purple.

"A very pretty little life, as you say," interrupted Gaston Lachaille. "You're forgetting one thing only, Gigi, and that is, I'm in love with you."

"Oh," she cried, "you never told me that!"

"Well," he admitted uneasily, "I'm telling you now."

She remained standing before him, silent and breathing fast. There was no concealing her embarrassment; the rise and fall of her bosom under the tight bodice, the hectic flush high on her cheeks, and the quivering of her closely pressed lips—albeit ready to open again and taste of life.

"That's quite another thing!" she cried at last. "But then you are a terrible man! You're in love with me, and you want to drag me into a life where I'll have nothing but worries, where everyone gossips about everyone else, where the papers print nasty stories. You're in love with me, and you don't care at all if you let me in for all sorts of horrible adventures, ending in separations, quarrels, Sandomirs, revolvers, and lau—and laudanum."

She burst into violent sobs, which made as much noise as a fit of coughing. Gaston put his arms around her to

bend her toward him like a branch, but she escaped and
took refuge between the wall and the piano.

"But listen, Gigi! Listen to me!"

"Never! I never want to see you again! I should never
have believed it of you. You're not in love with me.
You're a wicked man! Go away from here!"

She shut him out from sight by rubbing her eyes with
closed fists. Gaston had moved over to her and was trying to discover some place on her well-guarded face
where he could kiss her. But his lips found only the point
of a small chin wet with tears. At the sound of sobbing,
Madame Alvarez had hurried in. Pale and circumspect,
she had stopped in hesitation at the kitchen door.

"Good gracious, Gaston!" she said. "What on earth's
the matter with her?"

"The matter!" said Lachaille. "The matter is that she
doesn't want to."

"She doesn't want to!" repeated Madame Alvarez.
"What do you mean, she doesn't want to?"

"No, she doesn't want to. I speak plainly enough, don't
I?"

"No. I don't want to," whimpered Gigi.

Madame Alvarez looked at her granddaughter in a
sort of terror.

"Gigi! It's enough to drive one mad! But I told you,
Gigi. Gaston, as God is my witness, I told her——"

"You have told her too much!" cried Lachaille.

He turned his face toward the child, the face of a poor,
sad, love-sick creature, but all he saw of her was a slim
back shaken by sobs and a disheveled head of hair.

"Oh," he exclaimed hoarsely, "I've had enough of
this!" and he went out, banging the door.

The next day, at three o'clock, Aunt Alicia, summoned by *pneumatique,* stepped out of her hired
brougham. She climbed the stairs up to Alvarez' floor—
pretending to the shortness of breath proper to someone
with a weak heart—and noiselessly pushed open the
door, which her sister had left slightly ajar.

"Where's the child?"

"In her room. Do you want to see her?"

"There's plenty of time. How is she?"

"Very calm."

Alicia shook two angry little fists.

"Very calm! She has pulled the roof down about our heads, and she is very calm! These young people of today!"

Once again she raised her dotted veil and withered her sister with a single glance.

"And you, standing there, what do you propose doing?"

With a face like a crumpled rose, she sternly confronted the large pallid face of her sister, whose retort was extremely mild.

"What do I propose doing? How do you mean? I can't, after all, tie the child up!" Her burdened shoulders rose on a long sigh. "I surely have not deserved such children as these!"

"While you stand there wringing your hands Lachaille has rushed away from here and in such a state that he may do something idiotic!"

"And even without his straw hat," said Madame Alvarez. "He got into his car bareheaded! The whole street could have seen him!"

"If I were to be told that by this time he's already become engaged or is busy making it up with Liane, it would not surprise me in the least!"

"It is a moment fraught with destiny," said Madame Alvarez lugubriously.

"And afterward, how did you speak to that little brat?" Madame Alvarez pursed her lips.

"Gigi may be a bit scatterbrained in certain things and backward for her age, but she's not what you say. A young girl who has held the attention of Monsieur Lachaille is not a little brat."

A furious shrug of the shoulders set Alicia's black lace quivering.

"All right, all right! With all due respect, then, how did you handle your precious princess?"

"I talked sense to her. I spoke to her of the family. I tried to make her understand that we sink or swim together. I enumerated all the things she could do for herself and for us."

"And what about nonsense? Did you talk nonsense

to her? Didn't you talk to her of love, travel, moonlight,
Italy? You must know how to harp on every string.
Didn't you tell her that on the other side of the world
the sea is phosphorescent, that there are hummingbirds
in all the flowers, and that you make love under gar-
denias in full bloom beside a moonlit fountain?"

Madame Alvarez looked at her spirited elder sister
with sadness in her eyes.

"I couldn't tell her all that, Alicia, because I know
nothing about it. I've never been farther afield than Cabourg and Monte Carlo."

"Aren't you capable of inventing it?"

"No, Alicia."

Both fell silent. Alicia, with a gesture, made up her
mind.

"Call the kid in to me. We shall see."

When Gilberte came in, Aunt Alicia had resumed all
the airs and graces of a frivolous old lady and was smelling the tea rose pinned near her chin.

"Good afternoon, my little Gigi."

"Good afternoon, Aunt Alicia."

"What is this Inez has been telling me? You have an
admirer? And *what* an admirer! For your first attempt,
it's a masterstroke!"

Gilberte acquiesced with a guarded, resigned little
smile. She offered to Alicia's darting curiosity a fresh
young face, to which the violet-blue shadow on her eyelids and the high color of her mouth gave an almost artificial effect. For coolness' sake, she had dragged back
the hair off her temples with the help of two combs, and
this drew up the corners of her eyes.

"And it seems you have been playing the naughty girl
and tried your claws on Monsieur Lachaille! Bravo, my
brave little girl!"

Gilberte raised incredulous eyes to her aunt.

"Yes, indeed! Bravo! It will only make him all the
happier when you are nice to him again."

"But I am nice to him, Aunt. Only, I don't want to,
that's all."

"Yes, yes, we know. You've sent him packing to his
sugar refinery, that's perfect. But don't send him to the

Devil: he's quite capable of going. The fact is, you don't love him."

Gilberte gave a little childish shrug.

"Yes, Aunt, I'm very fond of him."

"Just what I said, you don't love him. Mind you, there's no harm in that—it leaves you free to act as you please. Ah, if you'd been head over heels in love with him, then I should have been a little anxious. Lachaille is a fine figure of a man. Well built—you've only to look at the photographs of him taken at Deauville in his bathing suit. He's famous for that. Yes, I would feel sorry for you, my poor Gigi. To start by having a passionate love affair—to go away all by your two selves to the other side of the world, forgetting everything in the arms of the man who adores you, listening to the song of love in an eternal spring—surely things of that sort must touch your heart! What does all that say to you?"

"It says to me that when the eternal spring is over, Monsieur Lachaille will go off with another lady. Or else that the lady—me, if you like—will leave Monsieur Lachaille, and Monsieur Lachaille will hurry off to blab the whole story. And then the lady—still me, if you like—will have nothing else to do but get into another gentleman's bed. I don't want that. I'm not changeable by nature, indeed I'm not."

She crossed her arms over her breasts and shivered slightly.

"Grandmama, may I have a *cachet faivre*? I want to go to bed. I feel cold."

"You great goose!" burst out Aunt Alicia. "A silly little milliner's shop is all you deserve! Go! Go marry a bank clerk!"

"If you wish it, Aunt. But right now, I want to go to bed."

Madame Alvarez put her hand on Gigi's forehead.

"Don't you feel well?"

"I'm all right, Grandmama. Only, I'm sad."

She leaned her head on Madame Alvarez' shoulder and, for the first time in her life, closed her eyes pathetically like a grown woman. The two sisters exchanged glances.

"You must know, my Gigi," said Madame Alvarez,

"that we won't torment you to that extent. If you say you really don't want to——"

"A failure is a failure," said Alicia caustically. "We can't go on discussing it forever."

"You'll never be able to say you didn't have good advice, and the very best at that," said Madame Alvarez.

"I know, Grandmama, but I'm sad all the same."

"Why?"

A tear trickled over Gilberte's downy cheek without wetting it, but she did not answer. A brisk ring of the doorbell made her jump where she stood.

"Oh, it must be him," she said. "It is him! Grandmama, I don't want to see him! Hide me, Grandmama!"

At the low, passionate tone of her voice, Aunt Alicia raised an attentive head and pricked an expert ear. Then she ran to open the door and came back a moment later. Gaston Lachaille, haggard, his eyes bloodshot, followed close behind her.

"Good afternoon, Mamita. Good afternoon, Gigi!" he said airily. "Please don't move. I've come to pick up my straw hat."

None of the three women replied, and his assurance left him.

"Well, you might at least say a word to me, even if it's only How-d'you-do?"

Gilberte took a step toward him.

"No," she said, "You haven't come to pick up your straw hat. You have another one in your hand. And you would never bother about a hat. You've come to make me more miserable than ever."

"Really!" burst out Madame Alvarez. "This is more than I can take. How can you, Gigi! Here is a man who, out of the goodness of his generous heart——"

"If you please, Grandmama, just a moment, and I'll be through."

Instinctively she straightened her dress, adjusted the buckle of her sash, and marched up to Gaston.

"I've been thinking, Gaston. In fact, I've been thinking a great deal——"

He interrupted her, to stop her saying what he was afraid to hear.

"I swear to you, my darling——"

"No, don't swear to me. I've been thinking I would
rather be miserable with you than without you. So . . ."

She tried twice to go on.

"So . . . There you are. How d'you do, Gaston, how
d'you do?"

She offered him her cheek in her usual way. He held
her, a little longer than usual, until he felt her relax
and become calm and gentle in his arms. Madame Alvarez seemed about to hurry forward, but Alicia's impatient little hand restrained her.

"Leave well enough alone. Don't meddle any more.
Can't you see she is way beyond us?"

She pointed to Gigi, who was resting a trusting head
and the rich abundance of her hair on Lachaille's shoulder.

The happy man turned to Madame Alvarez.

"Mamita," he said, "will you do me the honor, the
favor, give me the infinite joy, of bestowing on me the
hand . . ."

[TRANSLATED BY ROGER SENHOUSE]

The Photographer's Missus

When the woman they called "the photographer's Missus" decided to put an end to her life, she set about realizing her project with much sincerity and painstaking care. But, having no experience whatever of poisons, thank heaven, she failed. At which the inhabitants of the entire building rejoiced, and so did I, though I did not live in the neighborhood.

Madame Armand—of the Armand Studio, Art Photography and Enlargements—lived on the same landing as a pearl stringer, and it was rare for me not to meet the amiable "photographer's Missus" when I went up to visit Mademoiselle Devoidy. For in those far-off days I had, like everyone else, a pearl necklace. As all women wanted to wear them, there were pearls to suit all women and all purses. What bridegroom would have dared to omit a "string" from his wedding presents to his bride? The craze started at baptism, with the christening gift of a row of pearls no bigger than grains of rice. No fashion, since, has ever been so tyrannical. From a thousand francs upward, you could buy a "real" necklace. Mine had cost five thousand francs, that is to say, it did not attract attention. But its living luster and its gay orient were a proof of its excellent health and mine. When I sold it, during the great war, it was certainly not for an idle whim.

I didn't usually wait to have its silk thread renewed till it was really necessary. Having it restrung was an excuse for me to visit Mademoiselle Devoidy, who came from my part of the country, a few villages away. From being a saleswoman in a branch of *The Store of a Thousand Necklaces* where everything was sham, she had gone on to being a stringer of real pearls. This unmarried woman of about forty had kept, as I had, the accent

of our native parts, and delighted me furthermore by a
restrained sense of humor, which from the heights of
a punctilious honesty made fun of a great many people
and things.

When I went up to see her, I used to exchange greet-
ings with the photographer's Missus, who was often standing outside her wide-open door, opposite Mademoiselle
Devoidy's closed one. The photographer's furniture tres-
passed onto the landing, beginning with a "pedestal"
dating back to the infancy of the craft, a camera stand
of carved, beautifully grained walnut, itself a tripod. Its
bulk and its solid immobility made me think of those
massive wooden winepress screws that used to appear,
at about the same period, in "artistic" flats, supporting
some graceful statuette. A Gothic chair kept it company
and served as an accessory in photographs of First
Communicants. The little wicker kennel and its stuffed
Pomeranian, the pair of shrimp nets dear to children in
sailor suits, completed the store of accessories banished
from the studio.

An incurable smell of painted canvas dominated this
top landing. Yet the painting of a reversible canvas background, in monochrome gray on gray, certainly did not
date from yesterday. One side of it represented a bal-
ustrade at the edge of an English park; the other, a
small sea, bounded in the distance by a hazy port,
whose horizon dipped slightly to the right. As the front
door was frequently left open, it was against this stormy
background and this slanting sea that I used to see the
photographer's Missus encamped. From her air of vague
expectancy I presumed that she had come out there to
breathe the cool air of the top landing or to watch
for some customer coming up the stairs. I found out
later that I was wrong. I would go into her opposite
neighbor's and Mademoiselle Devoidy would offer me one
of her dry, pleasant hands, infallible hands, incapable
of hurrying or trembling, that never dropped a pearl
or a reel or a needle, that gummed the point of a strand
of silk by passing it, with one sure twist of the fingers,
through a half-moon of virgin wax, then aimed the
stiffened thread at the eye of a needle finer than any
sewing needle.

What I saw most clearly of Mademoiselle Devoidy was her bust, caught in the circle of light from her lamp, her coral necklace on her starched white collar, her discreetly mocking smile. As to her freckled, rather flat face, it merely served as a frame and a foil for her piercing brown, gold-spangled eyes, which needed neither spectacles nor magnifying glass and could count the tiny "seed pearls" used in making those skeins and twists that are known as "bayaderes" and are as dull as white bead trimming.

Mademoiselle Devoidy, living in cramped quarters, worked in the front room and slept in the back one, next door to the kitchen. A double door at the entrance made a tiny foyer. When a visitor knocked or rang, Mademoiselle Devoidy would call out, without getting up: "Come in! The key turns to the left!"

Did I feel the beginnings of a friendship with this fellow native of my own province? I most certainly liked her professional table, covered with green baize, with a raised edge like a billiard table, and scored with parallel troughs along which her fingers ranged and graded the pearls with the help of delicate tweezers, worthy of touching the most precious matter: pearls and the wings of dead butterflies.

I also had a friendly feeling for the details and peculiarities of a craft that demanded a two-year apprenticeship, a special manual dexterity, and a slightly contemptuous attitude toward jewels. The mania for pearls, which lasted a long time, allowed the expert stringer to work in her own home and to do as much as she chose. When Mademoiselle Devoidy told me, suppressing a yawn: "So and so brought me *masses* last night; I had to compose till two o'clock in the morning," my imagination swelled these "masses" to fairy-tale size and elevated the verb "compose" to the rank of creative labor.

In the afternoon and on dark mornings in winter, an electric bulb set in a metal morning glory was switched on above the table. Its strong light swept away all the shadows on the workbench, on which Mademoiselle Devoidy allowed nothing to stand; no little vase with a rose in it, no pin tray or ornament in which a stray pearl might hide. Even the scissors seemed to make themselves perfectly flat. Apart from this precaution, which kept the table in a permanent state of pearl-decked nudity, I never saw Mademoiselle Devoidy show the faintest sign of wariness. Chokers and necklaces lay dismembered on the table like stakes not worth picking up.

"You're not in a great hurry? I'll clear a little place for you. Amuse yourself with what's lying about while I rethread you. So it refuses to get any fatter, this string? You'll have to put it in the chicken coop. Ah, you'll never know your way about."

All the time Mademoiselle Devoidy was teasing, her smile was busy reminding me of our common origin, a village ringed with woods, the autumn rain dripping on the piles of apples on the edge of the fields, waiting to be taken to the cider press. . . . Meanwhile, I did, indeed, amuse myself with what was lying about on the table. Sometimes there were huge American necklaces, ostentatious and impersonal; Cécile Sorel's pearls mingled with Polaire's choker, thirty-seven famous pearls. There were jewelers' necklaces, milky and brand new, not yet warmed into life by long contact with women's skin. Here and there a diamond, mounted in a clasp, emitted rainbow sparks. A dog collar, a fourteen-row choker, stiffened with vertical bars of brilliants, spoke of wrinkled dewlaps, an old woman's sinewy neck, perhaps of scrofula. . . .

Has that curious craft changed? Does it still fling heaps of treasures, defenseless fortunes, into the laps of poor and incorruptible women?

When the day was drawing to a close, Madame Armand sometimes came and sat at the green baize table. Out of discretion, she refrained from handling the necklaces over which her birdlike gaze wandered with glittering indifference.

"Well, so your day's work's over, Madame Armand?" Mademoiselle Devoidy would say.

"Oh, me—mine doesn't have to be fitted into the day like my husband's. My dinner to warm up, the studio to tidy, little things here and there—it's easily done."

Rigid when she was standing, Madame Armand was no less rigid seated. Her bust, tightly encased in a red-

and-black tartan bodice with braided loops, visible between the stiff, half-open flaps of a jacket, made me
think of a little cupboard. She had something of the
fascination of a wooden ship's figurehead. At the same
time she suggested the well-mannered efficiency of a
good cashier and various other sterling virtues.

"And Monsieur Armand, what nice thing's he up to
at this moment?"

"He's still working. He's still on his last Saturday's
wedding. You see he has to do everything in a little
business like ours. That wedding procession on Saturday
is giving him a lot of trouble, but it means quite a good
profit. The couple in one picture, a group of the brides-
maids, the whole procession in four different poses, goodness knows what all. I can't help him as much as I'd
like to."

The photographer's Missus turned to me as if to
apologize. As soon as she spoke, all the various stiff
and starchy phenomena of the close-fitting bodice, the
jacket, the imitation gardenia pinned in her buttonhole,
melted in the warmth of a pleasant voice with hardly
any modulations in it, a voice made to recount local
gossip at great length.

"My husband gets tired because he's starting this
exophthalmic goiter—I call it his exo for short. The
year's been too bad for us to take on an assistant camera-
man. The bothersome thing is, I haven't got a steady
hand, I break things. A pot of glue here, a develop-
ing tank there, and bang, there goes a frame on the
floor. You can see what a loss that means at the end
of a day."

She stretched out a hand toward me that was, indeed, shaking.

"Nerves," she said. "So I stick to my own little domain: I do all the housework. In one way it seems to
be good for my nerves, but . . ."

She frequently paused on a "but," after which came
a sigh, and when I asked Mademoiselle Devoidy whether
this "but" and this sigh hid some melancholy story, my
fellow countrywoman retorted: "What an idea! She's a
woman who laces tightly to give herself a slim waist
so she has to fight every minute to catch her breath."

Madame Armand, who had regular features, remained faithful to the high military collar and the tight, curled fringe because she had been told she looked like Queen Alexandra, only saucier. Saucier, I cannot honestly say. Darker, definitely. Heads of blue-black hair accompanied by white skin and a straight little nose abound in Paris and are usually of pure Parisian origin with no trace of Mediterranean blood. Madame Armand had as many lashes as a Spanish woman and a bird's eyes—I mean black eyes rich with a luster that never varied. The neighborhood paid her a laconic and adequate tribute by murmuring, as she passed, the words "Handsome brunet." On this point, Mademoiselle Devoidy's opinion allowed itself one reservation: "Handsome brunet's the word—especially ten years ago."

"Have you known Madame Armand ten years?"

"No, because she and little old Big Eyes only moved into this place three years ago. I've been in the house much longer than they have. But I can very well imagine Madame Armand ten years ago. You can see she's a woman who's devouring herself."

"Devouring herself? That's a strong expression. Aren't you exaggerating?"

An offended look, the color of spangled iron ore, passed under the lamp and met my eyes in the shadow.

"Anyone may be mistaken. Madame Armand may be mistaken too. Just fancy, she's got it into her head that she leads a sedentary life. So every evening, either before dinner or after, she goes out on foot to take the air."

"It's a good healthy habit, don't you think?"

Mademoiselle Devoidy, as she pinched her lips, made the little colorless hairs of mustache at the corners of her mouth converge—just as diving seals do when they close their nostrils to the water.

"You know what I think of healthy habits. Now that the photographer's Missus has got a bee in her bonnet that she has breathless fits if she doesn't go out, the next thing will be she'll be found on the stairs one day, dead of suffocation."

"You very seldom go out, Mademoiselle Devoidy?"

"Never, you might say."

"And you don't feel any the worse for it?"

"You can see for yourself. But I don't stop other people from doing what they please."

She darted her malicious gaze, directed at an invisible Madame Armand, toward the closed door. And I thought of the tart, ill-natured remarks the women herding the cattle in my native countryside exchange over the hedges as they slap the blood-swollen horseflies under the heifers' sensitive bellies.

Mademoiselle Devoidy bent her head over the threading of some very tiny pearls; at the edge of her forehead, between the cheek and the ear, the chestnut hair ended in vigorous down, silver, like her little mustache. All the features of this Parisian recluse spoke to me of downy willows, ripe hazelnuts, the sandy bottom of springs, and silky husks. She aimed the point of her needle, pinched between the thumb and forefinger that rested on the table, at the almost invisible holes in the small, insipidly white pearls that she speared in fives, then slipped on to the silk thread.

A familiar fist banged at the door.

"That'll be Tigri-Cohen. I recognize his knock. The key's in the door, Monsieur Tigri!"

The ill-favored face of Tigri-Cohen entered the little arena of light. His ugliness was now gay and ironical, now sad and imploring, like that of certain overly intelligent monkeys who have equal reason to cherish the gifts of man and to shiver with fear at them. I have always thought that Tigri-Cohen took tremendous pains to appear crafty, reckless, and unscrupulous. He adopted, perhaps out of guilelessness, the style and manner of a moneylender who charged exorbitant rates. As I knew him, he was always ready to part with twenty francs or even a "banknote," so much so that he died poor, in the arms of his unsuspected honesty.

I had known him in the wings and dressing rooms of music halls, where Tigri-Cohen spent most of his evenings. The little variety actresses used to climb on his shoulders like tame parakeets and leave wet-white all over this black man. They knew his pockets were full of small jewels, flawed pearls and gems just good enough to make into hatpins. He excited his little friends' admiration by showing them badly colored stones with beautiful names, peridots, chalcedonies, chrysoprases, and pretentious zircons. On the friendliest terms with all the girls, Tigri-Cohen would sell a few of his glittering pebbles between ten P.M. and midnight. But to the rich stars, he presented himself mainly in the role of buyer.

His taste for beautiful pearls always seemed to me more sensual than commercial. I shall never forget the state of excitement I saw him in one day when, going into his shop, I found him alone with a small, unremarkable, expressionless little man who drew out of his shabby waistcoat a sky-blue silk handkerchief and, out of the handkerchief, a single pearl.

"So you've still got it?" asked Tigri.

"Yes," said the little man. "Not for long, though."

It was an unpierced pearl, round, big as a fine cherry, and, like a cherry, it seemed not to receive the cold light shed from the even-number side of the Rue Lafayette but to emit a steady, veiled radiance from within. Tigri contemplated it without saying a word and the little chap kept silence.

"It's—it's—" began Tigri-Cohen.

He searched in vain for words to praise it, then shrugged his shoulders.

"Can I have it a moment?" I asked.

I held it in the hollow of my palm, this marvelous, warm virgin, with its mystery of tremulous colors, its indefinable pink that picked up a snowy blue then exchanged it for a fleeting mauve.

Before giving back the glorious pearl, Tigri sighed. Then the little man extinguished the soft rays in the blue handkerchief, thrust the whole, carelessly, into a pocket, and went away.

"It's—" repeated Tigri "—it's the color of love."

"To whom does it belong?"

"To whom? To whom? Think *I* know? To black chaps in India! To an oyster-bed company! To savages, to people with no faith and no feelings, to—"

"How much is it worth?"

He gave me a look of contempt.

"How much? A pearl like that, in the dawn of its

life, that's still going about in its little blue satin chemise at the bottom of a broker's pocket? How much? Like a kilo of plums, eh? 'That'll be three francs, Madame. Here you are, Madame. Thank you, Madame.' Ah, to hear anyone ask *that*——!"

Every muscle of his ugly, passionate mime's face was working, that face that was always overloaded with too much expression, too much laughter, too much sadness. That evening, in Devoidy's room, I remember he was dripping with rain and seemed not to notice it. He was exploring his pockets with a mechanical gesture, pockets that were secret hoards of necklaces of colored stones, cabochon rings, little bags in which diamonds slept in tissue paper. He flung some ropes of pearls on the green baize.

"There, Devoidy, my love, do that for me for to-morrow. And that one. Don't you think it's hideous? If you pulled out the pigeon's feather stuffed in the middle of that nut, you could thread it on a cable. Anyway, change the stuffing."

From force of habit, he bent over my necklace, with one eye screwed up.

"The fourth one from the middle—I'll buy that. No? Just as you like. Good-bye, my pets. Tonight I'm going to the dress rehearsal of the Folies-Bergère."

"Should be a fine evening for business," said Mademoiselle Devoidy politely.

"That shows you don't know a thing about it. To-night my good ladies will be thinking of nothing but their parts, their costumes, the audience's reaction, and going off into faints behind a prop. See you soon, pets."

Other visitors, especially female ones, passed through the boltless door into the narrow circle of harsh light. I stared at them with the avid curiosity I have always felt for people I run no risk of seeing again. Richly dressed women thrust out hands filled with precious white grain into the glare of the lamp. Or else, with a proud, languid gesture acquired from constantly wear-ing pearls, they undid the clasps of their necklaces.

Among others, my memory retains the picture of a woman all silvered with chinchilla. She came in very agitated and she was such a sturdy daughter of the people under all her luxury that she was a joy to the eye. She plumped herself down rudely on the straw-seated stool and commanded: "Don't unstring the whole row. Just get me out that one, on the side, near the middle, yes, that beauty there."

Mademoiselle Devoidy, who did not like despots, calmly and unhurriedly cut the two silk knots and pushed the free pearl toward her client. The beautiful woman grabbed it and studied it from very close up. Under the lamp, I could have counted her long, fluttering eyelashes, which were stuck together with mascara. She held out the pearl to the stringer: "You, what's *your* idea about this here pearl?"

"I know nothing about pearls," said Mademoiselle Devoidy impassively.

"Sure you're not joking?"

The beautiful woman pointed to the table, with evident irony. Then her face changed; she seized a little lump of cast iron under which Mademoiselle Devoidy kept a set of ready-threaded needles and brought it down hard on the pearl, which crushed into tiny fragments. I exclaimed "Oh!" in spite of myself. Mademoiselle Devoidy permitted herself no other movement than to clutch an unfinished string and some scattered pearls close against her with her sure hands.

The customer contemplated her work without saying a word. Finally, she burst into vehement tears. She kept noisily sobbing: "The swine, the swine," and, at the same time, carefully collecting the black from her lashes on a corner of her handkerchief. Then she stuffed her necklace, amputated of one pearl, into her handbag, asked for "a little bit of tissue paper," stowed every single fragment of the sham pearl into it, and stood up. Before she left the room, she made a point of affirming loudly, "That's not the last of this business, not by a long shot." Then she carried away into the outside air the unpleasant whiff of a brand-new, very fashionable scent: synthetic lily of the valley.

"Is that the first time you've seen a thing like that happen, Mademoiselle Devoidy?"

Mademoiselle Devoidy was scrupulously tidying up her workbench with her careful hands, unshaking as usual.

"No, the second," she said. "With this difference, that the first time, the pearl resisted. It was real. So was the rest of the necklace."

"And what did the lady say?"

"It wasn't a lady, it was a gentleman. He said: 'Ah, the bitch!' "

"Why?"

"The necklace was his wife's. She'd made her husband believe it cost fifteen francs. Yes. Oh, you know, when it comes to pearls, it's very seldom there isn't some shady story behind them."

She touched her little coral necklace with two fingers. I was amazed to catch this slightly sneering skeptic making a gesture to avert bad luck and to see the cloud of superstition pass over her stubborn brow.

"So you wouldn't care to wear pearls?"

She raised one shoulder askew, torn between her commercial prudence and the desire not to lie.

"I don't know. One doesn't know one's own self. Down there, at Coulanges, there was a fellow who couldn't have been more of an anarchist—he frightened everyone out of their wits. And then he inherited a little house with a garden and a round dovecote and a pigsty. If you were to see the anarchist now! There's quite a change."

Almost at once, she recovered her restrained laugh, her pleasantly rebellious expression, and her way of approving without being sycophantic and criticizing without being rude.

One night when I had lingered late with her, she caught me yawning, and I apologized by saying: "I've got one of those hungers. I don't take tea and I had hardly any lunch; there was red meat—I can't eat underdone meat."

"Neither can I," said my fellow countrywoman. "In our part of the world, as you well know, they say raw meat is for cats and the English. But if you can be patient for five minutes, a *mille-feuille* will be wafted here to you, without my leaving my chair. What do you bet?"

"A pound of chocolate creams."

"Pig who backs out!" said Mademoiselle Devoidy, holding out her dry palm, quite flat, to me. I slapped it and said "Done!"

"Mademoiselle Devoidy, how is it that your flat never smells of fried whiting or onions or stew? Have you got a secret?"

She indicated "Yes" by fluttering her eyelids.

"Can I know?"

An accustomed hand knocked three times on the front door.

"There you are, here it comes, your *mille-feuille*. And my secret's revealed. Come in, Madame Armand, come in!"

Nevertheless, she fastened my little middle-class necklace at the back of my neck. Loaded with a basket, Madame Armand did not at once offer me her chronically trembling fingers and she spoke very hurriedly: "Careful, careful, don't upset it. I've got something breakable. To-day's chef's special is *bœuf à la bourguignonne* and I brought you a lovely bit of lettuce. As to *mille-feuille*, nothing doing! It's iced Genoese cakes."

Mademoiselle Devoidy made a comic grimace at me and attempted to unburden her obliging neighbor. But the latter exclaimed: "I'll carry it all into the kitchen for you!" and ran toward the dark room at the back. As quickly as she had crossed the lighted zone, I had caught sight of her face and so had Mademoiselle Devoidy.

"I must fly, I must fly, I've got some milk on the gas stove," Madame Armand cried out in tomboyish tones.

She crossed the front room again at a run and pulled the door closed behind her. Mademoiselle Devoidy went out into the kitchen and came back with two Genoese cakes, with pink icing, on a plate adorned with a flaming bomb and the inscription "Fire Brigade Alarm."

"As sure as eggs is eggs," she said with a thoughtful air, "the photographer's Missus has been crying. And she doesn't have any milk on her gas stove."

"Domestic scene?"

She shook her head.

"Poor little old Big Eyes! He's not capable of it. Neither is she, for that matter. Look here, you got through

that cake quickly. Would you like the other one? She's
spoiled my appetite, Monsieur Armand's good lady, with
that face all gone to pieces."

"Everything will be all right tomorrow," I said, my
mind elsewhere.

In exchange for that flat remark, I received a brief,
trenchant glance.

"Oh, of *course* it will, won't it? And, anyway, if it isn't
all right, *you* won't be upset."

"What's all this? You think I ought to be more passionately concerned over the Armand family's troubles?"

"The Armand family isn't asking you for anything. And
neither am I. It would most certainly be the first time
anyone had heard *me* asking anyone for anything. . . ."

Mademoiselle Devoidy had lowered her voice in the effort to control her irritation. We were, I imagine, utterly
ridiculous. It was this cloud of anger, rising suddenly
between two hot-blooded women, that fixed the details
of an absurd, unexpected scene in my memory. I had the
good sense to put an end to it at once by laying my hand
on her shoulder: "Now, now. Don't let's make ourselves
out blacker than we are! You know quite well that if I
can be of any use to this good lady. . . Are you frightened for her?"

Mademoiselle Devoidy flushed under her freckles and
covered the top of her face with one hand, with a simple and romantic gesture: "Now you're being too nice.
Don't be too nice to me. When anyone's too nice to me,
I don't know what I'm doing—I boil over like a soup."

She uncovered her beautiful, moist-spangled eyes and
pushed the straw-seated stool toward me.

"One minute, surely you've got a minute? That's rain
you can hear; wait till the rain's over."

She sat down opposite me in her working place and
vigorously rubbed her eyes with the back of her forefinger.

"Get this well into your head first—Madame Armand
isn't a gossip or a woman who goes in for confidences.
But she lives very near, right on my doorstep. This place
is just a little block of apartments, the old-fashioned
kind. Two rooms on the right, two rooms on the left,
little businesses that can be done in one room at home.

People who live so very near you, it isn't so much that you hear them—anyway, they don't make any noise—but I'm conscious of them. Especially of the fact that Madame Armand spends so much time out on the landing. In places like this, if anything's not going right, the neighbors are very soon aware of it, at least I am."

She lowered her voice and compressed her lips; her little mustache hairs glistened. She pricked her green table with the point of a needle as if she were cabalistically counting her words.

"When the photographer's Missus goes out shopping for herself or for me, you can always see the concierge or the flower seller under the archway or the woman in the little *bistro* coming out, one or another of them, to see where she's going. Where is she going? Why, she's going to the dairy or to buy hot rolls or to the hairdresser, just like anyone else! So then the pryers take their noses inside again, anything but pleased, as if they'd been promised something and not given it. And the next time, they start all over again. But when it's me who goes out or Madame Gâteroy downstairs or her daughter, people don't stop and stare after us as if they expected something extraordinary was going to happen."

"Madame Armand has a—a rather individual appearance," I risked suggesting. "Perhaps she does somewhat overdo the tartan, too."

Mademoiselle Devoidy shook her head and seemed to despair of making herself understood. It was getting late; from top to bottom of the building, doors were slamming one by one, on every floor chairs were being drawn up around a table and a soup tureen; I took my leave. The door of the photographic studio, unwontedly shut, turned the camera pedestal and the crossed shrimp nets under the gas jet into an important piece of decoration. On the ground floor the concierge raised her curtain to watch me going: I had never stayed so late.

The warm night was foggy around the gas lamps, and the unusual hour gave me that small, yet somehow rewarding, pang I used to experience in the old days when I came away from stage performances that had begun when the sun was at its zenith and finished when it was dark.

Do those transient figures of long-past periods of my
life deserve to live again in a handful of pages as I here
compel them to? They were important enough for me to
keep them secret, at least during the time I was involved
with them. For example, my husband, at home, did not
know of the existence of Mademoiselle Devoidy or of my
familiarity with Tigri-Cohen. The same was true of Monsieur Armand's "Missus" and of a certain sewing woman,
expert at repairing worn quilts and making multicolored
silk rags into patchwork baby-carriage covers. Did I like
her for her needlework, which disdained both fashion
and the sewing machine, or was it for her second profession? At six o'clock in the afternoon she abandoned her
hexagonal pieces of silk and went off to the Gaîté-Ly-
rique, where she sang a part in *Les Mousquetaires au
Couvent.*

For a long time, in the inner compartment of my handbag, between the leather and the lining, I kept a fifty-
centime "synthetic" pearl I had once lost in Tigri-Cohen's shop. He had found it, and before returning it to me,
he had amused himself by studding my initials on it in
little diamonds. But at home I never mentioned either
the charming mascot or Tigri himself, for the husband I
was married to then had formed such a rigid, block-
shaped idea of the jeweler, such a conventional notion
of a "dealer," that I could neither have pleaded the
cause of the latter nor rectified the error of the former.

Was I genuinely attached to the little needlewoman?
Did I feel real affection for the misunderstood Tigri-
Cohen? I do not know. The instinct to deceive has not
played a very large part in my different lives. It was essential to me, as it is to many women, to escape from
the opinions of certain people, which I knew to be subject to error and apt to be proclaimed dogmatically in a
feigned tone of indulgence. Treatment of this sort drives
us women to avoid the simple truth, as if it were a dull,
monotonous tune, to take pleasure in half lies, half dis-
tortions, half escapes from reality.

When the opportunity came, I made my way once
more to the narrow-fronted house over whose brow the

open blue pane of the photographic studio window slanted like a visor.

As soon as I entered the hall of the block of apartments, a cleaner's delivery man in a black apron and a woman carrying bread in a long wicker *cistera* barred my way. The first, without being asked, obligingly informed me: "It's nothing, just a chimney on fire." At the same moment, a "runner" from a fashion house came dashing down the stairs, banging her yellow box against all the banisters and screeching: "She's as white as a sheet! She hasn't an hour to live!"

Her scream magically attracted a dozen passersby who crowded around her, pressing her close on all sides. Desire to escape, slight nausea, and idle curiosity struggled within me, but in the end they gave way to a strange resignation. I knew perfectly well—already out of breath before I had begun to run—I knew perfectly well that I should not stop until I reached the top landing. Which of them was it? The photographer's Missus or Mademoiselle Devoidy? Mentally, I ruled out the latter as if no peril could ever endanger her mocking wisdom or the sureness of those hands, soft as silky wood shavings, or scatter the milky constellations of precious, tiny moons she pursued on the green baize table and impaled with such deadly aim.

All the while I was breathlessly climbing the stories, I was fighting to reassure myself. An accident? Why shouldn't it have happened to the knitting women on the fourth floor or the bookbinding couple? The steamy November afternoon preserved the full strength of the smells of cabbage and gas and of the hot, excited human beings who were showing me the way.

The unexpected sound of sobbing is demoralizing. Easy as it is to imitate, that retching, hiccuping noise remains crudely impressive. While I was being secretly crushed to death between the banisters and a telegraph boy who had pushed up too fast, we heard convulsive male sobs and the commentators on the staircase fell silent, avidly. The noise lasted only a moment; it was extinguished behind a door that someone up there had slammed again. Without having ever heard the man whom Mademoiselle Devoidy nicknamed little old Big

Eyes weep, I knew beyond a shadow of a doubt that it was he who was sobbing.

At last I reached the top floor, crammed with strangers between its two closed doors. One of them opened again and I heard the biting voice of Mademoiselle Devoidy.

"Ladies and gentlemen, where are you going like that? It doesn't make sense. If you want to have your photographs taken, it's too late. Why no, don't worry, there hasn't been any accident. A lady has sprained her ankle, they've put a crepe bandage on it and that's the beginning and end of the story."

A murmur of disappointment and a little laughter ran through the crowd flocking up the stairs. But it struck me that, in the harsh light, Mademoiselle Devoidy looked extremely ill. She proffered a few more words designed to discourage the invaders and went back into her flat.

"Well, if that's all—" said the telegraph boy.

To make up his lost time, he jostled a cellarman in a green baize apron and a few dim women and disappeared by leaps and bounds, and at last I was able to sit down on the Gothic chair reserved for First Communicants. As soon as I was alone, Mademoiselle Devoidy reappeared.

"Come in, I saw you all right. I couldn't make signs to you in front of everyone. Do you mind? I wouldn't be sorry to sit down for a moment."

As if there was no refuge except in her regular, everyday haunt, she collapsed into the chair she worked in.

"Ah, that's better!"

She smiled at me with a happy look.

"She's brought it all up, so we needn't worry any more."

"All what?"

"What she'd taken. Some stuff to kill herself. Some disgusting filth or other."

"But why did she do it?"

"There you go, asking why! You always have to have three dozen reasons, don't you? She'd left a letter for little old Big Eyes."

"A letter? Whatever did she confess?"

By degrees Mademoiselle Devoidy was recovering her composure and her easy, mocking way of treating me.

"You've got to know everything, haven't you? As to confessing, she confessed all. She confessed: 'My darling Geo, don't scold me. Forgive me for leaving you. In death, as in life, I remain your faithful Georgina.' Next to that, there was another scrap of paper, which said: 'Everything is paid except the washerwoman, who had no change on Wednesday.' It happened about a quarter-past two, twenty-past two—"

She broke off and stood up.

"Wait, there's some coffee left."

"If it's for me, don't bother."

"I want some myself," she said.

The panacea of the people appeared with the sacred vessels of its cult, its blue-marbled enamel jug, its two cups adorned with a red-and-gold key pattern, and its twisted glass sugar bowl. The smell of chicory faithfully escorted it, eloquent of ritual anxieties, of deathbed vigils and difficult labors, of whispered palavers, of a drug within reach of all.

"Well, as I was saying," Mademoiselle Devoidy went on, "about two or a quarter past, someone knocked at my door. It was my little old Big Eyes, looking ever so embarrassed and saying: 'You haven't happened to see my wife going downstairs?' 'No,' I says, 'but she might have gone down without my seeing her.' 'Yes,' he says to me. 'I ought to have been out myself by now, but, just as I was on the point of leaving, I broke a bottle of hyposulfite. You can see the state my hands are in.' 'That was bad luck,' I says to him. 'Yes,' he says to me, 'I need a duster, the dusters are in our bedroom, in the cupboard behind the bed.' 'If that's all,' I says, 'I'll go get you one. Don't touch anything.' 'That isn't all,' he says to me. 'What's worrying me is that the bedroom's locked and it never is locked.' I stared at him. I don't know what came into my head, but I got up, nearly pushing him over, and off I went and knocked at their bedroom door. He kept saying: 'Why, what's the matter with you? What's the matter with you?' I answered him tit for tat: 'Well, what about you? You haven't taken a look at yourself.' He stayed standing there with his hands spread out, all cov-

ered with hyposulfite. I come back in here, I snatch up
the hatchet I chop up my firewood with. I swear to you
the hinges and the lock bust right off at the same blow.
They're no better than matchwood, these doors."

She drank a few mouthfuls of tepid coffee.

"I'll get a safety chain put on mine," she went on.
"Now that I've seen what a fragile thing a door is."

I was waiting for her to continue her story, but she
was toying absently with the little metal shovel that gathered up the seed pearls on the cloth and seemed to have
nothing more to say.

"And then, Mademoiselle Devoidy?"

"Then what?"

"She—Madame Armand—was she in the room?"

"Of course she was. On her bed. Actually in her bed.
Wearing silk stockings and smart shoes, black satin ones,
embroidered with a little jet motif. That was what struck
me all at once, those shoes and those stockings. It struck
me so much that, while I was filling a hot-water bottle,
I said to her husband, 'Whatever was she up to, going to
bed in her shoes and stockings?' He was sobbing as he
explained to me: 'It's because of her corns and her
crooked third toe. She didn't want anyone to see her
bare feet, not even me. She used to go to bed in little
socks. She's so dainty in all her ways.'"

Mademoiselle Devoidy yawned, stretched, and began
to laugh: "Ah, you've got to admit a man's a total loss in
circumstances like that. *Him!* The only thing *he* could
think of doing was crying and keeping on saying: 'My
darling . . . My darling . . .' Lucky I acted quickly," she
added proudly. "Excuse the details, it makes me feel
queasy. Oh, she's saved all right! But Doctor Camescasse, who lives at number eleven, won't let her have
anything but a little milk and soda water till further or-
ders. Madame Armand swallowed enough poison to kill a
regiment—apparently that's what saved her. Little old
Big Eyes is on sentry duty at her bedside. But I'm just
going to run in and have a look at her. Will we be seeing
you again soon? Bring her a little bunch of violets—it'll
be more cheerful than if you'd had to take one to her in
the Montparnasse cemetery."

I was already on the pavement when, too late, a question crossed my mind: why had Madame Armand wanted to die? At the same moment, I realized that Mademoiselle Devoidy had omitted telling me.

During the following days, I thought of the photographer's Missus and her abortive suicide; this naturally led me on to thinking about death and, unnaturally for me, about my own. Suppose I were to die in a streetcar? Suppose I were to die while having dinner in a restaurant? Appalling possibilities, but so highly unlikely that I soon abandoned them. We women seldom die outside our own homes; as soon as pain puts a handful of blazing straw under our bellies, we behave like frightened horses and find enough strength to run for shelter. After three days, I lost the taste for choosing the pleasantest mode of departing. All the same, country funerals are charming, especially in June, because of the flowers. But roses so soon become overblown in hot weather. . . . I had reached this point when a note from Madame Armand—admirable spelling and a ravishing curly handwriting like lacework—reminded me of my "kind promise" and invited me to "tea."

On the top landing, I ran into an elderly married couple who were leaving the photographer's studio, arm in arm, all dressed up in braided jacket, necktie, and stiff black silk. Little old Big Eyes was showing them out and I scanned his heavy eyelids for traces of his passionate tears. He greeted me with a joyful nod that implied mutual understanding.

"The ladies are in the bedroom. Madame Armand is still suffering from slight general fatigue. She thought you would be kind enough to excuse her receiving you so informally."

He guided me through the studio, had a courteous word for my bunch of violets—"the Parma ones look so distinguished"—and left me on the threshold of the unknown room.

On this narrow planet, we have only the choice between two unknown worlds. One of them tempts us—ah, what a dream, to live in that!—the other stifles us at the first breath. In the matter of furnishing, I find a certain absence of ugliness far worse than ugliness. Without containing any monstrosity, the total effect of the room where Madame Armand was enjoying her convalescence made me lower my eyes, and I would not have the slightest pleasure describing it.

She was resting, with her feet up, on the made-up bed, the same bed she had untucked to die in. Her eagerness to welcome me would have made her rise had not Mademoiselle Devoidy restrained her with the firm hand of a guardian angel. November was mild only out of doors. Madame Armand was keeping herself warm under a little red-and-black coverlet, crocheted in what is called Tunisian stitch. I am not fond of Tunisian stitch. But Madame Armand looked well, her cheeks were less parched, and her eyes more brilliant than ever. The vivacity of her movements displaced the coverlet and revealed two slim feet shod in black satin, embroidered—just as Mademoiselle Devoidy had described them to me—with a motif in jet beads.

"Madame Armand, a little less movement, please," gravely ordered the guardian angel.

"But I'm not ill!" protested Madame Armand. "I'm coddling myself, that's all. My little Exo's paying a woman to come in and do the housework for me in the morning, Mademoiselle Devoidy's made us a lemon sponge cake, and you bring me some magnificent violets! A life of idle luxury! You will taste some of my raspberry and gooseberry jelly with the sponge cake, won't you? It's the last of last year's pots, and without boasting . . . This year I made a mess of them, and the plums in brandy too. It's a year when I've made a mess of everything."

She smiled, as if making some subtle allusion. The unvarying glitter of her black eyes still reminded me of some bird or other; but now the bird was tranquil and refreshed. At what dark spring had it slaked its thirst?

"In that affair, no matter how many were killed and wounded, nobody's dead," concluded Mademoiselle Devoidy.

I greeted the sentence that came straight out of our native province with a knowing wink and I swallowed, one on top of the other, a cup of very black tea and a glass of sweet wine that tasted of licorice: what must be, must be.

I felt ill at ease. One does not so quickly acquire the knack of conjuring up, in the straightforward light of afternoon, such a very recent suicide. True, it had been transformed into a purging, but it had been planned to prevent any return. I tried to adapt myself to the tone of the other two by saying playfully: "Who would believe that charming woman we see before us is the very same one who was so unreasonable the other day?"

The charming woman finished her wedge of lemon sponge before pantomiming a little confusion and answering, doubtfully and coquettishly: "So unreasonable —so unreasonable—there's a lot could be said about that."

Mademoiselle Devoidy cut her off short. She seemed to me to have acquired a military authority from her first act of lifesaving.

"Now, now! You're not going to start all over again, are you?"

"Start again? Oh, never!"

I applauded the spontaneity of that cry. Madame Armand raised her right hand for an oath.

"I swear it! The only thing I absolutely deny is what Doctor Camescasse said to me: 'In fact, you swallowed a poison during an attack of neurasthenia.' That infuriated me. For two cents I'd have answered him back: 'If you're so certain, there's no point in asking me a hundred questions. *I* know perfectly well in my own mind that I didn't commit suicide out of neurasthenia!' "

"Tst, tst," rebuked Mademoiselle Devoidy. "How long is it since I've seen for myself you were in a bad way? Madame Colette here can certify that I've mentioned it to her. As to neurasthenia, of course it was neurasthenia; there's nothing to be ashamed of in that."

The crocheted coverlet was flung aside; the cup and saucer narrowly escaped following suit.

"No, it wasn't! I think I might be allowed to have my own little opinion on the subject! I'm the person concerned, isn't that so?"

"I do take your opinion into account, Madame Armand. But it can't be compared with the opinion of a man of science like Doctor Camescasse!"

They were exchanging their retorts over my head, so

tensely that I slightly ducked my chin. It was the first time I had heard a would-be suicide arguing her case in my presence as if standing up for her lawful rights. Like so many saviors, heavenly or earthly, the angel tended to overdo her part. Her spangled eye lit up with a spark that was anything but angelic, while the color of the rescued one kindled under her too-white powder.

I have never turned up my nose at a heated argument between cronies. A lively taste for street scenes keeps me hovering on the outskirts of quarrels vented in the open air, which I find good occasions for enriching my vocabulary. I hoped, as I sat at Madame Armand's bedside, that the dialogue between the two women would blaze up with that virulence that characterizes feminine misunderstandings. But incomprehensible death, which teaches the living nothing; the memory of a nauseating poison; the rigorous devotion that tended its victim with a rod of iron; all this was too present, too massive, too oppressive to be replaced by a healthy exchange of abuses. What was I doing in this home timidly ruled by little old Big Eyes? What would remain to me of his "Missus," whom death had failed to ravish, beyond a stale, insipid mystery? As to Mademoiselle Devoidy, that perfect example of the dry, incorruptible spinster, I realized that I could no longer imagine she was anything of an enigma and that the attraction of the void cannot last forever.

Sorrow, fear, physical pain, excessive heat and excessive cold, I can still guarantee to stand up to all these with decent courage. But I abdicate in the face of boredom, which turns me into a wretched and, if necessary, ferocious creature. Its approach, its capricious presence that affects the muscles of the jaw, dances in the pit of the stomach, sings a monotonous refrain that one's feet beat time to; I do not merely dread these manifestations, I fly from them. What was wrong in my eyes about these two women, who from being gratitude and devotion incarnate were now putting up barriers between them, was that they did not proceed to adopt the classic attitudes. There was no accompaniment of scurrilous laughter, of insults as blinding as pepper, of fists dug well into the ribs. They did not even awaken minute old grievances,

kept alive and kicking by long stewing over and brood-
ing on. Nevertheless, I did hear dangerous exchanges
and words such as "neurotic . . . ingratitude . . . meddler
. . . poking your nose in . . ." I think it was on this last
insult that Mademoiselle Devoidy rose to her feet, flung
us a curt, bitter, ceremonious "good-bye," and left the
room.

Somewhat belatedly, I displayed suitable agitation.

"Well, really! But it's not serious. What childishness!
Who'd have expected—"

Madame Armand merely gave a faint shrug that
seemed to say "Forget it!" As the daylight was going
fast, she stretched out her arm and switched on the bedside lamp, which wore a crinoline of salmon-pink silk. At
once the depressing character of the room changed and I
did not hide my pleasure, for the lampshade, elaborately
ruched and pretentious as it was, filtered an enchanting
rosy light, like the lining of a seashell. Madame Armand
smiled.

"I think both of us are pleased," she said.

She saw I was about to mention the disagreeable inci-
dent again and stopped me.

"Forget it, madame, these little tiffs—the less one
thinks about them the better. Either they work themselves out of their own accord, or else they don't, and
that's even better. Have another drop of wine. Yes, yes,
have some more. It's pure unadulterated stuff."

She leaped from her couch, deftly pulling down her
dress. In those days women did not let themselves slide
off a sofa or out of a car revealing a wide margin of bare
thigh as they do nowadays with such cold and barbarous
indifference.

"You're not overtaxing your strength, Madame Armand?"

She was walking to and fro on her jet-and-satin-shod
feet, those feet that had been modest even in death. She
poured out the pseudoport, pulled an awning over the
ceiling skylight, displaying a briskness that was not without grace, as if she had grown lighter. A likable woman,
in fact, whose thirty-six years had left few traces. A
woman who had wanted to die.

She switched on a second pink lamp. The room, ex-

traordinary by its very ordinariness, exuded the false
cheerfulness of well-kept hotel bedrooms.

My hostess came and picked up the chair abandoned
by Mademoiselle Devoidy and planted it firmly beside me.

"No, madame, I won't allow people to believe that I
killed myself out of neurasthenia."

"But," I said, "I've never thought— Nothing gave me
any reason to believe—"

I was surprised to hear Madame Armand refer to her
unsuccessful attempt as an accomplished fact. Her eyes
were frankly presented to me, wide open and looking
straight into mine, but their extreme brightness and blackness revealed hardly anything. Her small, smooth, sensible forehead, under the curled fringe, really did look as
if it had never harbored the regrettable disorder called
neurasthenia between the two fine eyebrows. Before she
sat down, she straightened the violets in the vase with
her unsure hands; I saw their stalks tremble between her
fingers. "Nerves, you know." Hands that were too clumsy
even to measure out an effective dose of poison.

"Madame," she said, "I must tell you first of all that I
have always had a very trivial life."

Such a prelude threatened me with a long recital. Nevertheless, I stayed where I was.

It is easy to relate what is of no importance. My memory has not failed to register the idle words and the mild
absurdities of these two opposite neighbors, and I have
tried to reproduce them faithfully. But, beginning with
the words "I have always had a very trivial life" I feel
absolved from the tiresome meticulousness imposed on a
writer, such as carefully noting the too-frequent reitera-
tions of "in one way" and "what poor creatures we are"
that rose like bubbles to the surface of Madame Armand's story. Though they helped her to tell it, it is for
me to remove them. It is my duty as a writer to abridge
our conversation and also to suppress my own unimpor-
tant contribution to it.

"A very trivial life. I married such a good man. A man
as perfect and hardworking and devoted as all that really
shouldn't exist. Now, could you imagine anything unexpected happening to a man as perfect as that? And we

didn't have a child. To tell you the honest truth, I don't think I minded much.

"Once, a young man in the neighborhood— Oh, no, it's not what you're expecting. A young man who had the nerve to accost me on the staircase because it was dark there. Handsome, I have to admit he was handsome. Naturally, he promised me the moon and the stars. He told me: 'I'm not going to take you under false pretenses. With me, you'll see life in the raw. You can reckon I'm quite as likely to make you die of misery as of joy. Things will go my way, not yours.' And so on, and so on. One day he said to me: 'Let me have a look at your little wrist.' I wouldn't give it to him. He grabbed hold of it and twisted it. For more than ten days I couldn't use my hand and it was my little Exo who did it up for me. At night, after he'd put a clean crepe bandage on my wrist —I'd told him I'd had a fall—he would stare for a long time at that bandaged wrist. I was ashamed. I felt like a dog who's come home with a collar no one's ever seen it wearing and they say to it: 'But where on earth did you get a collar like that?' That shows the least evil-minded people can be sharp in their way.

"With this young man, it was all over before it began. Do you know what I couldn't stand? It was this gentleman I'd never spoken three words to daring to say to me 'tu'. He just sprang up before my feet as if he'd risen out of the earth. Well, he vanished back into it again.

"Since then? Why, nothing. Nothing worth mentioning. There's nothing to surprise you in that. Plenty of women, and not the ugliest ones either, would be in my state if they didn't lend a helping hand. You mustn't believe men throw themselves on women like cannibals. Certainly not, madame. It's women who spread that idea about. Men are much too anxious not to have their peace upset. But lots of women can't stand a man behaving decently. I know what I'm talking about.

"Personally, I'm not the kind that thinks much about men. It's not my temperament. In one way, it might have been better for me if I had thought of them. Instead of that, whatever do you think came into my head one morning when I was cutting up some breast of veal? I said to myself: 'I made breast of veal with green peas only last Saturday, all very nice, but one mustn't overdo it, a week goes by so fast. It's eleven already, my husband's got a christening group coming to pose at half-past one, I must get my washing up done before the clients arrive, my husband doesn't like to hear me through the wall rattling the dishes or poking the stove when clients are in the studio. . . . And after that I must go out, there's that cleaner who still hasn't finished taking the shine off my husband's black suit, I'll have to have a sharp word with her. If I get back to do my ironing before dark, I'll be lucky; never mind, I'll dampen my net window curtains again and I'll iron them tomorrow, sooner than scorch them today. After that, I've got nothing to do but the dinner to get ready and two or three odds and ends to see to and it'll be finished.'

"And instead of adding, as I often did, 'Finished—and none too soon,' I went on: 'Finished? How d'you mean, finished? Is that all? Is that the whole of my day, today, yesterday, tomorrow? But this is dreaming. I've got to have something else to my day, understand?' That night, when I was in bed, I was still going over and over all my idiotic thoughts. The next day, I felt better and I had to make some jam and pickle some gherkins, so you can imagine I sent Mademoiselle Devoidy out to do the shopping, it was well and truly her turn, so as to give all my time to hulling my strawberries and rubbing my gherkins in salt. I was deep in my work when suddenly it came over me again: 'The events of my life—so today's jam-making day? Be careful about the copper preserving pan, it's got a rounded bottom, if it tips over on the hole of the gas range, what a catastrophe! And I haven't got enough glass jam jars, I'll have to borrow the two jars Madame Gâteroy uses for her potted goose if she can spare them. And when I've finished my jam, what will come along in the way of a sensational event?' At last you can see the picture.

"It wasn't five o'clock by the time my jam was done. Done and very badly done. The worst failure I'd ever had, all the sugar burned to caramel. Luckily, the strawberries cost next to nothing. And there, off I went again: 'Tomorrow, let's see, tomorrow . . . Tomorrow we've got that lady who comes to mount the proofs on fiber-

oard.' Fiberboard was a novelty imitation felt that made
a lovely background for sports photos. But it needed a
special knack and special kind of glue. So once a week
this lady used to come and I used to keep her to lunch—
it made a change for me. We didn't lose by it, she made
good use of her time and it was better for her than running around to the little eating place. I added something
special in the way of a sweet or something good from
the pork butcher's.

"But this day I'm telling you about, I felt that it was
all the same to me, or rather that nothing satisfied me.
And the following days—I pass them over in silence.

"What did you say? Oh, no! Oh, you're quite wrong! I
didn't despise my occupations, on the contrary. I've
never put my mind to them so much. Nothing went
amiss. Except that I found the time long and at the same
time I kept looking about for something I could do to
fill it up. Reading? Yes. You're certainly right. Reading
makes a good distraction. But I've got such a twisted
character that everything I tried to read seemed to me—
a little thin, sort of poor. Always this mania for something big. When I'd done my housework and finished the
day's jobs, I used to go out and take a few breaths on
the landing—as if I'd been able to see farther from there.
But landing or no landing, I'd had enough and more
than enough.

"Pardon? Ah, you've put your finger right on the trouble. Enough of what, precisely? Such a happy woman, as
Madame Gâteroy used to say when she talked about me.
Such a happy woman, why exactly, that's what I would
have been if, here and there, in my trivial little life, I'd
had something great. What do I call great? I've no idea,
madame, because I've never had it! If I'd had it even
once, I guarantee I'd have realized at once, without a
shadow of doubt, that it *was* great!"

She rose from her chair, sat down on the bed, rested
her elbows on her knees, and propped up her chin. In
that way, she was facing me directly. With a wrinkle in-
cised between her eyebrows and one eye nervously
screwed up, she did not appear uglier to me; on the contrary.

"What queer things presentiments are, madame! Not

mine, I'm talking of my husband's. Just about that time he said to me point-blank: 'If you like, in July we'll go off for a month to Yport, as we did two years ago. That'll do you good.' Yport? Yes, it's not bad, mainly a family holiday place, but quite a lot of Paris celebrities go there. Fancy, when we were there before, we saw Guirand de Scevola, that painter who's become so famous, every single day. He was painting the sea in anger, from nature, with the legs of his easel in the foam of the waves. It was a real sight. Everyone used to stare at him. Naturally, I said to my little Exo: 'You're choosing a nice time to go and squander what little money we have at the seaside!' 'When it is a question of you,' he answered, 'nothing else counts.' That day and many days after, I absolutely swore to myself never to do anything to hurt a man like that. Anyway, it wasn't going to Yport that would have brought something great into my life. Unless saving a child who was drowning— But I can't swim.

"Little by little, I admit I made myself very unhappy. In the end, what did I go and imagine? I went and imagined that this thing life couldn't do for me, I'd find it in death. I told myself that when death is approaching, not too fast, not too violently, you must have sublime moments, that your thoughts would be lofty, that you'd leave behind everything that's petty, everything that cramps you, nights of bad sleep, bodily miseries. Ah, what a wonderful compensation I invented for myself! I pinned all my hopes on those last moments, you see.

"Oh! But yes indeed, madame, I did think of my husband! For days and days, for nights and nights. And about his unhappiness. Do me the honor of believing that I weighed it all and envisaged this, that, and the other before setting out on the road. But once I had set out, I was already far on my way."

Madame Armand looked down at her hands, which she had clasped, and gave an unexpected smile.

"Madame, people very seldom die because they've lost someone. I believe they die more often because they haven't had someone. But you think that by killing myself I was cruelly deserting my husband? Well, if the worst came to the worst, my beloved Geo could always have followed me if it had been too much for him to

dear. . . . Give me credit for this, before I set out on my
way, I worked everything out to the smallest detail. It may
seem nothing, but I had all sorts of complications. One
thinks it's ever so simple, just to lie down on one's
bed, swallow some horrible thing or other, and good-
bye! Just to procure this drug, goodness knows what
trouble I had and what lies I had to tell! I had to make
up my mind on the spur of the moment one day when
I got the chance—there'd been an accident to the red
light in the darkroom, which meant my husband had to
go out immediately after lunch. For two cents I'd have
chucked the whole thing. But I recovered my nerve, I
was sustained by my idea, by the thought of this—
this kind of—"

I risked suggesting a word, which Madame Armand
pounced on eagerly: "Yes, madame, apotheosis! That's
exactly it, apotheosis! That particular day I was uneasy.
I kept wondering what other hitch might still occur.
Well, the morning slipped by as easy as slipping a letter in the mailbox. Instead of lunch, I had some herb
tea. The embroidered sheets on the bed, all the housework properly done, the letter to my husband sealed up,
my husband in a hurry to go out. I called him back
to give him his lightweight overcoat and I thought he'd
gone when really he was still there: he'd broken the
bottle of hyposulfite, you remember?

"I think I'm alone at last, I lock the door, and I
get myself settled. Yes, here, but inside the bed, the
embroidered pillows behind my back, everything all
fresh and clean. Right! I'd hardly lain down when I
remembered the washerwoman. I get up, I scribble a
word on a slip of paper, and I lie down again. First
of all, I swallowed a pill to stop stomach spasms, and
I waited ten minutes, as I'd been told to do. And then
I swallowed the drug, all at once. And believe me"—
Madame Armand twisted her mouth a little—"it was
anything but delicious.

"And then? And then I wait. No, not for death, but
for what I'd promised myself before it. It was as if I
were on a quay, waiting to embark. No, no, I wasn't
in pain, but I could feel myself getting old. The last
straw was that my feet—I had my shoes on—were get-

ting hot at the bottom of the bed and hurt like fury wherever there was a bad spot on them. Even worse than that, I imagine I hear the doorbell ring! I think: 'It's happened on purpose. I'll never get through.' I sit up and try and remember if someone's made an appointment for a sitting. I listen hard. But I think it was the buzzings in my ears beginning. I lie down again and I say a little prayer, though I'm not particularly religious: 'My God, in your infinite goodness, take pity on an unhappy and guilty soul. . . .' Impossible to remember the rest, on my word. But that might have been enough, mightn't it?

"And I went on waiting. I was waiting for my reward, my great arrival of beautiful thoughts, a great pair of wings to carry me away, to sweep me right away from being myself any more. My head was going around and around. I thought I saw great circles all around me. For a second it was like when you dream you're falling from the top of a tower, but that was all. Nothing else, would you believe it, but all my everyday thoughts and fidgets, including that very day's? For example, I kept worrying like anything that my little Exo would only have cold meat and salad and warmed-up soup when he came in that night. At the same time, I thought: 'Even that will be too much. He'll be so upset over my death, it'll spoil his appetite. Everyone in the house will be so kind to him. My God, take pity on an unhappy and guilty soul. . . .' I'd never have believed that, when I was dying, it would be my feet that I suffered from most.

"The buzzings and the circles went on going around and around me, but I still kept on waiting. I waited lying down, as good as gold." She slid toward the middle of the bed, resumed the attitude and the stillness of her postponed death, and closed her eyes so that I could see nothing of them but the feathery, black line of the lashes.

"I didn't lose my head, I listened to all the noises on the staircase, I went over everything that I had forgotten, everything I had left in a muddle on the other side, I meant the side I was leaving. I reproached myself for those evening walks I used to take without bothering whether my husband might be bored all alone when his day's work was over. Trifles, petty little things, uninteresting thoughts that floated on the top of the buzzings and the circles. I remember vaguely that I wanted to put my hands over my face and cry and that I couldn't. It was as if I hadn't any arms. I said to myself: 'This is the end. How sad it is that I haven't had what I wanted in life even in my death.'

"Yes, I think that's all, madame. A terrible icy cold came and cut off the thread of my thoughts, and yet I'm not sure, even of that. What I am sure of is that never, never again will I commit suicide. I know now that suicide can't be the slightest use to me. I'm staying here. But, without wanting to offend Mademoiselle Devoidy, you can see for yourself that I'm in my right mind and that a neurotic woman and myself are two utterly different things."

With a jerk, Madame Armand sat up. Her story had left her with a feverish flush that animated her pale skin. Our conversation ended in "Good-bye, see you soon!" as if we were on a station platform, and after exclamations about the "shocking lateness" we parted for a very long time. She held the door of the apartment open behind me, so that the light in the studio should illuminate the landing for me. I left the photographer's Missus in her doorway, slender and solitary, but not wavering. I am sure she did not stumble a second time. Whenever I think of her, I always see her shored up by those scruples she modestly called fidgets and sustained by the sheer force of humble, everyday feminine greatness, that unrecognized greatness she had misnamed "a very trivial life."

[TRANSLATED BY ANTONIA WHITE]

Armande

"That girl? But, good heavens, she adores you! What's more, she's never done anything else for ten whole years. All the time you were on active service, she kept finding excuses for dropping in at the pharmacy and asking if I had received a letter."

"Did she?"

"She wouldn't leave the shop until she'd managed to slip in her 'How's your brother?' She used to wait. And while she was waiting she'd buy aspirin, cough lozenges, tubes of lanolin, toilet water, tincture of iodine."

"So naturally, you saw to it she was kept waiting?"

"Well, after all, why not? When I finally did tell her I had news from you, off she went. But not until then. You know what she's like."

"Yes—no, to be honest, I *don't* know what she's like."

"What do you expect, my poor pet? You make everything so complicated for yourself, you wear yourself out with all these wasted scruples. Armande is a very well-educated girl, we all know that. She takes her position as a comfortably rich orphan a shade too seriously. I grant you it's none too easy a one in a subprefecture like this. But just because of that, to let her put it over on you to that extent, *you*, Maxime, of all people! Look out—this is the new pavement. At least one can walk without getting one's feet wet now."

The September sky, black and moonless, glittered with stars that twinkled large in the damp air. The invisible river splashed under the single arch of the bridge. Maxime stopped and leaned on the parapet.

"The parapet's new too," he said.

"Yes. It was put up by the local tradesmen, with the consent of the Town Council. You know they did tremendously well here out of food and clothing, what with all the troops going through and the exodus."

"Out of food, clothes, footwear, medical supplies, and everything else. I also know that people talk about 'the exodus' as they do about 'the agricultural show' and 'the gala horse show and gymkhana.'"

"Anyway, they wanted to make a great sacrifice."

Madame Debove heard Maxime laugh under his breath at the word "sacrifice" and she prudently left her sentence unfinished to revert to Armande Fauconnier.

"In any case, she didn't let you down too badly during the war. She wrote to you, didn't she?"

"Postcards."

"She sent you food parcels and a marvelous pullover."

"To hell with her food parcels and her woolens" said Maxime Degouthe violently, "*and* her postcards! I've never begged charity from her, as far as I know?"

"Good gracious, what a savage character you are. . . . Don't spoil your last evening here, Maxime! Admit it was a charming party tonight. Armande is a very good hostess. All the Fauconniers have always been good hosts. Armande knows how to keep herself in the background. There was no chance of the conversation getting on to that children's clinic that Armande supports entirely out of her own money."

"Who hasn't organized something in the way of a children's clinic during the war?" growled Maxime.

"Why, lots of people, I assure you! In the first place, you've got to have the means. *She* really has the means."

Maxime made no reply. He hated it when his sister talked of Armande's "means."

"The river's low," he said after a moment or two.

"You've got good eyes!"

"It's not a question of eyes, it's a question of smell. When the water's low, it always smells of musk here. It's the mud, probably."

He suddenly remembered that, last year, he had said the very same words, on the very same spot, to Armande. She had wrinkled her nose in disgust and made an ugly grimace with her mouth. "As if *she* knew what mud was . . . Mud, that pearl-gray clay, so soft to the bare toes, so mysteriously musky, *she* imagines it's the same as excrement. She never misses an opportunity to shrink away from anything that can be tasted or touched or smelled."

Dancing owlet moths almost obscured the luminous globes at either end of the bridge. Maxime heard his sister yawn.

"Come on, let's go. What on earth are we doing here?"

"I'm asking *you*!" sighed Madame Debove. "Do you hear? Eleven o'clock! Hector's sure to have gone to bed without waiting up for me."

"Let him sleep. There's no need for us to hurry."

"Oh yes there is, my dear fellow. *I'm* sleepy."

"He took his sister's arm under his own, as he used to in the old days when they were students, sharing the same illusions, in that halcyon period when a brother and sister believe, quite genuinely, that they are perfectly content with being a chaste imitation of a pair of lovers. "Then a big, ginger-headed youth comes along and the devoted little sister goes off with him, for the pleasure and the advantages of marrying the Grand Central Pharmacy. After all, she did the right thing."

A passerby stepped off the pavement to make room for them and bowed to Jeanne.

"Good evening, Merle. Stopped having those pains of yours?"

"It's as if he'd said, 'Madame Debove. Good evening, Madame Debove.' "

"He's a customer," explained Jeanne.

"Good Lord, I might have guessed that," said her brother ironically. "When you put on your druggist's-wife voice."

"What about you when you put on your professional quack's voice? Just listen, am I exaggerating one bit? 'Above all, dear lady, endeavor as far as possible to control your nerves. The improvement is noticeable, I will even go so far as to say remarkable, but for the time being we must continue to be very firm about avoiding all forms of meat,' and I preach to you and I instruct you and I drown you in advice."

Maxime laughed wholeheartedly; the imitation of his slightly pontifical manner was so true to life.

"All women are monkeys. They're interested only in our absurdities and our love affairs and our illnesses. The other one can't be so very different from this one."

He could see her, the other one, as she had looked when he left her just now, standing at the top flight of steps that led up to the Fauconniers' house. The lighted chandelier in the hall behind her gave her a nimbus of blue glass convolvulus flowers and chromium hoops. "Good-bye, Armande." She had answered with only a nod. "You might call her a miser with words! If I had her in my arms, one day, between four walls or in the corner of a wood, I'd make her scream, and for good reason!" But he had never met Armande in the corner of a wood. As to his aggressive instincts, he lost all hope of gratifying them the moment he was in Armande's presence.

Eleven o'clock struck from the hospital, then from a small low church jostled by new buildings, last of all, in shrill, crystalline strokes from a dark ground-floor room whose window was open. As they crossed the Place d'Armes, Maxime sat down on one of the benches.

"Just for one minute, Jeanne! Let me relax my nerves. It's nice out of doors."

Jeanne Debove consented sulkily.

"You ought to have worked them off on Armande, those nerves of yours. But you haven't got the guts!"

He did not protest and she burst into a malicious laugh. He wondered why sexual shyness, which excites the desires of dissolute women, arouses the contempt of decent ones.

"She overawes you, that's it. Yes, she overawes you. I simply can't get over it!"

She elaborated her inability to get over it by inundating him with various scoffing remarks, accompanied now by a neighing laugh, now by a spurt of giggles.

"After all, you're not in your very, *very* first youth. You're not a greenhorn. Or a neurotic. Nor, thank heaven, physically deformed."

She enumerated all the things her brother was not and he was glad she omitted to mention the one quite simple thing he was—a man who had been in love for a very long time.

Maxime Degouthe's long-persisting love, though it preserved him from debauchery, turned into mere habit when he was far from Armande for a few months. When he was away from her, a kind of conjugal fidelity allowed him to amuse himself as much as he liked and even to forget her for a spell. So much so that when he had finished his medical studies, he had been paralyzed to find himself faced with a grown-up Armande Fauconnier when the Armande he remembered was a gawky, sharp-shouldered, overgrown adolescent, at once clumsy and noble like a bony filly full of promise.

Every time he saw her again, she completely took possession of him. His feeling for her was violent and suppressed, like a gardener's son's for the "young lady up at the big house." He would have liked to be rather brutal to this beautiful tall girl whom he admired from head to foot, who was just sufficiently dark, just sufficiently white and as smooth as a pear. "But I wouldn't dare. No, I don't dare," he fumed to himself every time he left.

"The back of the bench is all wet," said Madame Debove. "I'm going home. What are your plans for tomorrow? Are you going in to say good-bye to Armande? She's expecting you to, you know."

"She hasn't invited me."

"You mean you don't dare go on your own? You may as well admit it, that girl's got you completely buffaloed!"

"I do admit it," said Maxime, so mildly that his sister stopped cruelly teasing him.

They walked in silence till they reached the Grand Central Pharmacy.

"You'll lunch with us tomorrow, of course. Hector would have a fit if you didn't have your last meal with him. Your parcel of ampules will be all ready. No one can say when we'll be able to get those particular serums again. Well, shall I call up Armande and say you'll be coming over to say good-bye to her? But I needn't say definitely you're not coming?"

She was fumbling endlessly with a bunch of keys.

Maxime lent her the aid of his flashlight and its beam
fell full on Jeanne Debove's mischievous face and its
expression of mixed satisfaction and disapproval.

"She wants me to marry Armande. She's thinking of
the money, of the fine, rich house, of 'the excellent
effect,' of my career, as she says. But she'd also be
willing for me to marry Armande without being over-
enthusiastic about her. Everything's perfectly normal.
Everything except myself, because I can't endure the
idea that *she*, Armande, could marry me without being
in love with me."

He hurried back to his hotel. The town was asleep
but the hotel, close by the station, resounded with all
the noises that are hostile to sleep and blazed with
lights that aggravate human tiredness. Hobnailed boots,
shuddering ceiling lights, uncarpeted floors, the gates of
the elevator, the whinnyings of hydraulic pressure, the
rhythmic clatter of plates flung into a sink in the base-
ment, and the intermittent trilling of a bell never
stopped outraging the need for silence, which had driven
Maxime to his bedroom. Unable to stand any more, he
added his own contribution to the selfish human concert, dropped his shoes on the wooden floor, carried
them out into the corridor, and shut his door with a
loud slam.

He drenched himself with cold water, dried himself
carelessly, and got into bed quite naked, after having
studied himself in the looking glass. "Big bones, big
muscles, and four complete limbs, after all, that's not
too bad, these days. A large nose, large eyes, a cap of
hair as thick as a motorcyclist's helmet—girls who
weren't Mademoiselle Fauconnier have found all that
very much to their taste. I don't see Mademoiselle
Fauconnier sleeping with this naked, black-haired
chap. . . ."

On the contrary, he saw her only too well. Irritated
by fretful desire, he waited for the hotel to become
quiet. When—save for a sound of barking, a garage
door, the departure of a motorcar—silence was at last
established, a breeze sprang up, swept away the last insults inflicted by man on the night, and came in
through the open window like a reward.

"Tomorrow," Maxime vowed to himself. It was a muddled vow that concerned the conquest of Armande quite as much as the return to professional life and the daily, necessary triumph of forced activity over fundamental listlessness.

He reiterated "tomorrow," flung away his pillow, rolled over on his stomach, and fell asleep with his head between his folded arms in the same attitude as a small intimidated boy of long ago who used to dream of an Armande with long black curls. Later on, another Maxime had slept like that, the adolescent who had plucked up courage to invite "those Fauconnier ladies" as they were coming out from High Mass to have lemon ices at Peyrol's. "Really, Maxime, one doesn't eat lemon ices at a quarter to twelve in the morning!" Armande had said. In that one word "really," what a number of reproofs she could convey! "Really, Maxime, you needn't *always* stand right in front of the window. You shut out the daylight. Maxime, really! You've returned a ball *again* when it was '*out*.' "

But when a particular period was over, there had been no more "reallys" and no more reproaches showered on his head. Still not properly asleep, Maxime Degouthe groped around a memory, around a moment that had restored a little confidence to his twenty-five-year-old self and had marked the end of Armande's gracious condescension. That day, he had arrived with Jeanne at the foot of the steps just as Armande was opening the silvered wrought-iron door to go out. They had not seen each other for a very long time: "Hello, imagine seeing you! Yes, my sister insisted on bringing me with her, perhaps you'd rather I hadn't come. Now, really, you're joking. A friend of mine in Paris gave me a lift in his car and dropped me here this morning. How awfully nice! Are you going to be here for some time? No, the same friend's picking me up tomorrow after lunch and driving me back. Well, that *is* a short stay." In fact, such trivialities as to make either of them blush had either of them paid any attention to what they were saying. From the height of five or six steps, a wide, startled, offended gaze fell on Maxime. He also caught, at the level of his knees, the brush of a skirt

hem and a handbag, which Armande had dropped and
which he retrieved.

After a gloomy game of Ping-Pong, a tea composed
entirely of sugary things, a handshake—a strong, swift,
but promptly withdrawn hand had clasped his own—he
had left Armande once again, and on the way back,
Jeanne had given her cynical opinion of the situation:
"You know, you could have the fair Armande without
half trying. And I know what I'm talking about." She
added: "You don't know the right way to go about it."
But those had been the remarks of a twenty-year-old,
the infallibility of one girl judging another girl.

He thought he was only half asleep and fell into deep
but restless dreams. A nightmare tortured him with the
shaming illusion that he was dressing old Queny's incurable foot on the steps leading up to the Fauconniers'
house and that Armande was enthroned, impassive, at
the top of them. Didn't she owe part of her prestige
to those eight broad steps, almost like a series of ter-
races, that were famous throughout the town? "The
Fauconniers' flight of front steps is so impressive. Without these front steps, the Fauconniers' house wouldn't
have nearly such a grand air. . . ." As if insulted, the
sleeper sat up with a start. "Grand air indeed! That
cube! That block with its cast-iron balconies and bands
of tiles!" He woke up completely, and once again the
Fauconnier home inspired him with the old awed respect. The Fauconnier heliotropes, the Fauconnier polyg-
onums, the Fauconnier lobelias, recovered their status
of flowers adorning the altar where he worshiped. So,
to send himself to sleep again, Maxime soberly envisaged
the duties that awaited him the next day, the day after,
and all the rest of his life, in the guise of the faces of
old Queny, of the elder Madame Cauvain, of her
father, Monsieur Enfert, of "young" Mademoiselle Philippon, the one who was only seventy-two. . . . For old
people do not die off in wartime. He swallowed half
his bottle of mineral water at one gulp and fell heavily
asleep again, insensible to the mosquitoes coming up
from the shrunken river and the noises of the pale
dawn.

"My last day of idle luxury." He had his breakfast

in bed, feeling slightly ashamed, and ordered a bath, for which he had to wait a considerable time. "My last bath —I'm not going to get up till I've had my bath! I'm not leaving without my bath!" As a matter of fact, he preferred a very stiff shower or the chance plunges he had taken, straight into rivers and canals, these last months between April and August.

With some caution he made use of a toilet water concocted by his brother-in-law, the red-haired druggist. "Hector's perfumes, when they don't smell of squashed ants, smell of bad cognac." He chose his bluest shirt and his spotted foulard tie. "I wish I were handsome. And all I am is just so-so. Ah, how I wish I were handsome!" he kept thinking over and over again as he plastered down his brilliantined hair. But it was coarse, intractable, wavy hair, a vigorous bush that preferred standing up to lying down. When Maxime laughed, he wrinkled his nose, crinkled up his yellow-brown eyes and revealed his "lucky teeth," healthy and close set except for a gap between the two upper front ones. Coatless and buckled into his best belt, he had, at nearly thirty, the free and easy charm and slightly plebeian elegance of many an errand boy you see darting through the crowd on his bicycle, nimble as a bird in a bush. "But, in a jacket, I just look common," Maxime decided, as he straightened the lapels of the ready-made jacket. "It's also the fault of the jacket." He threw his reflection an angry glance. "Nevertheless, beautiful Armande, more than ten others have been quite satisfied with all that and have even said 'Thank you.'" He sighed and turned humble again. "But, seeing that it's to no one but Armande I'm appealing when I conjure up my poor little girlfriends, what on earth does it matter whether they thanked me or even asked for more? It's not about them I'm thinking."

He packed his suitcase with the care and dexterity of a man accustomed to using his hands for manipulating living substance, stopping the flow of blood, applying and pinning bandages. The September morning, with its flies and its warm yellow light, came in fresh through the open window; at the end of a narrow street a dancing shimmer showed where the river lay. "I won't go and say good-bye to Armande," Maxime Degouthe decided. "For one thing, lunch is always late at Jeanne's; for another, I've got my case of medical supplies to fill up at the last minute, and if I'm going to have time to get a bite of food before the train leaves, it'll be impossible, yes, physically impossible."

At four o'clock he opened the front gate, marched up the gravel path of the Fauconniers' garden, climbed the flight of steps, and rang the bell. A second time, he pressed his finger long and vainly on the bell button, sunk in a rosette of white marble. No one came and the blood rushed up into Maxime's ears. "She's probably gone out. But where are her two lazy sluts of servants and the gardener who looks like a drunkard?" He rang again, restraining himself with difficulty from giving the door a kick. At last he heard steps in the garden and saw Armande running toward him. She stopped in front of him, exclaiming "Ah" and he smiled at seeing her wearing a big blue apron with a bib that completely enveloped her. She swiftly untied the apron and flung it on a rose bush.

"But it looked very well on you," said Maxime.

Armande blushed and he blushed himself, thinking that perhaps he had hurt her feelings. "She would take it the wrong way, naturally. She's impossible, impossible! Pretty, those flecks of white soap in her black hair. I'd never noticed that the skin at the edge of her forehead, just under the hair, is slightly blue."

"I was at the end of the garden, in the washhouse," said Armande. "It's laundry day today, so—Léonie and Maria didn't even hear the bell."

"I won't keep you from your work. I only stopped by for a couple of minutes. . . . Since I'm leaving tomorrow morning. . . ."

He had followed her to the top of the steps, and Maxime waited for her to indicate which of the wicker chairs he should sit in. But she said: "From four to seven the sun just beats down on you here," and she led him into the drawing room, where they sat down opposite each other. Maxime seated himself in one of the armchairs tapestried with La Fontaine's fables—his was *The Cat, the Weasel and the little Rabbit*—and stared at the rest of the furniture. The baby-grand piano, the Revolution clock, the plants in pots—he gazed at them all with hostile reverence.

"It's nice in here, isn't it?" said Armande. "I keep the blinds down because it faces south. Jeanne wasn't able to come?"

"Goodness, is she frightened of me?" He was on the point of feeling flattered. But he looked at Armande and saw her sitting stiffly upright on *The Fox and the Stork,* one elbow on the hard arm of the chair, the other on her lap, with her hands clasped together. In the dusk of the lowered blinds, her cheeks and her neck took on the color of very pale terra-cotta, and she was looking straight at him with the steady gaze of a well-brought-up girl who knows she must not blink or look sideways or pretend to be shy so as to show off the length of her lashes. "What am I doing here?" thought Maxime furiously. "This is where I've got to, where we've both got to, after ten, fifteen years of what's called childhood friendship. This girl is made of wood. Or else she's choked with pride. You won't catch me again in the Fauconnier drawing room." Nevertheless, he replied to Armande's questions, he talked to her about his "practice" and the "inevitable difficulties" of this postwar period. Nor did he fail to remark: "But you know better than anyone what these difficulties are. Look at you, loaded down with responsibilities and all alone in the world!"

Armande's immobility was shattered by an unexpected movement; she unclasped her fingers and clutched the arms of her chair with both hands as if she were afraid of slipping off it.

"Oh, I'm used to it. You know my mother brought me up in a rather special way. At my age, one's no longer a child."

The sentence, begun with assurance, broke off on a childish note that belied the last words. She mastered herself and said in a different voice: "Won't you have a glass of port? Or would you prefer orangeade?"

Maxime saw there was a loaded tray within easy reach of her hand and frowned.

"You're expecting guests? Then I'll be on my way!"

He had stood up; she remained seated and laid her hand on Maxime's arm.

"I never invite anyone on washday. I assure you I don't. Since you'd told me you were going away again tomorrow, I thought you might possibly——"

She broke off, with a little grimace that displeased Maxime. "Ah, no! She's not to ruin that mouth for me! That outline of the lips, so clear-cut, so full; those corners of the mouth that are so—so— What's the matter with her today? You'd think she was burying the devil for good and all!"

He realized he was staring at her with unpardonable severity and forced himself to be gay.

"So you're heavily occupied in domestic chores? What a lovely laundress you make! And all those kids at your clinic, do you manage to keep them in order?"

He was laughing only with his lips. He knew very well that when he was with Armande, love made him gloomy, jealous, self-conscious, unable to break down an obstacle between the two of them that perhaps did not exist. Armande took a deep breath, squared her shoulders, and commanded her whole face to be nothing but the calm, regular countenance of a beautiful brunet. But three shadowy dimples, two at the corners of the mouth, one in the chin, appeared when she smiled and quivered at every hint of emotion.

"I've got twenty-eight children over at the clinic, did you know that?"

"Twenty-eight children? Don't you think that's a lot for a young unmarried girl?"

"I'm not frightened of children," said Armande seriously.

"Children. She loves children. She'd be magnificent, pregnant. Tall as she is, she would broaden at the hips without looking squat, like short women who are carrying babies. She'd take up an enormous amount of space in the garden, in bed, in my arms. And she'd have trusting eyes, the lovely, dark-ringed eyes of a pregnant woman. But for that to happen, mademoiselle has got to tolerate someone coming close to her, a little closer than offering her a ball at arm's length on a tennis racket. She doesn't look as if the idea had ever occurred to her, that girl doesn't! In any case, *I'm* giving up all thought of it!"

He stood up, resolutely.

"This time, Armande, it's serious."

"What is?" she said, very low.

"Why, the fact that it's five o'clock, that I've got two or three urgent things to do, a big parcel of medical supplies to get ready. My little village is out of everything in the way of serums and pills."

"I know," said Armande at once.

"You know?"

"Oh, I just accidentally heard them say so, at your brother-in-law's."

He had leaned toward her a little; she drew away with such a fierce movement that she knocked her elbow against a monumental lampstand.

"Have you hurt yourself?" said Maxime coldly.

"No," she said, equally coldly. "Not in the least."

She passed in front of him to open the front door, with its wrought-iron lacework. It resisted her efforts.

"The woodwork's warped. I keep telling Charost to fix it."

"Haven't I always known it to stick like that? Don't destroy my childhood memories!"

Pursing her lips tight, she shook the door with a stubborn violence that made its panes rattle. There was a loud crash of glass and metal behind her, and, turning around, she saw Maxime staggering among the splintered cups and chromium hoops of the chandelier that had just fallen from the ceiling. Then his knees went limp and he fell over on his side. Prone on the floor, he made an attempt to raise his hand to his ear, could not finish the gesture, and lay perfectly still. Armande, with her back against the front door she had not had time to open, stared at the man lying at her feet on his bed of broken glass. She said in a strangled, incredulous voice: "No!" The sight of a trickle of blood running down behind Maxime's left ear and stopping for a moment on the collar of the blue shirt, which it soaked, restored Armande's power of speech and movement. She squatted down, straightened herself up swiftly, opened the door, which was half obstructed by the injured body, and

screamed shrill summonses out into the garden: "Maria!
Léonie! Maria! Maria!"

The screams reached Maxime where he lay, unconscious. Along with the screams, he began to hear the
buzzing of hives of bees and the clanging of hammers,
and he half opened his eyes. But unconsciousness
promptly swallowed him up again, and he fell back among
the swarms of bees and the hammering to someplace
where pain, in its turn, tracked him down. "The top of
my head hurts. It hurts behind my ear and on my shoulder."

Once again, the loud screams disturbed him: "Léonie!
Maria!" He came to, very unwillingly, opened his eyes, and
received a sunbeam full in his face. The sunbeam appeared to be red; then it was cut off by a double moving
shadow. All at once, he realized that Armande's two
legs were passing to and fro across the light; he recognized Armande's feet, the white linen shoes trimmed
with black leather. The feet were moving about in all
directions on the carpet quite close to his head, sometimes open in a V and staggering, sometimes close together and crushing bits of broken glass. He felt an urge
to untie one of the white shoelaces for a joke, but at that
very moment, he was shot through with agonizing pain,
and without knowing it, he moaned.

"My darling, my darling," said a shaking voice.

"Her darling? What darling?" he asked himself. He
raised his cheek, which was lying heavily on fragments
of pale blue glass and the bottoms of electric light bulbs.
The blood spread out in a pool and his cheek was sticky
with it. At the pathetic sight of the precious red
spilled all about him, he came to completely and understood all. He took advantage of the fact that the two feet
had turned their heels to him and were running toward
the terrace to feel his aching head and bruised shoulder
and to discover that the source of the blood was behind
his ear. "Good, a big cut. Nothing broken. I might have
had my ear sliced off. It's a good thing to have hair like
mine. Lord, how my head does ache!"

"Maria! Léonie!"

The black-and-white shoes returned; two knees
sheathed in silk went down on the splintered glass. "She'll

cut herself!" He made a slight movement to raise himself, then decided instead to lie still and keep quiet, only turning his head over so as to show Armande where his wound was.

"Oh heavens, he's bleeding," said Armande's voice. "Maria! Léonie!"

There was no reply.

"Oh, the sluts," the same voice said violently.

Sheer astonishment made Maxime give a start.

"Speak to me, Maxime! Maxime, can you hear me? My darling, my darling——"

Sabots were heard running in the garden, then climbing the steps.

"Ah, there you are, Charost! Yes, the chandelier fell down. A person could die in this place without anyone's hearing! Where *are* those two wretched girls?"

"In the meadow, mademoiselle, spreading out the sheets. Ah, the poor unfortunate young man! He had a hundred years of life ahead of him!"

"I'm quite sure he still has! Run around to Doctor Pommier, tell him—— If he's not in, Doctor Tuloup. If *he's* not in, the druggist, yes, the ginger-haired one, Madame Jeanne's husband. Charost, go get the towels from my bathroom, the little hand towel from the cloakroom. You can *see* I can't leave him. And the brown box in the cupboard! Hurry up, will you! Get someone to tell those two idiots to leave their washing. Don't go yourself, send someone!"

The sabots clattered away.

"My darling, my darling," said the low, sweet voice.

"It really was me, the darling," Maxime told himself. Two hot hands feverishly massaged one of his, interrogating it. "There, there, my pulse is excellent! Don't get panicky! How beautiful she must be at this moment . . ." He groaned on purpose and slid the thread of a glance at Armande between his eyelids. She was unsightly, with huge, terrified eyes and her mouth gaping stupidly. He closed his lids again, enraptured.

The hands pressed a wet towel over his wound, pushed away the hair. "That's not right, my pet, that's not right. Isn't there any iodine in the place? She'll make me bleed unnecessarily, but what the hell does that matter as long

as she keeps working on me?" The ferruginous smell
of iodine rose in his nostrils. He was aware of the wholesome burning pain, and relaxed, content. "Well done!
But when it comes to putting on an efficient bandage, my
girl, I'm miles ahead of you. That one will never hold.
You should have shaved off a bit of my hair." He heard the
girl clucking her tongue against her teeth, "tst, tst," then
she became despairing.

"Oh, I'm too stupid! A lump of mud, in fact!"

He very nearly laughed but turned it into a vague,
pitiful mumbling.

"Maxime, Maxime!" she implored.

She untied his tie, opened his shirt, and, trying to find
his heart, brushed the masculine nipple, which swelled
with pride. For a moment the two of them were equally
and completely motionless. As the hand withdrew, after
receiving its reassuring answer from the heart, it slowly
went over the same ground on its way back. "Oh, to take
that hand that's stroking me in this startled way, to get
up, to hug that grand, beautiful girl I love, to turn *her*
into a wounded, moaning creature, and then to comfort her, to nurse her in my arms. I've waited so long for
that. But suppose she defends herself?" He decided to go
on with his ruse, stirred feebly, opened his arms, and fell
back into pretended unconsciousness.

"Oh," cried Armande, "he's fainted! Why don't those
imbeciles come!"

She leaped to her feet and ran off to fetch a fiber
cushion, which she tried to insert between Maxime's
head and the splinters of glass. As she did so the make-
shift bandage came off. Maxime could hear Armande
stamping her feet, walking away, and slapping her thighs
with a forceful plebeian despair. She returned to him,
sat down right in the litter of broken glass and the pool
of bloodstained water, and half lay down against the
wounded man. With exquisite pleasure he could feel she
had lost her head and was crying. He squeezed his eyelids together so as not to look at her. But he could not
shut out the smell of black hair and hot skin, the sandal-
wood smell that healthy brunets exude. She raised one of
his eyelids with her finger, and he rolled up his eyeball as
if in ecstasy or a swoon. With her sleeve, she wiped his

forehead and his mouth; furtively, she opened his lips and bent over him to look at the white teeth with the gap between the front ones. "Another minute of this sort of thing and—and I shall devour her!" She bent a little lower, put her mouth against Maxime's, then drew back at once, frightened at the sound of hurried footsteps and breathless voices. But her whole body remained close to him, knowing and alert, and there was still time for her to whisper the hackneyed words girls new to love stammer out before the man has taught them others or they invent more beautiful, more secret, ones: "Darling . . . My beloved boy. My very own Maxime."

When the rescue party arrived, she was still sitting on the ground in her soaked skirt and her torn stockings. Maxime was able to wake up, to complete his deception by a few incoherent words, to smile in a bewildered way at Armande, and to protest at all the fuss going on around him. The Grand Central Pharmacy had provided its stretcher and its pharmacist, who constructed a turban of bandages on Maxime's head. Then the stretcher and its escort set forth like a procession with the incense of a choir of voices.

"Open the other half of the door. Look out, it won't go through. I tell you it will go through if you veer a bit to the right. There—just a half inch to spare. You've got eight steps to go down."

At the top of the terrace, Armande remained alone, useless, and as if forgotten. But, at the bottom of the steps, Maxime summoned her with a gesture and a look: "Come—I know you now. I've got you. Come, we'll finish that timid little kiss you began. Stay with me. Acknowledge me. . . ." She walked down the steps and gave him her hand. Then she adapted her step to that of the stretcher-bearers and walked meekly beside him, all stained and disheveled, as if she were coming straight from the hands of love.

[TRANSLATED BY ANTONIA WHITE]

The Sick Child

The child who was going to die wanted to hoist himself a little higher against his big pillow, but he could not manage it. His mother heard his mute appeal and helped him. Once again the child who had been promised to death had his mother's face very close to his own, the face he thought he would never look at again, with its light brown hair drawn back from the temples like an old-fashioned little girl's, the long, rather thin cheeks with hardly a trace of powder, the very wide-open brown eyes, so sure of controlling their anxiety that they often forgot to keep guard over themselves.

"You're rosy tonight, my little boy," she said gaily.

But her brown eyes remained fixed in a steady, frightened look that the little boy knew well.

So as not to have to raise his feeble head, the little boy slid his pupils, with their big sea-green irises, into the corners of his lids and corrected her gravely: "I'm rosy because of the lampshade."

Madam Mama looked at her son sorrowfully, inwardly reproaching him for wiping out, with one word, that pink color she saw on his cheeks. He had shut his eyes again, and the appearance of being asleep gave him back the face of a child of ten.

"She thinks I'm asleep." His mother turned away from the white-faced little boy, very gently, as if afraid he might feel the thread of her gaze break off. "He thinks I think he's asleep." Sometimes they played at deceiving each other like this. "She thinks I'm not in pain," Jean would think, though the pain would be making his lashes flicker on his cheekbones. Nevertheless, Madam Mama would be thinking, "How well he can imitate a child who's not in pain! Any other mother would be taken in. But not me . . ."

"Do you like this smell of lavender I've sprayed about? Your room smells nice."

The child acquiesced without speaking; the habit and the necessity of preserving his strength had ended in his acquiring a repertory of very tiny signs, a delicate and complicated pantomime like the language of animals. He excelled in making a magic and paradoxical use of his senses.

For him, the white muslin curtains gave out a pink sound when the sun struck them about ten in the morning, and the scratched pale calf binding of an ancient *Journey on the Banks of the Amazon* smelled, to his mind, like hot pancakes. The desire to drink was expressed by three "claps" of the eyelids. To eat, oh, as to wanting to eat, he didn't think about that. The other needs of the small, limp, defeated body had their silent and modest telegraph code. But everything that in the existence of a child under sentence of death could still be called the capacity for pleasure and amusement retained a passionate interest in human speech. This faculty searched for exact and varied words to be employed by a musical voice, ripened, as it were, by the long illness and hardly sharper than a woman's. Jean had chosen the words employed in draughts, in "solitaire," with its glitter of glass marbles, in "nine holes," in a dozen other old-fashioned games that made use of ivory and lemonwood and were played on inlaid boards. Other words, mostly secret, applied to the Swiss "patience" pack, fifty-two little glazed cards, edged and picked out with gold like drawing-room paneling. The queens wore shepherdess hats, straw ones with a rose under the brim, and the shepherd knaves carried crooks. Because of the bearded kings with rubicund faces and the small, hard eyes of mountain smallholders, Jean had invented a patience that excluded the four rustic monarchs.

"No," he thought, "my room doesn't really smell nice. It isn't the same lavender. It seems to me that in the old days, when I was able to walk about . . . But I may have forgotten."

He mounted a cloud of fragrance that was passing within reach of his small, pinched, white nostrils and rode swiftly away. His life of being confined to bed provided him with all the pleasures of illness, including the spice of filial malice of which no child can bear to deprive himself, so he gave no hint of his secret delights.

Astride the scented cloud, he wandered through the air of the room; then he got bored and escaped through the frosted glass transom and went along the passage, followed in his flight by a big silver clothes moth who sneezed in the trail of lavender behind him. To outdistance it, he pressed his knees into the sides of the cloud of fragrance, riding with an ease and vigor that his long, inert, half-paralyzed legs refused to display in the presence of human beings. When he escaped from his passive life, he knew how to ride, how to pass through walls; best of all, he knew how to fly. With his body inclined like a diver's plunging down through the waves, his forehead passed with careless ease through an element whose currents and resistances he understood. With his arms outstretched, he had only to slant one or other of his shoulders to change the direction of his flight, and by a jerk of his loins he could avoid the shock of landing. In any case, he rarely did land. Once, he had rashly let himself come down too near the ground, over a meadow where cows were feeding.

So close to the ground that he had seen, right opposite his own face, the beautiful, astonished face of a cream-colored cow with crescent-shaped horns and eyes that mirrored the flying child like two magnifying glasses, while the dandelion flowers came up out of the grass to meet him, growing bigger and bigger, like little suns. He had only just had time to catch tight hold of the tall horns with both hands and thrust himself up into the air again; he could still remember the warmth of the smooth horns and their blunted, as it were, friendly, points. The barking of a dew-drenched sheepdog who ran up to protect his cow gradually faded away as the flying child soared up again into his familiar sky. Jean remembered very clearly that he had had to exert all the strength of his arm-wings that morning to make his way back through a periwinkle-colored dawn, glide over a sleeping town, and fall on his enameled iron bed, the contact of which had hurt him very much indeed. He had felt an agonizing pain burning his loins and tearing his thighs with red-hot pincers, a

pain so bad that he had not been able to hide two pearly
traces of tears from Madam Mama's sharp-eyed tenderness.

"Has my little boy been crying?"

"In a dream, Madam Mama, only in a dream . . ."

The cloud of pleasant scent suddenly reached the end
of the passage and butted its muzzle against the door
leading to the kitchen.

"Whoa! Whoa! What a brute! Ah, these lavender
half-breeds, with wild-thyme blood! They'd smash your
face for you if you didn't hold them. Is *that* how you
go through a kitchen door?"

He gripped the repentant cloud hard between his knees
and guided it into the upper region of the kitchen, into
the warmed air that was drying the washing near the
ceiling. As he lowered his head to pass between two
pieces of linen Jean deftly broke off an apron string and
slipped it into the cloud's mouth by way of a bit. A
mouth is not always a mouth, but a bit is always a bit,
and it matters little what it bridles.

"Where shall we go? We'll have to get back in time
for dinner and it's late already. We must go faster,
Lavender, faster. . . ."

Having gone through the service door, he decided, for
fun, to go down the staircase head first, then helped himself to a few slides on his back. The lavender cloud,
frightened by what was being asked of it, hung back a
little. "Oh, you great goof of a mountain filly!" said the
child, and this boy who never laughed at all in his
cloistered life burst out laughing. As he rode wildly
down he grabbed hold, in passing, of the tangled fur of
one of the house dogs, the one they told him was so
clever he could go down the steps and out onto the pavement, "do his business all by himself," then return to his
parents' house and scratch at the front door. Startled
by Jean's hand, he yelped and flattened himself against the
banisters.

"Coming with us, Riki? I'll take you up behind me!"

With a small, powerful hand he caught up the dog
and flung him onto the misty, ballooning rump of the
lavender mare, who, spurred by two bare heels, galloped
down the last two flights. But there the dog, panic-

stricken, jumped down from the eiderdown pillion and fled upstairs to his basket, howling.

"You don't know what you're missing!" Jean shouted to him. "*I* was frightened too, at first, but now . . . Watch, Riki!"

Rider and mount hurled themselves against the heavy street door. To Jean's amazement, they encountered not the malleable obstacle of yielding oak and melting ironwork and big bolts that said "Yes, yes" as they slid softly back, but the inflexible barrier of a firmly chiseled voice that was whispering: "See, he's fast asleep."

Numbed by the shock, harrowed from head to foot, Jean was aware of the cruel harshness of the two words "See he's, Seehees, Seeheeze." They were sharper than a knife blade. Beside them lay three severed syllables, "fasta-sleep."

"Fa . . . sta . . . sleep," repeated Jean. "That's the end of the ride, here comes Fa . . . sta . . . sleep, curled up in a ball! Good-bye. Good-bye . . ."

He had no time to wonder to whom he was saying good-bye. Time was running out horribly fast. He dreaded the landing. The foundered cloud missed its footing with all the four legs it never had; before it dispersed in tiny cold drops, it threw its rider, with a heave of its nonexistent hindquarters, into the valley of the lacquered bedstead, and once again Jean groaned at the brutal contact.

"You were sleeping so well," said the voice of Madam Mama.

A voice, thought her little boy, that was all a tangle of straight lines and curved lines—a curved one, a straight one—a dry line—a wet line. But never would he try to explain that to Madam Mama.

"You woke up moaning, darling. Were you in pain?"

He made a sign that he was not, waving his thin, white, well-groomed forefinger from right to left. Besides, the pain was calming down. As to falling onto this rather harsh little bed—after all, he was pretty used to it. And what could you expect of a big puffy cloud and its scented bumpkin's manners?

"The next time," thought Jean, "I'll ride the Big Skating Rink." In the hours when he lay with closed lids and they put a screen between the bright bulb and the lampshade, that was the name of the iimmmmmmense nickel-plated paper knife, so big that instead of two m's, it needed three or often four in its qualifying adjective.

"Madam Mama, would you bring the Big Skat—I mean the big paper knife—a little farther forward under the lampshade? Thanks a lot."

To prepare his next ride at leisure, Jean turned his head on the pillow. They had cut his fair hair very short at the back, to keep it from matting. The top of his head, his temples, and his ears were covered with curls of pale, faintly greenish-gold, the gold of a winter moon, which harmonized well with his sea-green eyes and his face as white as a petal.

"How exquisite he is!" murmured Madam Mama's female friends. "He looks quite astonishingly like L'Aiglon." Whereupon Madam Mama would smile with disdain, knowing well that the Duc de Reichstadt, slightly thick-lipped like his mother, the Empress, would have envied the firm, cupid's bow mouth with its fine-drawn corners that was one of Jean's beauties. She would say haughtily: "Possibly there is something—yes, in the forehead. But, heaven be praised, *Jean* isn't tubercular!"

When, with a practiced hand, she had brought the lamp and big paper knife closer together, Jean saw what he was waiting to see on the long chromium blade, a pink reflection like snow at dawn, flecked here and there with blue, a glittering landscape that tasted of peppermint. Then he laid his left temple on the firm pillow, listened to the music of waterdrops and fountains played by the strands of white horsehair inside the cushion under the pressure of his head, and half closed his eyes.

"But, my little boy, it's just about your dinner time. . . ." said Madam Mama hesitantly.

The sick child smiled indulgently at his mother. You have to forgive healthy people everything. Besides, he was still faintly concussed from his fall. "I've got plenty of time," he thought, and he accentuated his smile, at the risk of seeing Madam Mama—as she did, faced with certain smiles, too perfect, too full of a serenity that, for her, could only have one meaning—lose her equanimity and rush out of the room, knocking herself against the doorjamb.

"If you don't mind, darling, I'll have my dinner very quickly all by myself in the dining room while you're having yours on your tray."

"Why, of course, of course," answered the white, graciously condescending small forefinger, crooking itself twice.

"We know, we know," also observed the two lash-bordered eyelids, blinking twice. "We know what an oversensitive lady Mama is, and how a pair of tears suddenly come into her eyes, like a pair of precious stones. There are lots of precious stones for ears. . . . Eye-rings, Madam Mama has eye-rings when she thinks about me. Won't she ever get used to me? How illogical she is."

As Madam Mama was bending over him he raised his unfettered arms and gave her a ritual hug. His mother's neck raised itself proudly under the weight suspended on it, pulling up the child's thin, overly tall body; the slim torso followed by the long legs, inert now, yet capable of gripping and controlling the flanks of a shadowy cloud.

For a moment, Madam Mama contemplated her gracious invalid son, propped up against a hard pillow that sloped like a desk. Then she exclaimed: "I'll be back very soon! Your tray will be here in a minute. Besides, I must go and hurry up Mandora. She's never on time!"

Once again, she went out of the room.

"She goes out, she comes in. Above all, she goes out. She doesn't want to leave me but she keeps going out of my room all the time. She's going off to dry her pair of tears. She's got a hundred reasons for going out of my room; if by any chance she didn't have one, I could name a thousand. Mandora's never late."

Turning his head with precaution, he watched Mandora come in. Wasn't it right and inevitable that this fullbodied, golden, potbellied maid, with her musical, resonant voice and her shining eyes that were like the precious wood of a lute, should answer to the name of Mandora? "If it weren't for me," thought Jean, "she'd still be calling herself Angelina."

Mandora crossed the room and her brown-and-yellowstriped skirt, as it brushed against the furniture, gave out

rich cello notes that only Jean could perceive. She placed
the little short-legged table across the bed; on its embroidered linen cloth stood a steaming bowl.

"Here's this dinner of yours."

"What is it?"

"First course, phosphatine: there, you know that.
After—you'll see for yourself."

The sick child received all over his half-recumbent
body the comfort of a wide brown gaze, thirst quench-
ing and exhilarating. "How good it is, that brown ale of
Mandora's eyes! How kind to me she is, too! How kind
everyone is to me! If only they could restrain themselves
a little . . ." Exhausted under the burden of universal
kindness, he shut his eyes and opened them again at the
clink of spoons. Medicine spoons, soup spoons, dessert
spoons. Jean did not like spoons, with the exception of a
strange silver spoon with a long twisted stem, finished off
at one end with a little engine-turned disk. "It's a sugar
crusher," Madam Mama would say. "And the other end
of the spoon, Madam Mama?" "I'm not quite sure. I
think it used to be an absinthe spoon." And nearly always
at that moment her gaze would wander to a photograph
of Jean's father, the husband she had lost so young—
"Your dear papa, my own Jean"—and whom Jean coldly
and silently designated by the secret words "That man
hanging up in the drawing room."

Apart from the absinthe spoon—absinthe, absinthe,
absent, apse saint—Jean liked only forks, four-horned
demons on which things were impaled, a bit of mutton
cutlet, a tiny fish curled up in its fried breadcrumbs, a
round slice of apple and its two pips, a crescent of apricot
in its first quarter, frosted with sugar.

"Jean, darling, open your bill."

He obeyed, closing his eyes, and swallowed a medicine
that was almost tasteless except for a passing, hypocritical
sickliness that disguised something worse. In his secret
vocabulary, Jean called this potion "dead man's gully."
But nothing would have wrenched such appalling syllables
out of him and flung them gasping at the feet of Madam
Mama.

The phosphatized soup followed inevitably; a badly
swept hayloft, with its chinks stuffed with mildewed flour.

But you forgave it all that because of something that
floated impalpably over its clear liquid; a flowery breath,
the dusty fragrance of the cornflowers Mandora bought in
little bunches in the street for Jean, in July.

A little cube of grilled lamb went down quickly. "Run,
lamb, run, I'm putting on a good show, but go right
down into my stomach in a ball—I couldn't chew you for
anything in the world. Your flesh is still bleating and I
don't want to know that you're pink in the middle!"

"It seems to me you're eating very fast tonight, aren't
you, Jean?"

The voice of Madam Mama dropped from the height
of the dusk, perhaps from the molded plaster cornice,
perhaps from the big cupboard. By a special gracious
concession, Jean granted his mother permission to ascend
into the alpine world at the top of the cupboard, the
world of the household linen. She reached it by means
of the stepladder, became invisible behind the left-hand
door, and came down again loaded with great solid
slabs of snow, hewn straight out of the heights. This
harvest was the limit of her ambition. Jean went farther
and higher; he thrust up, alone, toward the white peaks,
slipping through an odd pair of sheets, reappearing in the
well-rounded fold of an even pair. And what giddy slides
between the stiff damask table napkins or on some alp of
starched curtains, slippery as glaciers, and edged with a
Greek key pattern, what nibbling of stalks of dried lavender, of their scattered flowers, of the fat and creamy
orris roots.

It was from there he would descend again into his bed
at dawn, stiff all over with cold, and pale, weak, and impish: "Jean! Oh, goodness, he must have uncovered himself again in his sleep! Mandora, quick, a hot-water bottle!"
Silently, Jean congratulated himself on having got back
just in time, as usual. Then he would note, on an invisible
page of the notebook hidden in the active, beating nook
in his side he called his "heart pocket," all the vicissitudes
of his ascent, the fall of the stars, and the orange tintin-
nabulation of the dawn-touched peaks.

"I'm eating fast, Madam Mama, because I'm hungry."

For he was an old hand at all kinds of deception and

didn't he know that the words "I'm hungry" made Madam Mama flush with pleasure?

"If that's true, darling, I'm sorry I gave you only stewed apples for your pudding. But I told Mandora to add a bit of lemon peel and a little stick of vanilla to make it taste nice."

Jean resolutely faced up to the stewed apples, an acid provincial girl aged about fifteen who, like other girls of the same age, had nothing but haughty disdain for the boy of ten. But didn't he feel the same toward her? Wasn't he armed against her? Wasn't he an agile cripple, leaning on the stick of vanilla? "It's always too short, *always,* that little stick," he murmured in his elusive way.

Mandora returned, and her billowing skirt with the broad stripes swelled up with as many ribs as a melon. As she walked she sounded—tzrromm, tzrromm, for Jean alone—the inner strings that were the very soul, the gorgeous music of Mandora.

"Finished your dinner already? If you eat so fast, you'll bring it up again. It's not your usual way."

Madam Mama on one side, Mandora on the other, were standing close by his bed. "How tall they are! Madam Mama doesn't take up much room in width in her little claret-colored dress. But Mandora, over and above her great sound box, makes herself bigger with two curved handles, standing with her arms akimbo." Jean resolutely defied the stewed apples, spread them all over the plate, pressed them down again in festoons on the gilded rim, and once again the question of dinner was settled.

The winter evening had long ago fallen. As he savored his half glass of mineral water—the thin, light furtive water that he thought was green because he drank it out of a pale green tumbler—Jean reckoned he still needed a little courage to conclude his invalid's day. There was still his nightly toilet, the inevitable, scrupulous details that demanded the aid of Madam Mama and even— tzrromm, tzrromm—the gay, sonorous assistance of Mandora; still the toothbrush, the washcloths and sponge, the good soap and warm water, the combined precautions for not getting the sheets the least bit wet; still the tender maternal inquiries.

"My little boy, you can't sleep like that. You've got the

binding of the big Gustave Doré digging right into your side, and that litter of little books with sharp corners all over your bed. Wouldn't you like me to bring the table nearer?"

"No, thanks, Madam Mama, I'm quite all right as I am."

When his toilet was finished, Jean struggled against the intoxication of tiredness. But he knew the limit of his strength and did not try to escape from the rites that ushered in the night and the marvels it might capriciously bring forth. His only fear was that Madam Mama's solicitude might prolong the duration of day longer than he could bear, might ruin a material edifice of books and furniture, a balance of light and shadows that Jean knew and revered. Building that edifice cost him his final efforts, and ten o'clock was the extreme limit of his endurance.

"If she stays, if she insists, if she still wants to go on watching over me when the big hand slants to the right of the XII, I'm going to feel myself turning white, whiter, whiter still, and my eyes will sink in and I won't even be able to keep answering the no-thank-you—quite-all-right-Madam-Mama—good-nights that are absolutely necessary to her and—and—it'll be awful. She'll sob."

He smiled at his mother, and the majesty that illness confers on children whom it strikes down wakened in the fiery glint of his hair, descended over his eyelids, and settled bitterly on his lips. It was the hour when Madam Mama would have liked to lose herself in contemplation of her mangled and exquisite work.

"Good night, Madam Mama," said the child, very low.

"Are you tired? Do you want me to leave you?"

He made one more effort, opened his eyes wide, the color of the sea off Brittany, manifested with his whole face the desire to be fit and hearty, and bravely lowered his high shoulders.

"Do I look like a tired boy? Madam Mama, I ask you now!"

She replied only with a roguish shake of her head, kissed her son, and went away, taking with her her choked-back cries of love, her strangled adjurations, her litanies that implored the disease to go away, to undo the fetters on the long, weak legs and the emaciated but not deformed loins, to set the impoverished blood running freely again through the green network of the veins.

"I've put two oranges on the plate. You don't want me to put out your lamp?"

"I'll put it out myself, Madam Mama."

"Good heavens, where's my head? We haven't taken your temperature tonight!"

A fog interposed itself between Madam Mama's garnet dress and her son. That night Jean was burning with fever but taking a thousand precautions to conceal it. A little fire was smoldering in the hollow of his palms, there was a drumming woo-woo-woo in his outer ear, and fragments of a hot crown were clinging to his temples.

"We'll take it tomorrow without fail, Madam Mama."

"The bell push is just under your wrist. You're quite sure you wouldn't rather have the company of a night-light during the hours you're alone, you know, one of those pretty night—"

The last syllable of the word stumbled into a pit of darkness and Jean collapsed with it. "Yet it was only a very tiny pit," he rebuked himself as he fell. "I must have a big bump at the back of my neck. I must look like a Zebu. But I zeed, yes I zaw that Madam Mama didn't zee, no, didn't see anything fall. She was much too absorbed in all the things she takes away every night gathered up in her skirt, her little prayers, the reports she's got to give the doctor, the way I hurt her so much by not wanting anyone near me at night. She carries all that away in the lap of her skirt and it spills over and rolls on the carpet, poor Madam Mama. How can I make her understand that I'm not unhappy? Apparently a boy of my age can't either live in bed or be pale and deprived of his legs or be in pain without being unhappy. Unhappy—I *was* unhappy when they still used to wheel me about in a chair. I was drenched with a shower of stares. I used to shrink so as to get a bit less of it. I was the target for a hail of 'How pretty he is!' and 'What a dreadful pity!' Now the only miseries I have are the visits of my cousin Charlie with his scratched knees and his nailed shoes and that word 'boy scout,' half steel, half india rubber, that he overwhelms me with . . . And that pretty little girl who was born the same day as me, whom they sometimes call my foster-sister and sometimes my fiancée. She's studying dancing. She sees me lying in bed and then she stands on the tips of her toes and says: 'Look, I'm on points.' But all that's only teasing. There comes a time at night when the teases go to sleep. That is the time when everything's all right."

He put out the lamp and peacefully watched his nocturnal companions, the choir of shapes and colors, rising up around him. He was waiting for the symphony to burst out, for the crowd Madam Mama called solitude. He drew the pear-shaped bell push, an invalid's toy of moonlight-colored enamel, from under his arm and laid it on the bedside table. "Now, light up!" he commanded.

It did not obey at once. The night outside was not so black that you could not make out the end of a leafless branch of a chestnut tree in the street swaying outside one of the panes and asking for help. Its swollen tip assumed the shape of a feeble rosebud. "Yes, you're trying to soften my heart by telling me you're next season's bud. Yet you know how ruthless I am to everything that talks to me about next year. Stay outside. Disappear. Vanish! As my cousin would say: skedaddle."

His fastidiousness about words reared up to its full height and poured one more dose of withering scorn on that cousin with his scratched, purple knees and his vocabulary plastered with expressions such as "And how!" "I put a spoke in his wheel," "I'm not having any," and "Golly!" Worst of all, Charlie was always saying "Just think!" and "I do understand!" as if those immensely learned crickets, thought and penetration, would not have fled in terror on all their delicate legs from a boy like that, shod in hobnails and dried mud.

At the mere sight of his cousin Charlie, Jean wiped his fingers on his handkerchief as if to rid them of some kind of coarse sand. For Madam Mama and Mandora, interposed between the child and ugliness, between the child and scurrilous words, between the child and the baser sorts of reading, had made it possible for him to know and cherish only two forms of luxury: fastidiousness and pain. Protected and precocious, he had quickly mastered the hieroglyphs of print, dashing as wildly through books as he galloped astride clouds. He could compel the landscapes to rise up before him from the smooth page or assemble around him all the things that, for those likewise privileged, secretly people the air.

He had never used the silver fountain pen engraved with his initials since the day when his rapid, mature writing had startled and, as it were, offended the doctor with the cold hands. "Is that really the handwriting of a young child, madame?" "Oh yes, Doctor, my son has a very definitely formed handwriting." And Madam Mama's anxious eyes had asked apologetically: "It's not dangerous, Doctor, is it?"

He also refrained from drawing, fearing all the things the eloquence of a sketch might give away. After having drawn the portrait of Mandora, with all her inner keyboard of resounding notes, the profile of an alabaster clock galloping full speed on its four supporting pillars, the dog Riki in the hands of the barber, with his hair done, like Jean's own, "à l'Aiglon," he had been terrified by the truth to life of his efforts and had wisely torn up his first works.

"Wouldn't you like a sketchbook, my young friend, and some colored chalk? It's an amusing game and just the thing for a boy of your age." At the suggestion, which he considered outside the province of medicine, Jean had only replied by a look between half-closed lashes, a serious, manly look that summed up the doctor who was giving him advice. "My nice barber wouldn't dream of making such a suggestion!" He could not forgive the doctor for having dared to ask him one day when his mother was out of the room: "And why the devil do you call your mother Madam?" The angry masculine glance and the weak, musical voice had answered with one accord: "I didn't think that was any business of the devil's."

The nice hair cutter performed his mission very differently and told Jean all about his Sunday life. Every Sunday he went fishing around about Paris. With a dazzling sweep of his scissors he would demonstrate the gesture that flings the float and the bait far out and Jean would shut his eyes under the chill of the waterdrops, splashing out in wheels when the fisherman triumphantly hauled up his loaded line. . . .

"When you're well again, Monsieur Jean, I'll take you with me to the riverbank."

"Yes, yes," agreed Jean, his eyes closed.

"Why do they all want me to be well again? I *am* on the riverbank. What would I do with a chub-as-big-as-my-hand-here and a pickerel-as-long-as-your-paper-knife-there?"

"Nice barber, tell me some more. . . ."

And he would listen to the story of the hawk moths clinging under the arch of a little bridge, impromptu bait that had caught a "wagonload" of trout with a hazel twig cut from the hedge and three bits of string knotted together.

To the cool, grating accompaniment of the twittering scissors, the story would begin:

"You go as far as a tiny little creek no-broader-than-my-thigh that widens out as it crosses a meadow. You see two-three willows together and a bit of brushwood: that's the place."

On the very first day Jean had transplanted other things around the two-three willows: the tall spikes of common agrimony extracted from the big botany album and pink-flowered hemp that attracts butterflies and tired children and sends them to sleep. The monstrous pruned head of the oldest willow, crowned with white convolvulus, pulled faces only for Jean. The leap of a fish burst the glittering skin of the river; then another fish leaped. . . . The nice hairdresser, busy with his bait, had heard them and turned around.

"Makin' game o' me, those two! But I'll get 'em."

"No, no," Jean protested. "It was me. I threw two little pebbles into the water."

The tree frog was singing, the imaginary afternoon was passing.

"Singing invisible on his water-lily raft," mused Jean. "Why tree frog? Why not lily frog?"

The shearer of golden fleece, the river, and the meadow faded away like a dream, leaving behind on Jean's forehead a sweet, commonplace scent and a wavy crest of fair hair. Jean, waking up, heard a whispering coming

from the drawing room, a long low colloquy between
Madam Mama and the doctor from which one word escaped, crisp and lively, and made a beeline for Jean, the
word "crisis." Sometimes it entered ceremoniously, like
a lady dressed up to give away prizes, with an *h* behind
its ear and a *y* tucked into its bodice: Chrysis, Chrysis
Salutari. "Really? Really?" said the urgent voice of Madam Mama. "I said: perhaps . . ." replied the doctor's
voice, an unsteady voice that halted on one foot. "A
crisis, salutary but severe . . ." Chrysis Salutari Sevea,
a young creole from tropical America, lissom in her
flounced white cotton dress.

The child's subtle ear also gathered the name of another person, which no doubt it was expedient to keep
secret. A name he couldn't quite catch, something like
Polly O'Miley or Olly O'Miall and he finally decided it
must refer to some little girl, also stricken with painful
immobility and possessed of two long useless legs, whom
they never mentioned in front of him for fear he should
be jealous.

Complying with the order it had received, the tip
of the chestnut branch and its message of coming spring
had foundered in the sea of night. Although Jean had a
second time requested it to do so, the pear-shaped bell
push had not yet lit up. Its dim opal flame was not shining
on the bedside table, which bore the mineral water, the
orange juice, the big nickel paper knife with the alpine
dawn in its hidden depths, the myopic watch with its
domed glass, and the thermometer . . . Not one book lay
on the table, waiting for Jean to choose it. Printed texts,
whatever their size and shape, slept inside and ready
open in the same bed as the invalid child. At the foot of
the bed, a great tile of binding sometimes weighed heavily
on his almost lifeless legs without his making any com-
plaint.

He groped about him with his still-active arms and
fished up some paperbound books, tattered and warm.
An ancient volume thrust out its friendly horn from under
the pillow. The paperbacks, heaped in a cushion, took
their place against one of the little boy's thin hips and
the soft childish cheek pressed against the light calf binding that was a century old. Under his armpit, Jean verified

the presence of a tough favorite comrade, a volume as hard and squat as a paving stone, a grumpy, robust fellow who found the bed too soft and usually went off to finish his night on the floor on the white goatskin rug.

Angular pasteboard shapes and the sockets and sinuses and cavities of a fragile anatomy interlocked in the friendliest way. The temporary bruising made the chronic pain easier to bear patiently. Certain wayward little tortures, inflicted between the ear and the shoulder by the horned light brown calf, displaced and relieved the torments endured by that region and by the wretched little back with its wings of prominent shoulder blades.

"Whatever is the matter with you?" Madam Mama would say. "It looks as if you'd had a blow. Really, I simply can't understand . . ." In perfect good faith, the bruised child would think for a moment, then inwardly reply to himself: "There—why, yes, of course. It was that tree I couldn't avoid. It was that little roof I leaned on to watch the sheep going back into the fold. It was that big rake that fell on the back of my neck when I was drinking at the fountain. Still, what luck Madam Mama didn't see the little nick at the corner of my eye, the mark of that swallow's beak I knocked up against in the air. I didn't have time to avoid it, and it was as hard as a scythe. Really, a sky is so small . . ."

The confused murmur of his nights began to rise, expected but not familiar. It varied according to his dreams, his degree of weakness, his temperature, and the fantasies of a day that Madam Mama supposed depressingly like all the other days. This new night bore no resemblance whatever to yesterday's night. The darkness was rich in innumerable blacks. "The black is all purple tonight. I've got such a pain in—in what? In my forehead. No, what am I saying? It's always my back. . . . But no, it's a weight, two weights that are hung on my hips, two weights shaped like pinecones, like the ones on the kitchen clock. *You* there, for the last time, will you light up?"

To communicate his order to the enamel bell push, he leaned his temple hard against the pale leather binding and shuddered to find it so cold. "If it's frozen, it means I'm burning." No light flowed from the enamel pear. "What's the matter with it? And what's the matter with

me? Only this afternoon, the front door wouldn't let me
go through it." He stretched out his hand into the inhabited night air and found the shadowy pear without
groping for it. Capriciously changing its usual source, the
light appeared on the fat, shortsighted face of the spher-
ical watch. "What are you sticking your nose in for?"
muttered Jean. "Be satisfied with knowing how to tell the
time."

The mortified watch put out its light and Jean heaved
a sigh of gratified power. But all he could get out of his
rigid sides was a groan. All at once, a wind he recognized
among all others, the wind that snaps the pine trees,
dishevels the tamaracks, and flattens and raises the sand
dunes, began to roar. It filled his ears, and the images,
forbidden to the more ordinary dream that does not
pierce the curtain of closed eyelids, rose up and longed
to run free, to take advantage of the limitless room. Some
of them, strangely horizontal, checkered the vertical
crowd who had reared straight up on end. "Scottish
visions," thought Jean.

His bed trembled slightly, shaken by the vibrating ascent of High Fever. He felt three or four years fall away
from him, and fear, to which he was almost a stranger,
clutched at him. He very nearly called out: "To the rescue,
Madam Mama! They're carrying off your little boy!"

Neither in his rides nor in the rich kingdom of the very
strangest sounds—humpbacked sounds carrying rever-
berating ampuls on their heads, on their May-beetle backs,
pointed sounds with snouts like mongooses—nowhere
had Jean ever seen such a swarm suddenly appear. His
hearing tasted it like a mouth; his eye laboriously spelled
it out, fascinated. "Help, Madam Mama! Help me! You
know I can't walk! I can only fly, swim, roll from cloud
to cloud. . . ." At the same moment, something indescribable and forgotten stirred in his body, infinitely far away,
right at the very end of his useless legs, a confused,
scattered crowd of crazy ants. "To the rescue, Madam
Mama!"

But another person, whose decisions depended neither
on impotence nor on motherly kindness, made a haughty
sign that imposed silence. A magical constraint kept Madam Mama on the other side of the wall, in the place

where she waited, modest and anxious, to become as great as her little son.

So he did not scream. In any case, the unknown beings, the fabulous strangers, were already beginning to abduct him by force. Rising up on all sides, they poured burning heat and icy cold on him, racked him with melodious torture, swathed him in color like a bandage, swung him in a hammock of palpitations. With his face already turned to flee, motionless, to his mother, he suddenly changed his mind and launched himself in full flight, letting his own impetus carry him where it would, through meteors and mists and lightnings that softly opened to let him through, closed behind him, opened again. . . . And, just as he was on the very verge of being perfectly content, ungrateful, and gay, exulting in his solitude as an only child, his privileges as an orphan and as an invalid, he was aware that a sad little crystalline crash separated him from a bliss whose beautiful, soft, airy name he had yet to learn: death. A little, light, melancholy crash, coming perhaps from some planet deserted forever . . . The clear and sorrowful sound, clinging to the child who was going to die, held on so staunchly that the dazzling escape tried in vain to shake it off and outdistance it.

Perhaps his journey lasted a long time. But having lost all sense of duration, he could only judge of its variety. Often he thought he was following a guide, an indistinct guide who had lost his way too. Then he would groan at not being able to take on the pilot's responsibility, and he would hear his own groan of humbled pride or of such weariness that he abandoned his voyage, left the wake of a spindle-shaped squall, and took refuge, exhausted, in a corner.

There he was pounced on by the anguish of living in a country where there were no corners, no square, solid shapes; where there was only a dark current of icy air, a night in whose depths he was no longer anything but a small boy, lost and in tears. Then he would rear himself upright on a great many suddenly multiplied legs, promoted to the rank of stilts, which a searing pain was slicing off in rattling bundles, like faggots. Then everything would go dark and only the blind wind told him how fast he was traveling. Passing from a familiar continent to an unfamiliar sea, he caught a few words in a language he was surprised to find he understood: "The sound of the glass mug breaking woke me up."

"Madam can see he's smacking his lips. Doesn't Madam think he wants something to drink?"

He would have liked to know the name of that voice. "Madam . . . Madam . . . What Madam?" But already the speed at which he was going had swallowed up the words and the memory of them.

One pale night, thanks to a stop that jarred through his temples, he again gathered a few human syllables and would have liked to repeat them. The sudden stop had brought him painfully face to face with a harsh, solid object interposed between two noble and inhabited worlds. An object with no destination, finely striped, bristling with very tiny hairs and mysteriously associated—he discovered this afterward—with horrible "my-young-friends." "It's a—I know—a—sleeve. . . ." Promptly, he opened his wings and flung himself head first into reassuring chaos.

Another time, he saw a hand. Armed with slender fingers, with slightly chapped skin and white-spotted nails, it was pushing back a marvelous zebra-striped mass that was rushing up from the depths of the horizon. Jean began to laugh: "Poor little hand, the mass will make one mouthful of it. Just imagine, a mass that's all striped in black and yellow and has such an intelligent expression!" The feeble little hand struggled with all its outspread fingers and the parallel stripes began to broaden and bend and diverge like soft bars. A great gap opened between them and swallowed up the frail hand and Jean found himself regretting it. This regret was delaying his journey, and with an effort, he launched himself off again. But he carried the regret with him, just as once, very, very long ago, he had carried the tenacious tinkle of a broken mug. After that, through whatever whirlpools and troughs he swirled and dipped, drowsy and rather pleasantly giddy, his journey was disturbed by echoes, by sounds of tears, by an anxious attempt at something that resembled a thought, by an importunate feeling of pity.

A harsh barking suddenly rent the great spaces, and Jean murmured: "Riki . . ." In the distance, he heard a kind of sob that kept repeating: "Riki! Madam, he said Riki!" Another stammering reiterated: "He said Riki! He said Riki."

A little hard, quivering force, whose double grip he could feel under his armpits, seemed to want to hoist him up to the top of a peak. It was bruising him and he grumbled. If he had been able to transmit his instructions to the little force and its sharp corners, he would have taught it that this was no way to treat a famous traveler who uses only immaterial vehicles, unshod steeds, sledges that trace seven-colored tracks on the rainbow. That he only allowed himself to be molested by those—those elements whose power only the night can unleash and control. That, for example, the bird's belly that had just laid itself against the whole length of his cheek had no right at all. And, moreover, it was not a bird's belly because it was not feathered, but only edged with a strand of long hair. "That," he thought, "would be a cheek if there were any other cheek in the universe except mine. I want to speak, I want to send away this—this sham cheek. I forbid anyone to touch me, I forbid . . ."

To acquire the strength to speak, he breathed the air in through his nostrils. With the air, there entered in the marvel, the magic of memory, the smell of certain hair, certain skin he had forgotten on the other side of the world and that started up a wild rush of recollections. He coughed, fighting against the rise of something that tightened his throat, quenched a thirst lurking in the parched corners of his lips, salted his overflowing eyelids, and mercifully veiled from him his return to the hard landing-bed. Over an endless stretch, a voice said, re-echoing to infinity: "He's crying, dear God, he's crying. . . ." The voice foundered in a kind of storm from which there arose disjointed syllables, sobs, calls to some-one present, but concealed. "Come quick, quick!"

"What a noise, what a noise," thought the child re-proachfully. But more and more, he kept pressing his cheek unconsciously against the soft, smooth surface bordered by someone's hair and drinking up a bitter dew on it that welled out, drop by drop. He turned away his head and, as he did so, encountered a narrow valley, a nest molded exactly to his measure. He had just time to name it to himself—"Madam Mama's shoulder"—before he lost consciousness or else fell asleep on it.

He came to himself to hear his own voice, light and faintly mocking, saying: "Wherever have you come from, Madam Mama?"

There was no answer, but the deliciousness of a quarter of an orange, slipped between his lips, made him conscious of the return, of the presence of the person he was searching for. He knew that she was bending over him in that submissive attitude that flexed her waist and tired her back. Soon exhausted, he fell silent. But already a thousand questions were worrying him and he conquered his weakness to satisfy the most urgent one: "Did you change my pajamas while I was asleep, Madam Mama? When I lay down, last night, I had blue ones and these are pink."

"Madam, it's past believing! He remembers he had blue pajamas, the first night when—"

He did not listen to the rest of the sentence that a big, warm voice had just whispered and abandoned himself to the hands that were taking off his wet garments. Hands as deft as the waves between which he rocked, weightless and aimless . . .

"He's soaked. Wrap him up in the big dressing gown, Mandora, without putting his arms through the sleeves."

"The heat's all the way up, madam, don't be afraid. And I've just put in a new hot-water bottle for him. My goodness, he's positively drenched."

"If they knew where I've come from . . . Anyone would expect to be drenched," thought Jean. "I wish to goodness I could scratch my legs or that someone would take those ants off."

"Madam Mama."

He took hold of the muteness, the vigilant stillness, that were Madam Mama's answer when she was strained and on the alert.

"Would you please—scratch my calves a little because these ants . . ."

From the depths of silence, someone whispered with a

strange respectfulness: "He can feel ants. . . . He said ants. . . ."

Swathed in the dressing gown that was too big for him, he tried to shrug his shoulders. Why, yes, he had said ants? What was there astonishing about his having said Riki and ants? A reverie carried him away, relieved, to the margin between waking and sleeping; the rustle of some material brought him back again. Between his lashes, he recognized the hateful sleeve, the blue stripes, the little hairs of wool, and his resentment restored his strength. He refused to see any more of it but a voice came and opened his closed lids, a voice that said: "Well, my-young-friend . . ."

"I abolish him, I abolish him!" shrieked Jean inside himself. "Him, his sleeve, his my-young-friend, his little eyes, I curse them, I abolish them!" Beside himself with irritation, he was panting.

"Well, well. What's the matter? You're very restless. There . . . there . . ."

A hand laid itself on Jean's head. Powerless to revolt, he hoped to strike the aggressor down with one thunderbolt from his eye. But all he could see, sitting on the bedside chair reserved for Madam Mama, was a worthy, rather fat, rather bald man, whose eyes, as they met his own, filled with tears.

"Little one, little one. Is it true you've got ants in your legs? Is it true? That's splendid, honestly, that's really splendid. Could you manage to drink half a glass of lemonade? Wouldn't you like to suck a spoonful of lemon ices? A mouthful of milk and water?"

Jean's hand yielded itself up to some thick, very soft fingers and a warm palm. He murmured a vague acquiescence, not quite sure himself whether he was apologizing or whether he wanted the lemon ices, the drink, the "watered" milk. His eyes, paled to a tired gray between the great black rings and the dark eyebrows, gazed amicably into two small eyes of a cheerful blue that were moist and blinking and tender.

The rest of the new era was nothing but a series of muddled moments; a medley of different kinds of sleep, now short, now long, now hermetically sealed, inter-

spersed with sudden sharp awakenings and vague tremors.
The worthy doctor indulged in an orgy of great satisfied
coughs, ahem, ahem, and exclamations of "Dear lady,
this is wonderful! We're safe now!" All this din was
so cheerful that Jean, if he had not been sunk in apathy,
would have asked himself what happy event had occurred in the house.

The hours passed inexplicably, signposted by fruits in
jelly and milk flavored with vanilla. A boiled egg raised
its little lid and revealed its buttercup yolk. The window,
left ajar, let in a breath of spring, heady as wine.

The nice barber was not yet permitted to return. Jean's
hair hung down over his forehead and neck like a little
girl's and Madam Mama risked tying it back with a pink
ribbon, which Jean tore off with the gesture of an insulted boy.

Behind the pane, the chestnut branch's roselike buds
were swelling day by day, and all up and down Jean's legs
there ran ants armed with little nipping jaws. "This time
I've caught one, Madam Mama!" But all he was pinching
was his own transparent skin and the ant had fled inside
a tree of veins the color of spring grass. On the eighth
day of the new era, a great scarf of sunlight lying across
his bed moved him more than he could bear and he
decided that this very night the daily fever would bring
him what he had been vainly awaiting for a whole week.
Everything that profound weariness and sleep hewn out
of a solid block of black repose had robbed him of would
be restored: his faceless companions, his rides, the ac-
cessible skies, his security of an angel in full flight.

"Madam Mama, I'd like my books, please."

"My darling, the doctor said that——"

"It's not to read them, Madam Mama, it's so that they'll
get used to me again."

She said nothing and, with some apprehension, brought
back the tattered volumes, the big badly bound paving
stone, the light calf soft as a human skin, a *Pomology*
with colored plates of chubby fruits, the Guérin mot-
tled with flat-faced lions and duckbilled platypuses with
beetles big as islands flying over them.

When night came, having eaten his fill—food was now
something magical and interesting that he ate with the

avidity of children who have come back to life—he
pretended to be overcome with sleep and murmured his
good nights and a vague, mischievous song he had recently improvised. Having secretly watched the departure
of Madam Mama and Mandora, he took command of his
raft of folio and atlas and set sail. A young moon, behind
the chestnut branch, showed that the buds, thanks to the
warmer weather, were about to open in leafy fingers.

He sat up without assistance in bed, towing his still-
heavy legs that were overrun with ants. In the depths of
the window, in the celestial waters of night, swam the
curved moon and the dim reflection of a long-haired
child, to whom he beckoned. He raised one arm, and the
other child obediently copied his summoning gesture.
Slightly intoxicated with the power to work marvels, he
called up his boon companions of the cruel but privileged hours: the visible sounds; the tangible images; the
breathable seas; the nourishing, navigable air; the wings
that mocked feet; the laughing suns.

In particular, he called up a certain spirited little boy
who chuckled with inward laughter as he left the earth,
who took advantage of Madam Mama and, lord of her
sorrows and joys, kept her prisoner of a hundred loving
lies.

Then he waited, but nothing came. Nothing came that
night or the following ones, nothing ever again. The landscape of pink snow had vanished from the nickel paper
knife, and never again would Jean fly in a periwinkle dawn
between the sharp horns and the beautiful bulging eyes
of cattle azure with dew. Never again would brown-and-
yellow Mandora reverberate with all the strings—tzromm,
tzromm—humming beneath her vast, generous skirt. Was
it possible that the damask alp, piled high in the big
cupboard, would henceforth refuse to allow a child who
was nearly well to perform the feats that a small cripple
had achieved on the slopes of imaginary glaciers?

A time comes when one is forced to concentrate on
living. A time comes when one has to renounce dying in
full flight. With a wave of his hand, Jean said farewell
to his angel-haired reflection. The other returned his greet-

ing from the depths of an earthly night shorn of all marvels, the only night allowed to children whom death lets go and who fall asleep, assenting, cured, and disappointed.

[TRANSLATED BY ANTONIA WHITE]

Orchid

I can see before me a small, pointed wooden shoe, very pointed. It is made of some green material like jade, and on the tip of the shoe is painted in reddish-brown a minute nocturnal bird—two huge eyes, a beak. Inside the wooden shoe, along the whole length of the sole, someone—but who?—has sown a silver plant, slantwise. The point of the shoe is not empty, a hand—but whose? —has there upset a drop, which, shimmering like glass, acts as a mirror and is as different from a natural moist dewdrop as the artificial moisture vaporized by florists. I have scraped some of it off with the tip of my workaday blade, the trusty servitor that shrinks from no task, sharpens pencils, peels chestnuts, cuts my periwinkle-blue paper into rectangles and dark red radishes into rings. To gain a better knowledge of this translucid, stuck-on nip, I put it in my mouth. At once my very good friend raised hands and voice to heaven, "Poor doomed creature!" He then added some excellent advice concerning Malayan vegetable poisons and the brewing of the curare, an unsolved mystery. While waiting for the threatened death throes, I began, with the aid of my large magnifying glass, to decipher the orchid. This was a gift from my daughter, whom I had reproved in lieu of thanks. "Didn't you ask the florist the name of this monstrosity?" "Of course, Maman." "What did she say?" "What she said was, 'On my word, I'd be hard put to it to tell you. But for an uncommon name, it's not very common.'"

The tiny drop has not dissolved on my tongue. All I noticed was a very faint taste of raw potato.

All around the small shoe are five asymmetrical arms, green, speckled with brown, diverging. A beautiful lower lip with a white foundation, not unlike the tongue of an

249

iris in form, spread-eagled below them, stamped with a violet stipple, and the shape, yes, the shape of the pod of a cuttlefish, for in fact my orchid is an octopus: if not the eight arms, it does have the parrot beak of the octopods, the beak I called a moment ago the tip of the shoe.

Five arms only. Who has amputated the other three? Who? Where? Under what skies? With what purpose? By what license is this mimesis permitted?

I must remain calm. Why such excitement over a flower from the antipodes, the extravagant cousin of our own vernal hornet orchis, of our ophrys, which so pleasingly imitates a corset in its elegant waist and bee's wings! The more the wonders of the visible world become inaccessible, the more intensely do its curiosities affect us. I am far from complaining about it; my orchid of today is an ugly dream and full of attraction. To me it carries a suggestion of octopus, wooden shoe, silvery beard, owl, dried blood. It would have fascinated and beguiled many far wiser than myself, and, to mention but one, a big-game hunter of the last century, a quiet little fellow who killed bureaucratically, in impossible countries, the jaguars in their flowered dresses. He shot jaguars only, and now and again plump doves for the pot.

One day, while waiting at the spot chosen for him by the native beaters beside a jaguar track, he became bored. Raising his head, he caught sight of an orchid—a special kind of orchid. One that could be said to resemble a bird, a crab, a butterfly, an evil spell, a sexual organ, and, perhaps, even a flower. Dazzled, the big-game hunter propped up his rifle and started to climb, not without risk to his life. He captured the orchid and came down just in time to see coming toward his weaponless hands a lordly jaguar, in splendid fettle, wet with dew, which looked him over dreamily, then passed on its way.

I have heard that this same man, who was hunting about 1860, later turned botanist. All I should like to know is whether he was converted out of gratitude to the kindly jaguar or whether the orchid, more powerfully spellbinding than any other game, had once and for all

cast him deep into those regions where a man finding
himself between the devil and the deep blue sea does
not fail to choose the worse alternative.

[TRANSLATED BY ROGER SENHOUSE]

From *The Blue Lantern**

My only remaining property is a living beast, the fire.
It is my host and my creation. I know how to bank the
fire and how to protect the fire. I know how to surround it, outdoors, with a circular trench, so that it may
thrive without "burrowing" into the thatch and setting
fire to the haystacks. I know that it dislikes even numbers,
that three logs burn better than two and seven better
than four, and that, like all other beasts, it likes to have
its belly scratched from underneath.

Between me and the fire there is an old question that
I take my time about solving because the fire burns for
three-quarters of the year in my room, which has
adopted its red and black colors and its presence. I
consume it unceasingly. Unceasingly, but with a shade of
excessive economy. I nourish it generously, but I pretend
to be doing this out of charity. I show it that I come from
far away, from the provinces, where one learns not to
waste wood or bread. I ration its intake of splinters, twigs,
and dry leaves and I want to have the last word with it,
an ancient need of the tamer acquired in dealing with
animals. The fire rewards me by throwing itself on the
smallest of my offerings; it flatters me and facilitates my
short incantation, which has become mechanical: the
magic loses none of its force.

The fireplace in which I celebrate my fire is an old
construction that required only, if I judge rightly, the
hand of a simple mason. Within the walls of the Palais
Royal we have here and there door handles, panels made
for drawing rooms, and beautiful fireplaces. Mine has
lost its marble, which has been replaced by a kind of
beige and pinkish jelly. No matter; my fireplace has kept

its own character, its appetite for passion—the obedience of a machine that, closely tied to man's life, contributed to his rudimentary comfort.

Those who have meditated near a fire when night, fallen on the other side of the window, guaranteed them a secure enclosure need not fear that the dusky twilight, the shudder and the sudden start, will join them around the fire. Only novices feel so intensely the presence of a weight, of age, of fear, of evil. Let me murmur my short incantation:

> How pleasant a companion, the fire is
> To the prisoner, during the long winter evenings!
> Very near me a benevolent spirit warms itself
> Who drinks or smokes or sings an old tune. . . .

Who wrote these lines? With a little prodding I would say I did, because a reading contest in my district forced those of us who were twelve and thirteen to read aloud, with feeling, poetry and prose. A well-meaning man from the country town, having realized that no child in our district could read without hemming and hawing, became indignant, indicated the great peril in which the ignorance of the Department of Yonne would certainly plunge all France, and founded a reading prize. A red and gold tome and a diploma corroborated the fact that at twelve and a half years of age, Gabrielle-Sidonie Colette knew how to read and rewarded me for having stuttered while reading and said "who drinks sor smokes," thereby inadvertently correcting Madame de Sévigné's prose.

> How pleasant a companion the fire is
> To the prisoner . . .

After all, these mediocre lines are perhaps my creation. Mine, like the fire, like everything that surrounds me during the night.

A line of verse need not necessarily be beautiful for it to remain in the depths of our memory and occupy maliciously the place overrun by certain condemnable but unerasable melodies.

> How pleasant . . .

Night reading is a treacherous aid. More reliable than a book is the decor I have arranged in honor of the minutes and the hours. I am not always able to cope with my insomnia, but it is rare that I do not succeed in adapting to it by a kind of mental recovery that chases from this room and from me the fear of the unusual. It is not more than three o'clock in the morning; nothing as yet grows pale at the level of the rooftops. Because every pillar has a lantern, I can count, from my bed, the arcades of the Palais Royal. The house is so peacefully inhabited that I do not hear anyone sleeping, but if the fire tongs in my fireplace were to fall, they would disturb the uneasy rest of the man who sleeps two doors away. Now, if I am immobile this evening, I am not without plans because within me there moves—aside from this twisting pain, like the large screw in a winepress—a torture much less familiar than pain, a rebellion that during the course of my life I often denied, attempted to confound, and finally accepted; for writing leads only to writing. With humility, I shall go on writing. There is no other fate for me. But when does one stop writing? What is the warning sign? A trembling hand? I used to believe that the task of writing was like other tasks: you put down the tool and shout with joy "Finished"—and you clap your hands, from which rain down the grains of a sand considered precious. . . . It is then that in the pattern formed by the grains of sand you read the words "To be continued . . ."

[TRANSLATED BY ELAINE MARKS]

Selected Bibliography

(*Oeuvres complètes.* 15 vols. Paris: Flammarion, 1948–1950. This is the definitive edition of Colette's works, which is being translated and published in England by Secker & Warburg, Ltd., and distributed in the United States by Farrar, Straus & Company, Inc.)

Works by Colette (the dates in parentheses are those of the original French publication):

Claudine at School (1900)
Claudine in Paris (1901)
Claudine Married (1902)
Creatures Great and Small (1904, 1905, 1908, 1917, 1921)
The Vagabond (1910)
Music-Hall Sidelights (1913)
Mitsou (1919)
Chéri (1920)
My Mother's House (1922)
The Ripening Seed (1923)
The Last of Chéri (1926)
Break of Day (1928)
Sido (1929)
The Cat (1933)
My Apprenticeship (1936)
Bella-Vista (1937)
Chance Acquaintances (1940)
Julie de Carneilhan (1941)
The Kepi (1944)
Gigi (1944)
Armande (1944)
The Photographer's Missus (1944)
The Sick Child (1944)
The Blue Lantern (1949)
For a Flower Album (1949)

Selected Biography and Criticism

Beaumont, Germaine. "Présentation," *Colette par elle-même.* Paris: Éditions du Seuil, 1956, pp. 5–50.
Cocteau, Jean. *Colette.* Paris: Grasset, 1955.

Crosland, Margaret. *Madame Colette, A Provincial in Paris.* London: Peter Owen, Ltd., 1953; New York: British Book Centre, Inc., 1954.

Davies, Margaret. *Colette.* Edinburgh: Oliver & Boyd, Ltd., 1961.

Goudeket, Maurice. *Close to Colette.* Translated by Enid McLeod. New York: Farrar, Straus & Cudahy, Inc.; London: Secker & Warburg, Ltd., 1957.

Le Hardouin, Maria. *Colette.* Paris: Éditions Universitaires, 1956.

Houssa, Nicole. *Le Souci de l'expression chez Colette.* Brussels: Palais des Académies, 1958.

Marks, Elaine. *Colette.* New Brunswick, N. J.: Rutgers University Press, 1960.

Maulnier, Thierry. *Introduction à Colette.* Paris: La Palme, 1954.

Roy, Claude. "Classique Colette," *Point.* Souillac: Éditions le Point, 1951.